The Side Effects of Loving You

The Side Effects Of Loving You

Kaylha Karrington

www.urbanbooks.net

Urban Books, LLC
300 Farmingdale Road,NY-Route 109
Farmingdale, NY 11735

The Side Effects of Loving You

ISBN 13: 978-1-64556-533-8
EBOOK ISBN: 978-1-64556-534-5

First Trade Paperback Printing November 2023
Printed in the United States of America

10 9 8 7 6 5 4 3 2 1

Distributed by Kensington Publishing Corp.
Submit orders to:
Customer Service
400 Hahn Road
Westminster, MD 21157-4627
Phone: 1-800-733-3000
Fax: 1-800-659-2436

Part 1

Chapter One

Draya

Un-Break My Heart

"Another day," I told my ex-mother-in-law, Adella. Here I was, dropping my son KJ off at her house so that his father could come to pick him up for his week. I made sure I made this arrangement when we broke up so I didn't have to see his face again. He had made a fool out of me for the last time, and I'd had enough. I put up with his shit for so long that I actually forgot what it was like to be happy, like genuinely happy. It was like when I was away from him, I was smiling, giggling, and blushing. And when I was with him, he had me the same way, but he pissed me off even more.

"I wish that you and my son would get it together for the sake of KJ. I know it isn't easy, but I'm too old to be playing the middleman between the two of you," she said as I handed her Korey Jr.

I knew she wanted us to work things out, but she needed to understand that I needed a break. I needed to be able to go through life without him to see if I could be without him for real. It had been a hard year, but I made it, and so did my son. I never cried in front of him. I saved all my tears for my pillow like my old dance instructor used to say.

"It's been a year," she added, snapping me out of my thoughts.

"I know, but I'm just not ready to face him, Momma."

Just as those words left my mouth, the front door opened, and I was staring right into the eyes of Korey Sr.

"I'll see you Sunday, little man," I said in baby talk while kissing my son on the cheek and sidestepping him.

"You do know you can't avoid me forever, Julia," he said, calling me by my middle name, something only he did.

"Draya. Please call me Draya. I don't know how many times I have to tell you that. And I'm not avoiding you," I lied.

Closing my eyes, I pulled the door open to my car and climbed inside. Looking back at him, I started the engine, smiled, and backed out of the driveway. As soon as I was out of eyesight of them at the house, I took a deep breath. I didn't know why I was so nervous seeing this man, and I knew his mother was the reason he showed up that early. He would usually wait an hour before picking KJ up.

When I finally made it back to my house, I couldn't help but sit there for a second and think. Was I doing too much by avoiding my ex-fiancé and not trying to have a conversation with him? Was I out of line for not telling him how I was feeling and just leaving the way that I did?

I literally packed KJ and myself up and left the house with no questions. I didn't stay for an explanation or nothing. When you put up with a man for as long as I put up with Korey, then you didn't need proof of anything. If somebody said he did something, nine times out of ten, he did that shit. It never failed. When I minded my business and stayed in the house, somebody had a story each time that man went to the club, and he sat in my face and lied about it each time. It didn't matter if I had pictures. Hell, the FBI could give me all the evidence I needed, and this man would still say they were lying. It didn't make any sense, and I was tired of trying to make it.

I loved that man. Shit, it'd been a year, and I still couldn't see myself without him. But if he couldn't get himself together, we didn't have anything to talk about. That was the only reason I'd been avoiding him. I needed him to see that I didn't have to talk to him. I left him, not the other way around. I made sure he still got to see his son. I had never tried to keep him away from his son. I wasn't that type of mother. And when I needed a break, honey, I needed that shit.

My son was only 1 year old, and he already was in everything he could put his hands on. I could have shit hiding from his little ass, and he would crawl and dig until he couldn't anymore. Fucking with KJ, I cleaned up every day. Shit, not a day went by that my house didn't need my attention, whether it was in my room, his room, or the living room. If he could grab it, you could guarantee it was coming down along with whatever else.

When I pulled up to the house, I got out and went inside. Putting my music on, I cleaned top to bottom while it played, until Megan Thee Stallion came on. I started twerking and dancing.

"Ay!" I yelled out while throwing my hands in the air and rapping along with her.

Bitch, I'm a star, got these niggas wishin'
He say he hungry, this pussy the kitchen
Yeah, that's my dog, he gon' sit down and listen
Call him a trick, and he don't get it, hold up
Bitch, I'm a star, got these niggas wishin'

Looking back in the full-length mirror I had in my bedroom, I turned to the side and started watching my ass bounce up and down. I hadn't had a nigga inside of me since the day I gave birth to my son. There wasn't a nigga in Houston who could make me drop my panties. All these niggas were on some bullshit, and I didn't have time for that shit in my life. I was a mother first and a single bitch shortly afterward.

The sound of the music cutting off and my phone ringing made me stand up and cuss in my head.

"Bitches always calling when I'm having a concert," I said to myself while making my way to it. Picking it up, I looked at it and saw that it was my sister, Junie.

"Hey, baby girl."

"Hey, boo, what are you doing?" she asked.

"Nothing, cleaning up. You know how I do when KJ goes with his father."

"That's all your ass do. Let's go out tonight," she suggested, but it was almost as if she was begging. She quit her job and everything just to stay at home with their child. I didn't blame her, because nowadays, you couldn't trust anybody with your child, but she should have done all her research about staying home with a baby all the time. That shit will have you depressed, cranky, and you be snapping on everybody just because.

"I'm down with it. Who else coming?"

"I'm thinking Dreux."

When she said that, I said nothing. I knew for a fact that Dreux's ass was gonna be ready to go out. Her ass was hot in the drawers. Junie and I had been friends with her for about ten years. We all grew up with one another and made sure to keep in touch even after we graduated high school. Not once did I think we would all have kids for major drug dealers in Houston, but look at God.

"A'ight. You riding with me, or we meeting up?"

"Pregaming at your house."

"Okay. Let me finish cleaning up, and then I'll text you," I said and hung up the phone.

It didn't take me long to finish cleaning my bedroom and KJ's nursery. Once I was finished, I went downstairs and started to cook some shrimp nachos. Pulling out my phone, I was about to text my sister to let her know that she could come when my phone started to ring. Looking at it, I rolled my eyes when I noticed the number belonged to Korey's ass.

"Yeah?" I answered.

"What's with the attitude? I'm just calling to tell you we made it to the house just in case you wanted to know."

"How did you get my number?"

"My momma gave it to me."

"I told her ass not to give you my number. If I wanted you to have it, I would have given it to you."

"You need to get over the shit that happened between us. You know you love me, and I love you. You need to stop punishing me for something I didn't do."

"I don't know what you're talking about," I lied.

I knew exactly what he was talking about. I just didn't want to talk about it. I hated thinking about what got us to where we were, and I just wanted to forget about it. Sometimes it was on my mind, and I wished I had gotten that explanation, but then I changed my mind. The last thing I needed was for this man to come in and hurt my feelings any more than he already had. Korey could tell anybody else that he didn't cheat on me, but the way I felt, didn't no bitch have a reason to lie to me about this nigga.

"You know exactly what I'm talking about, but I see you're still on that childish shit and want to be petty."

"I'm not being anything. I just don't have anything to say to you. I don't understand why you don't get that," I said. The phone clicking in my ear told me that he had hung up.

Shaking my head, I sent my sister a come on text and rolled a blunt. It was a little hard for me with these long nails on, but I got it done. Once it was rolled, I grabbed a brush, put my long, jet-black hair up into a ponytail, and brushed my edges down. I was looking raggedy as hell and didn't even care. On my worst day, I could take a bitch's man and give him back when I was finished with him, but that was not who I was. Putting the blunt to my mouth, I lit it and took a long drag from it before getting up and making my way to the back porch.

Stepping outside, I closed my eyes as the sun blazed down on me. The weather out here was bipolar. One minute it was cold, and the next it was hot as hell. Sitting down, I hit the blunt a few more times before the doorbell rang. I strolled through the house and made my way to the door. My sister and Dreux were standing there with smiles and bags in their hands.

"You partying without us?" Junie asked with a frown on her face.

"I'm not partying. I just had to smoke me one to get my mind right before you hoes got here and worked my nerves."

"Girl, fuck you!" Dreux snapped, making both me and Junie laugh.

"Are you gonna let us in or just stand there like we're strangers?" Junie inquired.

Moving to the side, I watched their feet. "Uh-uh, take them damn shoes off, bitches!" I yelled, running and blocking their path.

I did not play when it came to people wearing shoes in my house. I had all-white carpet and marble floors that I liked to keep clean. No mud tracking went on in this bitch. I had cleaning bad, especially since having my son. Although he made the most messes, I had to clean the whole house all the time. The house could already be clean, and if I felt like it was dirty, I would clean everything all over again.

"Oh, bitch, you act like our shoes dirty," Dreux said, looking at me with a smirk on her face.

"I couldn't give a damn if they were new shoes. Take them hoes off," I told them, and they both giggled. They took them damn shoes off, though.

Nodding my head, I locked the door, and we all went into the living room so that we could drink and catch up.

Chapter Two

Junie

Dirty Laundry

I was sitting here listening to my sister and best friend talk, and I couldn't help but think about the shit I was going through with Jace, my man of three years. That man was everything to me, but he had a habit of putting his hands on me when I didn't do anything wrong. I was so sick of it, and I wanted so badly to leave. But it wasn't that simple when you had a man threatening to kill you if you left him. He didn't appreciate me, but he couldn't think about me being with somebody else. That shit was sad as fuck. Sometimes I could nag him and bitch about little shit, but it was because I was always in the house with our 3-year-old daughter. And he didn't seem to understand that was a full-time job just like his job.

He didn't even do much. His ass went to check on traps and was in the streets with his crew day in and day out. This was the first time I'd been able to get a break from Montana, and I needed it, but here he went texting my phone, trying to ruin my time.

"Junie? What's wrong?" Dreux asked, snapping me out of the thoughts that were going crazy in my head.

"Nothing, I'm fine. What are we talking about?"

"Me coming face-to-face with Korey after all this time," Draya said.

"Girl, you need to give my brother another chance. I know that you think he fucked up, but he was adamant that the girl was lying, so you should have believed your man."

"Even if his history makes it hard? You would rather your big sister be unhappy with him?"

"You weren't always unhappy, and you know that. You love that man's dirty drawers." I kept it real with her.

My sister and Korey had the perfect relationship. I didn't know where it went wrong, but he treated her like a queen. Even though they weren't together, he still wouldn't speak ill of her. He made sure he showed her the utmost respect, which I respected more than anything in the world. He was a way better man than Jace, but I was stuck with this nigga.

"How are things with you and Jace?"

"Not good. He's texting me right now, telling me that I need to come home and spend time with him. He doesn't want me to go to the club, but he has to understand that I'm sick of being locked in the house like I'm on house arrest. Montana is with Mommy for the night, so I'm going to have me some girl fun with my favorite girls," I told them, but I knew that when I got home, I would be getting my ass beat. He had warned me already that if I left, he was gonna hurt me.

"I never liked his ass. He's possessive and acts like just because you have a baby with him and that y'all are together, it means you belong to him. He needs to get it through his head that's not the way it works," Draya chimed in.

I nodded my head in agreement. "He doesn't care about none of that. I've told him numerous times that I'm not his property."

I couldn't tell them what was really going on behind those double doors that led to the horror house I lived in with this man. I knew that my sister would try to kill him or send him to jail. The last thing I needed was for him to go after the people I loved all because he wanted me in the house.

"That nigga is insecure. That's what you call that. But he is out there . . . never mind." Dreux stopped. I knew she knew something that I didn't know, and I wished that she would tell me so that I could ask him about it. I'd put up with so much dealing with this man. I needed a break from him. Shit, a long-ass break. *A break I may not come back from.*

"What?"

"I was just about to say, the way he treats you is bullshit. The way he's out here acting like he's single when he's not. I don't know how you put up with it, but I guarantee I wouldn't be able to."

"Oh, well, I kind of knew what I was getting myself into when I got with him."

"That doesn't mean he has to treat you the way he does. I don't know how you put up with that, because I would have been gone upside his head," Draya chimed in while putting another blunt to her mouth and lighting it.

The whole time I was thinking, *y'all don't know the half of it.* I kept it to myself because I didn't want any-body to judge me for staying with him. My sister didn't know what I went through. Shit, I didn't even open up to my mother and father about it. They would all be pissed if they found out the shit I really went through in that house.

My phone dinged, making me pick it up and look at it.

Jace: I'm going to be at the club tonight just to drag yo' ass out. You got me fucked up if you think you just about to be in the fucking club.

I had to get myself together before responding because I didn't want to say anything that would make him go crazy and pop up at my sister's house.

Me: Jace, you act like I go out all the time. You're the one who's all the way in the club, and it's been years since I went out. Shit, you won't even let me go out with you.

Those three dots popping up let me know that he was responding, and I was scared of what he might say.

Jace: I wouldn't give a fuck.

Setting my phone down, I decided not to respond.

"Jace must be texting you," Draya said, leaning forward and grabbing my ringing phone. Once she had it in her hand, I knew there was no stopping her from answering. And when she did, I could hear Jace yelling threats.

"Nah, you ain't gon' do shit to my sister, nigga. You got her fucked up. You can come to that club and act a fool if you want to, but I can guarantee that you won't be walking away!" she snapped at him.

Getting up, I tried to grab the phone from her, and she looked at me like I was crazy. "Don't go back and forth with him. That's what he wants," I tried to convince her so that she wouldn't argue with him. She was only making the situation worse. I knew when I got home he was gonna make me hurt.

"Is he putting his hands on you or something? I don't like how scared you are right now."

"No, he's not, but I know he's gonna come here," I said, obviously scared. I knew the shit was written all over my face.

"And he won't leave this bitch alive. I love my niece, but I can tell you that if he comes here with his shit, I will leave Montana fatherless."

I knew she was serious, and that was why I loved my sister. She would never let a man do me any kind of way if she could stop it. This here Jace, though, was somebody she couldn't stop. That man would do whatever he could to get to me, and he let it be known that he wouldn't care who he had to go through. If he couldn't get to me, then he would make me pay by going after those I loved. That was the shit I didn't want, so it was another reason for me to stay. I knew for a fact that his ass didn't have it all.

For the rest of the evening, we got loaded and talked until it was time to go. Standing from the sofa, I went upstairs to a guest bedroom and went straight into the restroom so that I could take a quick shower. I was in and out in ten minutes. Putting my short, ruffled blue off-the-shoulder dress on, I sat down and put on some matching heels, then looked in the mirror. Seeing that the slight bruise from that black eye he had given me was still visible, I put some makeup on, then added some nude lip gloss and walked right back out of the room. On the way downstairs, I stopped at my sister's bedroom and walked inside.

"Bitch, you don't know how to knock when you come in somebody's room?" she asked, sitting on the bed with no clothes on.

"Don't act like you have nothing I haven't seen before."

Rolling her eyes, she got off the bed and started to get dressed. By the time she was finished, she had on a black miniskirt and a short red blouse, and she'd donned some strapped heels that had fur on the end of them. We both got in front of her full-length mirror. We stared at each other with smiles on our faces, knowing we were some bad bitches.

"You bitches looking cute," Dreux said, stepping into the room, dressed in some ripped skinny jeans, a shirt that stopped just underneath her breasts, and some knee-high boots.

"I need a brush."

"Here," Draya said, handing me hers.

I brushed my hair before parting it in the middle. I was now ready to go have me some fun. I was a little worried about the shit that Jace had said, but I knew for a fact that if he tried to drag me out of that club, my sister would have my back. She wouldn't let it go down like that.

"Let's go."

We all walked out of the bedroom, then headed downstairs and out the front door. I hopped right in the front seat, and Dreux got in the back. Putting a pre-rolled blunt to my full lips, I lit it and took a long pull from it before holding the smoke in. I wanted to be lit. That way I didn't have to worry about Jace being there. Maybe Dreux was right and the nigga was insecure. I didn't know why because there wasn't another nigga I wanted to be with. Shit, I didn't even know if I wanted to stay with his ass.

"I pray to God that Jace don't be there acting a fool."

"He can try that shit if he wants to, but I can guarantee you he's gonna see another side of me. One that he hasn't seen in a long-ass time. He knows how I give it up," Draya chimed.

"And if he does act a fool, you need to be doing the same thing. Why the fuck he trying to check you, and he's in the club as well?" Dreux said, making me nod my head.

"I hate acting up in public. It always gives the woman a fucked-up reputation. Y'all know I'm not the confrontational kind."

"And that's why bitches always coming to you with shit about that nigga, because you don't do anything about it. He would have me fucked all the way up, and that's on everything I love."

I knew they were telling me the truth, but it didn't stop the way I felt. I didn't know why, but I felt like shit was about to go down tonight, and I didn't even want to be around when it did. I was slowly regretting going out tonight.

Chapter Three

Dreux

Be Careful

I wasn't the type to ever let a nigga do me any kind of way. I always made sure I let them know from jump that I was not the one to be played with. I may have been pretty on the outside and sweet and quiet on the inside, but one thing I would not tolerate was a nigga doing me the way my friend was sitting up here letting her baby daddy do her. Jace would have some issues on his hands if I were her.

As soon as we walked into the club, all eyes fell on us, and it felt good. I knew I looked good, and that was something nobody could ever take from me. I was a mixed breed, my momma black and my father white. I grew up getting bullied most of my life because people called me a half-and-half pit bull. That was until I got cool with Draya and Junie, the craziest bitches in Houston. They didn't take no shit, and they taught me not to as well. Now I was confused as to why Junie was letting Jace do her any kind of way and she wasn't doing anything about it. That was the exact reason I didn't have a man now. I just was not that bitch.

"This ho is crazy lit," Draya whispered in my ear while her hand was on the small of my back. We were trying to stick together until we reached our section, but with how rowdy the dance floor was, I didn't think we were going to be able to.

"I swear, I'm about to smack a bitch if one more bumps into me," I said, and we both laughed, knowing I was telling the truth. I could understand motherfuckers having fun and shit, but the least they could do was make sure they were dancing to where they didn't touch or bump into anyone else.

When we finally made it to our section, I plopped down on the sofa, immediately grabbed the bottle that was waiting for us, and popped it. I needed this.

"Shots for everybody!" I yelled, pouring us each a shot.

"Bitch, you stay trying to get a nigga drunk." Junie giggled, taking the cup.

Putting mine in the air, I toasted, "I know that this has been a busy year for all of us, but we're back. We have to keep having nights like this because I miss you hoes."

We all downed our shots. Clearing my throat, I coughed a little bit because of the burning sensation as it went down my throat. I looked out to the dance floor. Seeing Jace and Korey in a section with women dancing in front of them made me shake my head. I touched both Draya and Junie while throwing a nod in their direction. You could tell that Jace's mind was elsewhere. He was probably looking for Junie.

"I know this nigga not in the club when he's supposed to have his son," Draya said. In a split second, she was out of the section exit and walking up to Korey.

I followed closely behind her, but Junie stayed put. Stepping inside of their section, all I could hear was Draya going off on Korey. He was sitting there, nodding his head and licking his lips while she talked.

"Where's your girl?" Jace asked.

"Minding her business, something you don't want her to do. All you want is for her to sit in the house with Montana. Yeah, which reminds me, what was all that shit you were talking on that phone about what you were gonna do to my sister?"

"I was heated. I'm not gonna put my hands on her, but the least she could have done was let me know that she was going out."

"She doesn't have to let you know shit. Just like you're grown, so is she!" I snapped. This nigga had the game all the way fucked up. And if Junie didn't want to come in here and face this nigga, then you can best believe both Draya and I would.

"Man, this doesn't have nothing to do with neither one of y'all. That's why y'all don't have men. Y'all can't listen," he had the nerve to say. I wanted to knock his two front teeth right out of his mouth.

"You're an asshole, you know that?" I asked, and he smiled.

"I think I've heard that once or twice."

Rolling my eyes to the top of my head, I grabbed Draya by the arm, and we both walked out of the section and headed back to ours. Making my way through the dance floor, I accidentally bumped into this guy, and he turned around.

"You good, ma?"

"I'm fine, thanks."

"No problem. Can I get your name?"

"Dreux."

"I'm Deion."

"Nice to meet you, Deion. I'd better go."

He moved to the side, and I made my way through the crowd, back to the section. Sitting down, I stared at him. He raised his glass and threw me a nod while flashing his perfect smile. Pouring me another shot, I downed it and took the blunt that Junie was handing to me.

"What did Jace say?"

"Nothing. He was looking for you, which tells me that he didn't see you walk in here."

"But he saw y'all come back up here, because here he comes," she said, making me look in the direction of the section door. Lo and behold, this nigga and Korey were both walking in with the nigga Deion.

I did nothing but shake my head because I knew some shit was about to pop off. That was just the kind of niggas Korey and Jace were. Deion must've felt it as well, because he came and sat next to me.

"Damn, I didn't know you knew my niggas," he said.

"That's because you don't know me. And why you sitting all up on me? Back up." I grimaced with a frown on my face, making him chuckle.

"I can't sit close to you? Don't act like you don't feel the attraction."

"I don't. I just met yo' ass."

"So? We can still get to know one another," he urged, putting his arm around my shoulder and looking me dead in the eyes.

I couldn't even sit here and front. This nigga was fine as hell to me. His chocolate skin, broad shoulders, and muscles that bulged through the white turtleneck sweater he had on were everything to me.

"Deion, get your hands off me," I joked, moving out of his grasp. "I know your kind all too well. The last thing I need is for you to be all up on me when all you probably want is a fuck."

"Don't act like you know me, because you don't. I'm nothing like the niggas you used to, and I can promise you that."

"I call bullshit," I joked, and we both laughed.

"A'ight, you may be on to something, but I haven't mentioned fucking you once. Nor has the thought of bending you over and giving you long strokes crossed my mind."

I could tell this nigga was lying, but I decided to play along with him. He didn't know what he was getting himself into. If he was that kind who would fuck a bitch and not call, then he would be sick. I knew for a fact that he would want to call me once I was done with him.

"I know niggas. You're not the first to spit that shit, and I'm sure you won't be the last."

"You think you know me?"

"Nah, I know I do. You see, it's niggas like the ones you hang with that lets me know everything I need to know about a man. They're cheaters, liars, and they can't commit for nothing in the world."

"So you're pushing what your girls are going through off on me instead of giving a nigga a chance to get to know you?"

I couldn't help but look in his eyes to see if he was telling me the truth or playing with me. I didn't have time for that. I was a businesswoman, and the last thing I needed was a distraction from what I had going on in my life. So if he wasn't trying to be serious, then we had nothing to talk about.

"Do you have a girlfriend? Wife? Baby momma? Fiancée?"

"Nah, nope, hell nah, and shit no," he answered, making me laugh even more. His ass was silly.

"All you had to say was no to all."

"I know, but I wanted you to know that I wasn't bullshitting. Do you have a husband? Boyfriend? Baby daddy? Fiancé?"

"I do have a baby daddy, but he's not worried about me."

"How old is your son or daughter?"

"My daughter is eight."

"Okay, I see you. You say your baby daddy not worried about you, but I'm sure as soon as he catches wind of you fucking with me, he will be."

"What makes you think that?"

"Because I'm that nigga."

Rolling my eyes to the top of my head, I couldn't stop thinking about how fine this nigga was. He wasn't the normal type I would go for, but shit, it wouldn't hurt to try something new. Maybe I would have a different outcome than I did with the other niggas I fucked with. I'm not gonna lie and make it seem like I never wanted what Draya and Junie both had, because I did. That was just before I knew they were so in love and getting cheated and beat on. Those were things I could never go through and be okay with. I was too petty for that shit, and I liked to fight.

My daughter's father, Max, and I hadn't been to-gether since before she was born. He was my one fuckup through the years, and I never wanted to go through or experience the shit I did with him. He was disrespectful, had no issues with telling me how it was, and had no regard for my feelings when I needed him to. He wanted me to let him raise my child alone, and when I wouldn't agree, he tried everything in his power to get her taken from me. When none of that worked, I made it my business to keep his ass on a long leash. I would never fuck with that nigga the way I used to. Yeah, he was older than me, much older, but he still acted like a little-ass boy. That was something I couldn't stand, and it was why the relationship never lasted.

"Let me get your number before I get out of here," he suggested, pulling his phone out and handing it to me.

Not wasting any time, I put my number in his phone and saved it under my name before giving it back to him.

"If you hit me after two, you won't get a response," I let him know. He nodded his head and backpedaled out of the section toward the exit.

I watched him stroll. The way people moved out of his way showed that he had respect in the streets. Draya and Junie were both engrossed in the conversation they were having. I got up and made my way to the dance floor. I was not about to be cooped up in this section just because these niggas were in here. I came out to have fun, and that was exactly what I was finna do, because I didn't have a nigga to answer to.

Chapter Four

Korey Sr.

Commitment

Maybe I'm tripping, maybe I'm afraid of commitment
Maybe I'm afraid of spending my whole life with that same one woman
And every day something different, I can't keep slayin' them bitching
And some people say I'm addicted, but if it ain't what it is
Anyway, it's been a minute, so we hang, and we kicked it

I didn't know what it was about Draya, but I couldn't get over her and the way things ended for us. She meant the world to me, but I'd learned to just let her go through her moods and not interrupt it. She had it in her head that I was cheating on her even when I told her I wasn't. She didn't want to believe me, so I didn't know what to do. She wanted me out of the house, and I told her I wasn't leaving. The day she decided to pack up herself and my son and move out of the house hurt me to the core because, like everybody else, I thought that she and I would have been able to work out our issues.

My commitment issues had been a lot for me to handle since the day I watched my father disrespect and hurt my mother in a way I never thought he would. Shit fucked me up in the head. And because I didn't know any better, I thought that was how niggas were supposed to treat women.

"But why are you in the club when my son was supposed to be with you? Where is he? Go get my fucking child and bring him back the fuck home!" Draya yelled, snapping me out of the thoughts I was having.

"You need to calm the fuck down. He's with my momma. She knew I had to handle some business tonight, so I spent the day with him, then dropped him back off. I'm going to get him in the morning."

"No, I'm going to get him in the morning. You can kiss his and my black ass."

"I would love to kiss yours." I smirked, making her slap me in the back of the head.

She hated when I made jokes about shit when she was visibly pissed off, but that was how I'd been dealing with shit. This woman had my heart to the point where I couldn't even think about wanting to be with another woman without thinking about her. She was the only one I wanted to be with. I wished that she would just give me another chance to prove to her that I wasn't cheating on her. I had the proof and everything, but the fact that she left without giving me the chance to explain the shit told me she didn't care.

"You're so stupid. Bring my son home when you get him, 'cause I don't have time for this shit."

"I'm not bringing him nowhere. When you gon' stop frontin' and have a conversation with me? I mean, a real adult conversation."

"Korey, I don't think we have anything to talk about. It's not that I'm not trying to talk to you. I would if I felt like you had something to say that would be worth listening to. But all you do is lie, and I don't have time for that shit."

"You don't know what I'm going to say because you're not in my mind, and you can't read my shit. You didn't want to listen to me when I told your ass I wasn't cheating. I don't know why you think I would jeopardize my engagement to you for another bitch."

"Because you did it in the past, whether we were engaged or not. I was feeling you more than you were feeling me, and I don't like feeling like that. I need to know that I'm the only woman you want to be with. It's crazy, because not one bitch didn't know we were together, and the number of those who didn't care is ridiculous, and you let them."

"Lies. I've never made it seem like I was single. I can admit that, before we got engaged, I did some fucked-up shit. That's because I didn't know how to love you, but now I'm ready. After I popped that question, it was all about you and nobody else."

"And I'm supposed to believe you why?"

"Because you know when I'm lying, and you know when I'm telling you the truth. Look into my eyes, ma. You know I'm being real."

She looked into my eyes, and I could tell she was really trying to believe me. When she shook her head, I knew then that it didn't matter how real I was with this woman. She would never believe shit a nigga had to say. That was why, this past year, I'd been okay with keeping my distance with her, but that shit hurt. Our son was my everything, but I won't be like other niggas and say he was the best thing to come from us, because he wasn't. It was up there, but the love I had for this woman was something that could never be matched. Draya Julia was it for me, and that was the way it would always be.

I wasn't one of them niggas who would tell her, "If I can't have you, no nigga will," though. I just was not that type. But I would fight and work hard to get her back.

"Korey, I wish I could believe you. You don't know how bad I want to, but my gut is telling me that you're not being real."

"I am, though. I could understand following your woman's intuition, but you need to understand that shit is wrong about me right now. I never cheated on you with another woman once I popped that question. You became the only woman I wanted."

"I wish y'all would go back to y'all own section, shit. This is supposed to be our night out, not our night with these thirsty-ass niggas!" her friend, Dreux, yelled over the music, making Draya laugh.

"Right, get out," she chimed in.

Getting up, I walked out and made my way out the door until I noticed Jace wasn't behind me. Turning around, I went to his side and put my hand on his shoulder.

"Let's go, bro. We're not wanted in this ho."

"Aw, your feelings hurt," Draya joked, and she and Dreux laughed.

I helped that nigga up, and we walked out of the section and went back to ours. I was pissed because I was really trying to take her home and give her some of this good loving. I missed that wet, tight pink pussy of hers. I missed eating and beating it.

"You good, bro?" I asked Jace when we made it back to our section and sat down.

"I'm good. I just hate when she doesn't listen to me. The whole point in her staying home is so that she could be with the baby, not send her off with her mom so that she could go out."

This nigga was tripping, and I didn't know why. "Bro, you can't think that girl is going to stay in the house just because you want her to. That's not how that shit works. She's grown. I can understand her needing some time away from the baby, especially when you're always out and never home with her and the baby."

"I can understand that shit, but when she doesn't ask me if it's okay for her to go out, it makes it hard for me to trust her. It's like she has something to hide."

I couldn't help but laugh at this nigga. He was on some other shit. "My nigga, you act like you her master or some shit. She's grown. She doesn't have to tell you anything, bro."

He didn't say anything to me, just looked at me because he knew I was telling him the truth. It didn't matter if he got mad. He needed to chill the fuck out when it came to that woman. I didn't know how niggas were that controlling. *I would never be that way with Draya.* Shit, even when we were together, I wouldn't do no shit like that. She would have cussed me the fuck out if I tried.

"I hear you, bro, but it is what it is."

"Yeah," I said, putting a pre-rolled blunt to my mouth and lighting it.

Taking a long drag from it, I held the smoke in for a while, then blew it out. I needed to calm my nerves for me to not become the nigga I used to be. I would have had another bitch in my lap if this were me five years ago, but it wasn't.

"Hey, is anybody sitting here?" a female voice asked, making me look up.

"Yeah," I lied.

"He's lying. Take a seat, ma."

As soon as she did, I got up and moved to the other side of the section. I didn't want Draya to see no bitch sitting next to me because then she would start some more shit. She could say that she didn't want to be with me all she wanted to or tried to act like it, but one thing I knew was that she did. She wanted me just as much as I wanted her ass. I'm not gonna make it seem like she couldn't get another nigga, because she could. But the fact that she wasn't even paying none of the niggas attention who tried to talk to her told me that she was still feeling me in some way. I just wanted her to give me that chance.

"Why you sitting all the way over there?" the girl asked.

"I'm good. I don't have any conversation for you."

"Why not? It's not like you have a girl sitting in here with you. Your boy already told me you don't have a woman."

"What's your name?" I inquired.

She wasn't ugly, but she wasn't Draya either. She had a fat ass from the looks of it, and her titties sat up in the tight dress she had on. Her long hair was flowing past her shoulders, and she had some of the most gorgeous eyes I had ever seen.

"Emeka."

"Nice to meet you. I'm Korey. As I've said before, I don't have any conversation for you." I smirked at her.

"Well, we can go somewhere and not talk."

This bitch wasn't taking no for an answer, but she wasn't about to have a choice.

"I'm good," I said. *Damn.* Now I was starting to see how females felt when a nigga they weren't interested in kept trying to holla at them.

"You ain't that cute anyway, nigga!" she snapped, making me chuckle.

"You tried that shit, ma."

"I did. I just had to see how you were gonna react. I'm not looking for nothing that would get either of us in trouble. I like having male friends. Less drama."

"I feel you, but I'm not the one. I don't have female friends because it always ends up in me fucking them." I kept it real with her. I didn't know what she was looking for, but I already told her that I wasn't looking for all that. She had it, and if Jace wanted to be friendly, then she could be his friend, but I was straight on it. There was only one woman I wanted to be friends with, and she was staring right back at me with a frown on her face.

Chapter Five

Jace

About Love

I had been trying my hardest to make shit work with my girl. I loved Junie's ass to death, and I do mean death. She didn't know how long I had been waiting to find a woman like her. I knew I had been on some other shit with putting my hands on her, but I couldn't help it. Sometimes I would be good, and then I wouldn't be. I had a disorder that she didn't know about, and I wasn't taking the medication for it. I just felt like I didn't need that shit, and it made me feel hella weird when I put that shit in my body. I didn't feel like myself. I knew that being bipolar was not something to play with, and I didn't. I told the doctors and my mother when I was younger that I didn't like how that shit made me feel. Back then, I didn't have a choice but to take it. Now that I was grown, I could make my own decisions.

When I left the club, I sat in my car behind Junie, waiting for her to drive off so that we could go back home. I knew that I was doing a lot, but I needed her to know that I was serious when I told her I didn't want her in the club. The last thing I needed was for anybody to think that they could take advantage or try to hit on her when I wasn't around, and that was how niggas did.

As soon as she started her car, she pulled away from the driveway. I was close behind her but not too close. I didn't want to hit her brand-new Range Rover I had copped her last week. Turning my music up, I smoked the rest of my blunt and jammed along with the music until we reached the golden gates of our home.

One thing nobody could say was that I didn't have my girl and baby living good. I always made sure they had nothing but the best. Sometimes it came at the cost of me having a breakdown and putting my hands on her. It wasn't that I wanted to do those types of things, and I was getting better at it. It was just that, sometimes, some of the shit she did got on my nerves, and I hated when she didn't listen to me.

Watching as she got out of her car, I did the same and went inside. She was already halfway up the stairs when I called out to her.

"Let me talk to you in the kitchen."

Turning, she followed me in there. I stood at one end of the counter, and she stood at the other end. This was something we did so that I wouldn't put my hands on her if she said anything out of pocket. It didn't work all the time, but it did mostly.

"Yes?"

"Didn't I tell you to tell me if you were going out? I don't need to be surprised by walking in the club and seeing you or sitting down and seeing you. You made it your business not to come to my and Korey's section because you knew I was gonna get on your ass."

"I did, but it's not like I was hiding either. I don't understand the big deal in me going out. You act like I go to the club all the time or like I'm always dropping Montana off at your mother's. I barely bring her there because you always want me home."

Looking at her, I bit my bottom lip. "It's not a big deal, but what I want is for you to understand that anything could have popped off. Anything could have happened to you. What if I hadn't been there?"

"But you were. I'm sorry for not telling you, but it's not a big deal. Korey isn't all over Draya like you are over me, and she has his child as well. I just want to go out and have fun."

I didn't say anything to her. I walked around and stood next to her. Grabbing her by the back of the neck, I pulled her close to me and whispered in her ear. "Do you know why I act the way I do? It's because I care for you," I said, squeezing her neck as hard as I could.

"You're hurting me, Jace." She grimaced. She was trying to pry my hands off her neck as I guided her upstairs and into our bedroom.

Pushing her back on the bed, I leaned down close to her. "Next time, listen to what the fuck I say."

I knew she was scared just by the look on her face. She didn't have to worry about me putting my hands on her again if she listened to me. I didn't have anything against her having fun. I just wanted her to let me know so that I wouldn't be looking stupid when I caught her in the club.

Going into the bathroom, I shut the door behind me and started the shower. I wanted her to get in with me so I could fuck, but I knew she wasn't gonna want to, so I just took my clothes off and stepped inside by myself. Closing the door behind me, I turned my back and closed my eyes when the sound of it sliding open got my attention. Turning around, I watched as Junie climbed in, and I licked my lips. The sight of her shaved pussy and perky nipples had my dick rising for the occasion. Pulling her by the waist close to me, I picked her up and put her back on the wall behind us. Kissing her lips, I slid my tongue into her mouth and moved it around.

"Mm," she moaned.

Backing away, I sat her down and got on my knees in front of her. Putting her leg over my shoulder, I licked the slit of her opening, then reached behind her and held her ass cheeks tightly in my hands. Latching on to her clit, I sucked on it with no mercy, making sure I savored her goodness.

"Ooh, shit."

She started rotating her hips, and each time she put her pussy on my lips, I sucked on it furiously.

"You like that?" I asked, and she nodded her head.

Turning her over, I watched as she jiggled her ass in my face, and I bit her cheeks. Standing up behind her, I grabbed my dick and slid it up and down her opening before sliding it deep inside of her.

"Oooooh, Jace!" she screamed.

The steam that was surrounding us from the shower did nothing but make me want to fuck her even harder. Slowly, I slid my dick in and out of her, making sure not to miss the rhythm she had going on. She threw her head back on my shoulder, and I reached up and grabbed her hair. Holding her tightly, I kept feeding her all my dick until I felt her legs drop.

"Fuck," I groaned in her ear before kissing the back of it and sucking on it. Leaning her forward just a little bit, I rammed my dick in and out of her at a fast pace. "I want you in the bed. I'm trying to make another baby," I let her know, and she nodded her head.

I pulled out, and we showered and got out. As soon as we got into the bedroom, she lay back in the bed and opened her legs as wide as they would go. Climbing up, I wasted no time going down and tasting her juices again. I loved this woman with everything in me, and I wanted her to know that. This didn't make up for me reacting the way I did to seeing her in the club, but it was what it was.

I wasn't going to apologize for that because she should have stayed her ass at home.

I looked up into her eyes, and she licked her lips, then bit down on the bottom one while her eyes rolled to the back of her head. I knew she was feeling good just by the way she couldn't keep up with the rhythm.

"Mm, baby. That feelsssssss so good," she moaned, putting her hand on the back of my head and rotating her hips. "I'm about to cum."

Not wanting that, I moved up and slid my dick back inside of her wetness. Rising up, I put both of her legs over my forearms and started to pound her.

"Damn, you feel so good."

She said nothing, so I kept stroking her as hard and as fast as I could. I wasn't trying to cum fast, but the feeling of her pussy tightening around my dick had me about to bust all inside of her. I told her I had been wanting another baby for the longest, and now it was time. She was about to give me my son whether she wanted to or not.

"You gon' have me a baby?" I asked.

"Yes," she moaned out while putting her nails deep into my back.

She was pulling me closer to her, and I was feeding her all ten inches of my dick. She didn't know what she was getting herself into, but since she said yes, I was sure enough about to nut deep inside of her. As I pounded her, the headboard started to hit the back of the wall. I focused on that sound, and before I knew it, I was shooting all my seeds deep inside of her.

Once we finished, I climbed out of her and went back into the restroom so that I could take another shower. I was in and out in ten minutes and went back into the bedroom with a towel around my waist. Seeing her sleeping the way she was, I smirked, then walked to her side and kissed her on the cheek before making my way out the door and down the stairs.

Going into the living room, I turned the TV to ESPN and started to watch it while rolling a blunt. I didn't know why, but I felt like weed was the cure to all my issues. Well, most of them anyway. The vibrating of my phone ringing made me grab it off the coffee table and look at it. When I saw that it was Victoria, a female I had been seeing on the side, I quickly picked up.

"Yeah, what I tell you about calling me this late? You know I'm home."

"I know, but I had something to tell you."

"Which is?"

"I'm expecting, and the baby is yours."

"I'm not about to play these games with you. Get rid of it," I replied. I didn't know why the fuck she thought shit was sweet, like I was just going to be okay with her telling me she was pregnant. *Nah, get rid of that shit. The sooner the better, because Junie is the only woman I want carrying my children.*

"You're such an asshole. I'm not getting rid of nothing. If you didn't want any kids, you should have worn a condom, nigga," she said and hung up in my face.

I hated when side bitches did this shit. They knew their place until they got pregnant, and then they suddenly wanted to make it seem like they were better than the next bitch.

Looking at the screen, I had to make sure she hung up before calling her back. She sent me to voicemail, so I made a mental note to go by her crib and check her tomorrow. Tonight I was about to get in the bed and hold my woman until I went to sleep.

Chapter Six

Deion

Leave You Alone

When I finally pulled up to my house, it was going on eight in the morning, and I had a lot on my mind. *Dreux.* She was so fucking bad. I had been thinking about her from the moment I left the club to pulling up here. Now I was about to have to go in here and deal with my crazy-ass ex, Breann. I hated that she had to stay with me until she got her place renovated, but it was what it was. *As long as she don't try to check me for shit I do, then we good.* Getting out of the car, I made my way to the front door. I put my key in and swiftly turned it before pushing the door open and stepping inside.

"So where were you?" she asked when I turned around.

"Minding my business, something you should try. When yo' house gon' be ready?"

"Soon enough."

"It's not fast enough. You need to call them and tell them to hurry the fuck up. I want you gone, man."

"You don't have to be rude about it. You must've met a little bitch, and that's why you came in this late."

Sighing, I looked over at her. "Again, none of your business," I nonchalantly said and went upstairs, straight to my bedroom. Shutting the door behind me, I made a mental note to go by her new house and make sure those workers were doing their job so this girl could get the fuck out of mine. It was a shame when you had to prepare yourself just to come in the house because you knew a bitch was gon' try you.

Looking at the time on my phone, I decided to shoot Dreux a message. I was gonna make it my business to be around her because she was my type, from her light skin to her short haircut, beautiful smile, wide hips, big ass, and perky titties. I would be lying if I said I didn't think about what it would feel like to have her legs wrapped around my waist last night. But I knew I was gonna have to wait until Breann was out of my fucking house before inviting anybody over here. I rarely let motherfuckers know where I laid my head because, like other big homies in the streets, I had some niggas who wanted to see me gone. Jealous niggas. However, Dreux was someone I thought I could let be in my crib. She didn't strike me as a sheisty bitch, and I wanted to get to know her.

Going into the private restroom, I started the shower and stripped out of my clothes. Stepping inside, I turned my back toward the water and closed my eyes, letting the memory of the reason Breann and I broke up play out like always.

"I hate when you're not home, babe," she whined.

We were sitting on the living room sofa cuddled up. I didn't know why she always brought this conversation up, because she knew I was always busy. I had to make money, and in order to do that, I couldn't be in the house up under her ass all day.

"Breann, you know how I feel about my money. I have to get it if I don't want another nigga to. You don't have an issue with spending the shit, but you have one with me making it? I'm not the 'sit in the house' kind of guy."

"But you have men who make sure everything is good, and then you get your cut every week. So why not just do that?"

"Because it's not who I am or who I desire to be."

I never wanted to take over this organization for my big brother after he died, but my father made it perfectly clear that I didn't have a choice. Either I took it over willingly or unwillingly. Either way, it was mine to take over. The organization had been in my family for years, even when my father was a teen and his father ran it. We all had to do our time. The only difference was I wasn't like my brother, father, or grandfather. I always had to make sure I was seen so motherfuckers wouldn't think I was somebody to play with. In the time that my father and brother took over, motherfuckers got it through their heads that they could do what they wanted to do because these niggas weren't doing what they were supposed to do. I made a promise that wouldn't be me.

"I'm just saying, it wouldn't hurt to spend a little more time at home with me than with ya niggas."

"And I'm just saying, if you want to keep living the good life the way that you do, then you have to get used to me working all the time. It's not that I like to, but it is what it is. I've come to the realization that it's not gonna change, and that's where it is."

"Whatever."

"If you don't want to be here, you do know I'm not holding you hostage, right? I will never make a bitch stay with me, especially when they don't want to."

"First of all, watch that 'bitch' word. And secondly, the only reason you feel that way is because I'm letting you know that you on some bullshit. You don't think I hear the stories in the streets about you and your boys always getting together and fucking random bitches?"

At that point, I was done with the conversation. She had me fucked up. I didn't have time for this childish shit. One thing I didn't do was cheat when I was in a relationship. I was faithful as long as the bitch was faithful to me. I'd never been the type to go off the hype, but if this was what she thought about me, then we didn't need to be together at all.

"You know what? I'm good. This ain't gon' work. As much as I like you, one thing I told you that pisses me off is a woman showing her disregard and putting cheating on me when I don't do that shit. You don't trust me, and I can't be with somebody like that. Show yourself out," I said, getting up and walking out of the living room.

That was the last time she and I were together, and I didn't regret breaking up with her at all. She tried to make it seem like she was only saying that because she had heard things, but nobody should be able to make you think nothing about your significant other. You should have a mind of your own to know that a nigga won't cheat on you, especially when they let you know that shit. Don't get me wrong, I knew there were a lot of dudes who would make it seem like they were not cheaters, then when you got in a relationship with them, it was something totally different. But that wasn't me. My mother and father taught me to be honest. They told me that it helped if you were honest, and maybe you wouldn't have to put up with shit like most of these niggas did. I'd always been honest and never had to deal with a bitch fucking me over.

After showering, I got out and walked right out of the restroom with nothing on. I liked to air-dry my dick and balls. Sitting on the edge of the bed, I grabbed my weed tray and rolled a blunt. I was about to put it to my mouth when the door started to creak open. Looking at it, I saw Breann sticking her head in.

"I'm heading . . ." she started but stopped when she saw my dick hard. Opening the door a little wider, she walked in and stood in front of me. "Can we fuck one last time before I walk out of that door?"

"Breann, go 'head, ma. You can't handle just fucking me and you know that. You would want to fuck and be back together. Then when I say that's not gonna happen, you're gonna be in your feelings and want to ruin whatever relationships I may have."

"That's not true. Stop acting like you know me."

"I do."

Breann and I were together for a year and a half before I dumped her. I knew everything there was to know about her. She was insecure, grimy, and petty as fuck. She even tried to fuck one of my homies after I broke up with her, but he told me he didn't do it. She wasn't the type who would just get dick and forget all about it. She was the type who would want to be with me when I hit her with this good dick. She loved me and she knew it. That was why I couldn't have sex with her. The last thing I wanted was for her to think that this was something when it wasn't. We were not getting back together.

"I can't do it, ma. I mean, I would because you're here, but that would be wrong for me to fuck you, knowing you still want to be with me."

Getting up, I went over to my dresser and grabbed some boxer briefs, sliding them on. I then put some sweats on and decided to go shirtless since it wasn't that cold outside or in here. Once I had my blunt rolled, I sat back on the bed and turned the TV on.

"So you really not gon' fuck me when I'm standing right here willingly?"

"No, I'm not. I don't need pussy that bad that I would put up with your deranged moments that you go through. I know you better than you know yourself, and I know that you wouldn't be okay with us just fucking," I assured her, then put the blunt in my mouth and lit it. Taking a long drag from it, I held the smoke in, then turned her way and blew it in her direction.

"Asshole."

"Nah, I'm being real, and you don't like that shit. You're used to niggas jumping through hoops to get pussy, and I'm not that nigga," I let her know.

She walked out of the bedroom and slammed the door behind her. I knew she was mad, and I didn't give a fuck. That was something she needed to get through her head. I wasn't a normal nigga. That was the same shit I told Dreux, but she would soon find out that I was nothing like the lames she was probably used to fucking with. I just didn't have it in me to be out here arguing with a female about nothing. If she wasn't trying to grow old and get this money with me, then we didn't have anything to talk about.

I had a feeling that Dreux wasn't used to a nigga who was all about his money and didn't have time for the bullshit. I had my head on straight, and when I say that, I mean both of them. I wasn't out here trying to just fuck around. I didn't have it in me to be trying to prove myself to a female who was just gonna do what she wanted to do and believe what she wanted at the end of the day. I needed somebody who was secure with herself and would understand and know where she stood with me at the end of the day. I wanted a woman I didn't have to keep assuring I was all hers because she should already know that. And last but not least, I did not want a woman who was all about drama. I wanted one who was about me because I was gonna be the same way.

Chapter Seven

Draya

Type of Way

I could sit here and lie by saying I didn't miss Korey or that seeing him in the club last night didn't make my lady parts yearn for him, but it did. I didn't know how, after all this time, he was able to make me feel the way I was feeling. Rolling over in the bed, I saw Dreux lying next to me, and I viciously shook her.

"Mm, just five more minutes, Ma," she groaned, making me laugh.

"Girl, I am not your momma. And how the hell did you end up in my bed?"

"I don't remember. We had fun last night." She giggled and opened her eyes.

Sitting up in bed, I looked around the room, trying to find out what the hell happened. From the looks of it, our clothes were on the floor. Raising the covers, I sighed in relief when I saw that we both had on our pajamas. We must've been super drunk, and instead of having sex, we got in our nightclothes and went to bed.

"You thought we fucked, huh?" she asked, sitting up next to me.

"I'm not gonna lie, I got scared seeing our clothes on the floor." I chuckled, and she joined in.

"No, we would have remembered that shit. Let me get up. I have to be at the office in"—she looked at the clock hanging above the bathroom door—"shit, thirty minutes ago."

She jumped out of the bed and hurriedly went into the restroom. Hearing the shower start, I got up and made my way to the kitchen so that I could take something for the banging sensation I had going on in my head. After taking the medication, I went back into my bedroom at the same time Dreux was going through my closet, looking for something to put on.

"So you just gon' wear my clothes?"

"I mean, we are the same size. I just need something to wear today. Then I will get it dry-cleaned and sent back over here."

"Whatever, girl, have a good day."

"Thank you," she said, getting dressed, then brushing her short hair to make it look good.

Once she was gone, I cleaned my room and put our clothes in the hamper before going downstairs and fixing something to eat for breakfast. Sitting at the table with a grilled chicken salad, I poured some ranch dressing on it. I was about to eat when my phone started to ring. Looking at it, I saw that it was Korey's number.

"I really need to save his number," I said to no one in particular before answering. "Hello?"

"What you doing?"

"Nothing. How is my son?"

"He's good. I was wondering if you wanted to come to the park with us today. I just want to get him out of the house and spend some time with him."

"Uh, and you want me to come with you?"

"Yeah. I mean, that will give us some time to spend together so that we can talk a little bit more. I feel like the more we talk, the more we might come to understand one another, and maybe you can forgive me for the things I didn't do."

I couldn't help but let out a frustrated sigh. "I'm sick of talking about that. It's not like we're going to get anywhere with it. I forgave you a long time ago. Right now, I just want to move forward and be friends for the sake of our child."

"So you don't miss me?"

"Korey, why do you do this to me? I've spent a year trying to suppress my feelings for you, and it hasn't helped. Each time I think about you, they come back. I don't want either of us to think we have to be together in order for us to take care of our child and make sure he's good. We don't need each other for that, Korey. You know you don't want to be settled down, and I don't want to make a man do what he don't want to do."

"I do want to settle down, with you and nobody else. I don't know how many times I have to tell you that you mean the world to me. You're it for me. I know that in the past I fucked up and made you feel like I didn't appreciate you, and I'm sorry for that. I've learned my lesson. And from all the talks I've had with my mother, she has taught me that I need to stop depending on you to always be here for me and actually treat you like you're my equal, because you are."

Everything he was saying sounded good, but how realistic was it for him to deliver the shit he was saying? He could easily say it, then turn around and make it seem like I was tripping.

"I don't know, Korey. However, I will come to the park with you and my son."

"Bet," he said, and we hung up.

Finishing my food, I made sure I washed my plate. I went into the bedroom and straight to my private restroom. Starting the shower, I stripped out of my clothes and got inside. Leaning my head back, I decided to wash it, then put some conditioner in it before showering and stepping right back out. I had plans on letting this conditioner sit for a while because I needed it to. Rolling a blunt, I got dressed in a sundress, grabbed some brown sandals out of the closet, and set them on the floor in front of my bed.

Going into the restroom, I grabbed the showerhead, which stretched, and I leaned my head down. Washing the conditioner out of my hair, I brushed it up into a bun on top of my head, then put some hoop earrings on and a matching necklace. Once I was dressed, I put my sandals on and made my way downstairs. Grabbing my car keys, I grabbed my wallet and walked out of the house, then got into my car.

The entire drive to the park was long. I had my music on blast and was enjoying the sun that was blazing down on me. I had enough time to think about what I wanted. As much as I would love to hold Korey down for the rest of my life, I needed his actions to speak louder than his words. I needed him to know that I wasn't for none of that bullshit that I put up with a long time ago. I wanted him to know that if he didn't appreciate me, then we wouldn't be together. I was willing to give him another try, but not until he showed me that I could take him seriously this time around.

Pulling my car into the parking lot, I looked out to see Korey playing with KJ on the slide, and I couldn't help but smile. Seeing my baby happy gave me all the courage to get out of the car and walk over to them.

"Hey, Momma's baby," I said. KJ got out of his father's grasp and walked over to me. Leaning down, I picked him up and held him in my arms while kissing his little cheek, causing him to laugh and twist and turn in my arms.

"What's up, baby momma?" Korey asked.

"Don't call me that. You know how I feel about that term. I'm not just your baby momma."

"I know you're not, but I knew that would get the ice to break. You always acting like you don't have time to have a conversation with me, and the last thing I need is for you to be around here acting like you don't want to talk to me."

"Korey, I don't have nothing against you. That's something you have to realize. I know why you did what you did, but do you?"

"I didn't do anything. I don't know how many times I have to tell you I didn't cheat on you, girl. I was too scared to lose you and my son again, and I don't want to go through that shit again. I want to make sure that you and he are good forever if you would let me. I mean, I know that we haven't always been good, but you know that I've never tried to embarrass or humiliate you on purpose."

"But you did. You don't know how it feels to have to get messages or private phone calls from women who are not supposed to have your number and tell you that they're sleeping with your fiancé."

"What I want you to understand is that I didn't cheat on you after I proposed. Now, I know that you don't have a reason to believe me, but I'm not lying to you," he tried to assure me. I knew that he was telling me the truth, but my heart didn't want to believe it.

"I don't know, Korey. I want to believe you, I really do, but I'm scared that you might hurt me again, and I don't think I could handle that. I mean, look at the things my sister is going through with Jace. That man isn't good for her, and I wish that she would realize that before it's too late."

"What you mean? He loves her."

"Yeah. If love means controlling, then I don't want it," I said, and he looked at me with his head cocked to the side.

He could act like he didn't know what I was talking about all he wanted, but he did. Jace wasn't good for my sister. And now that I had this situation with me and Korey almost together, I was going to focus on figuring out why my sister was so scared to leave Jace. I didn't want to believe that he was putting his hands on her, but if he was, then I would have to hurt that nigga.

"You don't need to worry about your sister. She's grown."

"I hear what you saying, but I don't comprehend. You know how I am about my sister, and that's never going to change. Now, what are we doing?"

"I want to be with you if you would give me that chance. I don't want to have to be out here lonely, because you're the only one I want to be with. For the last year, I've been thinking about what I would do differently if I got you back in my life, and I plan on making sure I do everything differently this time. You don't have to worry about anything because it's all about you and our son."

"Actions speak louder than words, boo."

"Well, can I at least get a kiss for good luck?"

I had to think about it for a second before leaning in and kissing him on the lips. As soon as they touched, I felt that same spark I felt the first time we kissed.

"Mm," I moaned, holding on to his neck and sliding my tongue into his mouth.

"A'ight, you'd better chill," he said, moving back.

Looking into his eyes, I smirked and got up with KJ. We went on the slide and played for a little while before he and his father got into his car and I got into mine, and we headed back to my place. I didn't know what he thought was about to go down, but I knew for a fact what I wanted to go down, and that was my pussy in his mouth.

Chapter Eight

Korey Sr.

Blessing

When we made it back to Draya's, I had so much on my mind, but how she was all up on me made it hard for me to have a conversation with her. The feeling of her full lips on mine, making their way down to my chest, had me in a trance. This was the shit I missed so much.

"Bae, do you think it's a good idea for us to take it there already?" I asked.

"I mean, it's been a while for me. How about you?"

"Me too, but do you want to go into this new relationship with us having sex already? I don't want you to think that's the only reason we got back together. I also want to make sure that's not the only reason you're fucking with me. Because you don't want your body count to go up."

"Fuck you, Korey!" she snapped, sitting up in the bed.

KJ was lying in his room for a nap, and I was in the bedroom with her. I didn't try to ruin the mood, but I wanted to make sure she knew what she was getting herself into.

"I'm sorry. I'm just not trying to take it there with you only for you to hurt me in the end. I don't have time for that shit. I want you to make sure you're ready for this shit."

"I am ready. Why do you think we're here? If I didn't want to give you another chance, or if you think it's because I don't want to get my body count up, it's not that. I just really want you to be with me but not play with me in the end. The way you feel about me playing you is the same way I feel about you. I don't want to be hurt in the end either. We have to make sure we take care of one another. We have to make sure we don't play with one another's feelings because, like I told you, I don't think I can handle you hurting me again."

"I know you can't, and you won't have to worry about that happening again."

Pulling me closer to her, she kissed my lips and climbed on top of me. Straddling my lap, she laid her head on my chest, and I just held her around the waist while my head rested in the crook of her neck.

"Do you think we got this?"

"I do, honestly. Neither of us could see the other without each other, so I believe we can make this shit work for the better. Plus, our son deserves to have us both in the same house."

"Same house? Oh, I don't think we're ready to move back in with one another. I miss you so much, but I don't want us to rush into getting back together because that's how people end up hurt in the end. We couldn't really handle being around one another all the time, and that's probably why you got on my nerves a lot. Like, I literally couldn't stand being around you, and the last thing I want is for me to feel that way again."

"Well, tell me how you feel," I said with a chuckle.

"I don't mean it like that. I just mean I don't want us to get on each other's nerves to the point where we don't want to be around one another at all."

"I feel you. It's cool for you to feel that way. Also, when we do move back in together, I want us to get a new place.

I don't want to move in here with you, and I know you don't want to move back into the old house with me. I just want us to get a neutral place. I'm working and making sure I handle my money aspect of the business so that I can focus on the relationship."

She nodded her head. "I can understand that, and I know that you will always make sure your money is good above all. I'm gonna be doing the same, but you also have to remember you have a child. Make sure you're worried about him as well."

"I know that. I'll never put nothing above him. My son means the world to me, so it's a must that I make sure he's good as well as you. I'm happy that you're willing to give me another chance, and you won't have to worry about me doing anything to fuck this shit up."

"Uh-huh. Also, I want you to know that can't nobody fuck this up but me and you. So, if you ever feel like you can't be faithful, I would rather you break up with me because I don't have time for the bullshit. I know you're probably tired of me saying the same thing, but I have to just let you know I'm not playing with you."

Looking into her eyes, I grabbed her by the back of the neck and pulled her close to me. Kissing her on the lips, I slid my tongue into her mouth while she gyrated her pussy on my hips, causing my dick to get hard. I was adamant about not fucking her right now. I had to make sure I had my head on right so that when I did get up, I could go handle my business.

"Do you have to go?"

"Yeah, I do."

"Okay." She frowned.

I kissed her lips once again before sliding her off my lap and standing from the bed. After putting my shoes back on, I strolled out of the bedroom, downstairs, and out the door.

***

When I pulled up to my office building, I parked, then got out of the car. Making my way inside, I went straight up to my office and sat behind the desk to take a look at the books for the string of clubs I had throughout Houston. I wanted to make sure everything was on the up-and-up.

"Boss, we have a problem," Laila, one of my workers, said.

I motioned for her to come into the room, and she did and shut the door behind her, not saying anything. I waited for her to speak, but she didn't.

"So what's the issue?"

"Some of the women are fighting and making it hard for the newbies to make money."

"A little competition never hurt nobody."

"But it did. Kacey was taken to the emergency room from being hit with a bottle. She was getting the best of Minnie, who couldn't stand for that, so she hit her," she told me, making me shake my head.

This was the shit I didn't stand for. Like I said, a little competition never hurt anybody. But to hear that one of the workers got hit with a bottle in the head had me fucked up. I knew that I was going to have to go down to Lady Rouge to make sure these females knew that money was to be made, not lost.

"Is she talking about suing the company?" That was the first thing on my mind because one thing I didn't want to be was in the courtrooms behind this shit.

"Not yet, but if you don't get up to that hospital and talk to her before the cops come, she might. I don't want you to be in court, but that shit was gruesome. And you could tell Minnie meant harm when she hit her with that bottle."

"I want you to round up all the girls for a meeting."

"Gotcha, boss," she said and let herself out of the office. As soon as the door shut, I threw my head back on the headrest of the chair and closed my eyes. Just thinking about having to make an appearance at the club for the first time in a long time had my mind racing. I barely went there because I liked to have Laila run things without having to worry about it. Now I saw I was going to have to go up there at least twice a month to make sure shit was running smoothly.

Getting up from the chair, I put all the books in a drawer on the desk and locked it before exiting the room and shutting then locking the door. Making my way down the three stairs that led to the office, I walked right back out of the building, got into my Aston Martin, and pulled out of the parking lot. The entire drive to the hospital had me on edge. I didn't want to see nobody laid up in there, but I had no choice. I had to let Kacey know that this shit would be handled. This was a business, and that was the way I ran things. I would never let anybody jeopardize my money. I didn't care how much they brought me. When you put somebody in harm's way, shit was bound to get ugly.

Pulling into the parking lot at the hospital, I got out and strolled inside. Everybody in that bitch stopped and looked at me. My demeanor made everybody respect me, and the scowl on my face let everybody in this bitch know I wasn't for no bullshit.

"I need to see Kacey Carmichael."

"Only family can visit her."

"I am family, her brother."

"Oh, okay. Well, here you go. She's in room 256," the nurse told me, handing me the badge.

Sticking it to my blazer, I walked through the double doors and paced myself with each step I took, making sure I paid attention to the numbers on the doors. When

I reached her room, I took a deep breath before pushing the door open and stepping inside.

"Korey? What are you doing up here?" Wynter asked while caressing Kacey's hand.

"I came to see my worker. What are you doing up here?"

"I had to make sure she was okay. The way Minnie hit her with that bottle had all of us worried. None of us thought things were going to get out of hand like that."

"But they did, and now I have to talk to her in private. So if you don't mind . . ." I said.

She got up and walked out of the room without another word.

"You didn't have to come up here. It's just a minor concussion. I'll be fine."

"I know you will be. You're a fighter, but I had to make sure for myself. How are you feeling?"

"Woozy, but I think it's because of the pain medication they gave me."

"Yeah, that'll do that to you. You don't have to worry about anything. I'll handle the bill and everything. As far as Minnie, what would you like me to do about her?"

"What do you mean? I don't have no say-so in that part of your business."

"Usually no worker would, but since she hit you with that bottle, I would like to know what you think I should do about it. Suspend her? Fire her? It's up to you, ma."

"If this is about me suing the club, I would never do that. I knew what I was getting myself into when I first started working there."

"That doesn't mean you have to stand for shit to happen like a bottle being thrown at you."

"I would say suspend her only because I do know she has kids she needs to feed, and I would never want to take food from a child's mouth. Also, schedule her to work when I'm not working. I don't want to see her face."

"You don't have to worry about that part. She's about to feel my wrath. I'ma make sure she knows that she can't be around here putting her hands on people and think there are no consequences. When are they letting you out of here?"

"Tomorrow."

"Okay, well, I'll see you for the meeting I have set up if you want to come. If you just want to take a few days, then come back, that's fine with me as well."

"Yeah, I think that would be best. I need to be at my best if I want to make my coins." She smiled, making me chuckle and nod my head.

"That's all I need to hear. Get better, ma," I told her before turning and disappearing as fast as I had come.

Chapter Nine

Junie

I Remember

Jace and I hadn't said a word to one another since the day we had sex in the shower. I didn't know what it was about him, but I was starting to hate him with every fiber I had in my body. It didn't make any sense for me to hate somebody as much as I hated this man, but what could I do about it? My mother had been trying to get me to talk about the bruise I had under my eye, but I was so adamant about covering up for this man when I didn't have to. Not to my family. They should have known what was going on, but the threats my father spewed from his mouth the moment my mother asked was enough to make me keep my answer the same: I fell and hit my face. I had a feeling they knew I was lying, but neither said anything. They just nodded their heads and looked at one another.

"All I'm saying is if he is putting his hands on you, that's not a safe environment for you or my grandbaby. I want you back home before you can't come back."

"What you mean by that?" I asked.

"You don't watch *Crime Daily* and how many women put up with abuse then try to leave and end up missing? I don't want that to be you, sweetie."

"Oh, you don't have to worry about that. It won't be me. Jace is not putting his hands on me, I swear." I gave her a half-smile.

I knew for a fact she knew I was lying just by the look that she gave me, but she didn't say anything else, thank God.

"You know me and your mother raised you better than to be dealing with somebody if they're putting their hands on you. Now, you're saying he's not, and I'll take your word for it, but if you come back around with any more bruises, I'm going to have another conversation, and it won't be with you," my father said, walking into the living room with Montana next to him. She had a handful of cookies and a mouthful of them as well.

"I know, Daddy, and you know I wouldn't lie to y'all. Thank you again for keeping her," I told them before standing and picking her up.

I made my way to the front door, and my father kissed me on the cheek, and my mother hugged me.

"You always have a home here, you know that," she said, and I nodded my head. I knew why she was saying that, but I still wasn't ready to let them know what was going on in my home.

I was just happy that if he was going to put his hands on me, he would wait until Montana was sleeping or something before he took it there. One thing I couldn't deny was that Jace was a good father to our daughter, and he would never do anything to make himself look bad in front of her. She thought the world of him. That was an image he wanted to keep portraying, and I let him. I wouldn't even cry in front of my daughter because I was so scared that she would start to ask questions.

Montana was very smart for her age, and I knew when she started school, she was going to be the smartest in the class. She was only 3 and she already knew her ABCs and numbers, and she'd been learning how to read on *ABC Mouse.*

"Did you have fun with Momo and Papa?" I asked her, and she nodded her head.

"We went to Chuck E. Cheese."

"I bet y'all did," I laughed.

Chuck E. Cheese was like a kids' gambling spot. They would go there and spend all your money if you let them. She only went maybe once a month with me and her father, but my mother and father took her all the time just to get her out of the house. The entire ride back home was quiet since she went to sleep. She must've been tired with the way she was snoring and slobbering.

Pulling up to the house, I sat in the car for a while and contemplated just driving off with my sleeping baby and never coming back home. He wouldn't be able to do anything if he didn't know where we were, right? His car was sitting in the driveway, making me shake my head. But when he opened the front door and came out, it told me that I would never be able to drive off. Opening my car door, I reached over and grabbed my purse and her bag before getting all the way out and shutting my door. He pulled the back one open, picked her up, and held her close to his chest.

"Damn, my baby 'sleep," he said.

"Yeah, I think she was tired from all the fun she had with my parents."

"What did she do while she was there?"

"You know they took her behind to Chuck E. Cheese."

"Her spot." He chuckled, putting his hand around my waist and leading me into the house.

As soon as the door shut, he went upstairs, and I went into the kitchen to start dinner. I knew that she was gonna be keeping me up all night, so I was gonna make it my mission to go wake her up in a few minutes so that she would at least be tired tonight. Mommy did not feel like being up all night with her while Jace was getting good rest.

Once I had the food on, I went into the living room where Jace was and sat down.

"Here," he offered, handing me the blunt that was in his hand.

Putting it to my mouth, I took a long drag from it and held the smoke in before blowing it out and hitting it again. I handed it back to him, and he looked at me.

"I have to make a run, so you can have that," he said, leaning over and kissing me on the lips. "I swear I'm trying to do better by you and my child. I don't want to lose you, Junie."

Nodding my head, I said nothing because it was always the same thing, just a different day. He would act a fool, then come with that sob-ass apology like it was supposed to make me feel better about getting my ass beat. Nah, it didn't make me feel any better. It actually made me feel like he didn't care. *How do you put your hands on me, call me all kinds of bitches and hoes, then turn around and expect me to forgive you like it never happened?*

I was getting tired of having to deal with it day in and day out. I loved him with every breath in my body but hated him at the same time, if that was even possible. This Jace was not the man I fell in love with three years ago. He was actually something different, I just didn't know what. Watching as he walked out the door, I stood and went into the kitchen. Grabbing a glass, I poured some wine and went out on the back porch to smoke and drink. I needed this if I was gonna be able to sit in this house with him any longer.

You don't know how bad I wanted to jump at the opportunity of moving back home, but that was not where I wanted to be. I didn't want to be 25 years old and staying back with my parents all because of my poor choice in men. Jace wasn't the first bad choice I made, but at least they didn't put their hands on me. All they did was cheat and lie too much for my liking. I was a loyal girlfriend, and I would never do anyone the way I'd been done. It was just, for me, I would rather leave a nigga before I cheated on him, so I didn't understand why men did that to me. I didn't know if Jace was cheating on me, but I was sure that if he was, it would come out like it always did.

Taking the last swig of the wine, I set the cup down and finished the blunt, then went back inside. Deciding to go upstairs and check on Montana, I peeked through her bedroom door and saw that she was sleeping like she had a job. Shaking my head, I left her alone, then went into my and Jace's bedroom and took a shower. I needed to make sure I had myself together before she woke up. The only reason I wasn't gonna wake her up right now was that I wanted to enjoy my high and being tipsy.

When I got out, I went into the bedroom and quickly dressed in some black lace panties, a long-sleeved shirt, and some flannel pajama pants. As I walked out of the bedroom, the doorbell started to ring, causing me to rush out of the room and go downstairs. When I got there, I stood on my tiptoes and looked through the peephole. Seeing that it was one of the many men I had seen Jace with, I pulled back the door open and looked at him.

"What's up, ma? Is Jace here?" he asked, eyeing me up and down.

"No, he just left to make a run."

"Oh, a'ight. Can you tell him that Ace is looking for him?"

"I got you."

He smirked and leaned into me. "It's nice to finally meet you."

"You as well. I'm Junie."

"I know. I've seen you around but never said anything because I knew you was Jace's girl. You need to tell that nigga to keep his hands to himself. You're too beautiful to be walking around with scars like that one under your eye."

"He didn't do that."

"Whatever you say, but I know the truth of a black eye when I see one," he whispered and backed away from me.

Our eyes never left each other's until he got into his car and left the house. I didn't know him personally, but if he knew I was lying about the black eye, I wondered who else knew. Shit, I was happy I was able to cover it up before Draya, Dreux, and I went out. I knew if they had seen that, there wouldn't be no lying to them hoes. They would run with that and probably beat his ass.

Stepping back into the house, I shut and locked the door before going back into the kitchen and checking on my food. Fixing a small bowl, I hurriedly tasted the food before nodding my head and turning the fire down. I went back into the living room. The door opened at the same time, and Jace came in. His shirt was ripped, and he had a few scratches on his face and neck. He looked like he was in a fight with a cat or something.

"Oh, my God! Are you okay?" I asked, rushing to his aid.

"I'm good. It's nothing," he nonchalantly said, pushing past me and going up the stairs without another word.

Shaking my head, I didn't even bother to follow him. Instead, I sat on the couch and flipped through the channels, looking for something to watch.

Chapter Ten

Jace

Time for That

When I made it back to the house, I just knew Junie was going to be all over me about the scratches I had on my neck and face. That was the outcome of me going to talk to Victoria to reason with her about this abortion. She kept saying she wanted the baby and it was her first child, but she didn't understand that a baby was a lot of responsibility. On top of that, it wasn't like she just wanted to have the baby and take care of it herself. She wanted me to be in the child's life. And like I told her, that wasn't an issue, but I would want my child full-time, not part-time. I would take my baby away from her if she decided to have it, and that was when all hell broke loose. She hit me in the eye, scratched me up, and almost tried to strangle me with an extension cord. It took me really putting my hands on her for her to understand that I wasn't one to be played with. I let her get off a few licks because I knew she was hurt, but she took that shit too far.

After I got out of the shower, I threw on some boxers and basketball shorts. Walking out of the bedroom, I went downstairs and into the kitchen where Junie was fixing my plate. When she handed it to me, she wouldn't even look at my face, which told me that she knew something was wrong. I had to let her know something before she read too much into it.

"I got into a little scuffle with one of the workers. He scratched me like a bitch."

"I see. You might want to put something on that." She pointed to the big one I had on my neck and strolled out of the kitchen.

From the table, I could see her walking up the stairs and knew she was probably about to go wake up Montana so that she could eat and get ready for bed like the rest of us. It seemed like everything could easily start falling apart for me if I didn't nip this baby shit in the bud with Victoria's ass.

When she came back down, Montana was whining until she saw me, and then she reached for me. Right when I grabbed her, the waterworks stopped. She knew I didn't play that. Crying was for babies. And although she was only 3 years old, I didn't want her to think that crying was going to get her whatever she wanted. I wanted her to be tough.

"Stop all that crying, princess. Don't you want to eat some of this good food Mommy cooked?" I asked, and she nodded her head.

Junie shook her head and went to the stove. When she came back, she had Montana's plate and set it in front of us. Sitting her in her high chair, I placed her bowl in front of her and watched as she ate in silence while giving me two thumbs-up as if it were the best food ever. Junie then sat down, and I looked over at her.

"I think we should go on a family vacation soon. What do you think? I know that we don't spend enough time together, but it's time for that to change. I know that I haven't been the best man, but I'm working on changing that. I just need time."

"Okay, and I think a family vacation will be good for us."

"Also, I wanted to know what you felt about marrying me."

"Oh, I don't know."

"Be honest with me."

"You sure about that? Whenever I say what's on my mind, your hands make me regret that."

"I'm not going to put my hands on you, I promise."

"I just don't think we're ready for marriage, not until you learn to stop putting your hands on me. I love you so much, but sometimes I don't know if I can put up with it any longer."

"I know, and I'm sorry for that. You have no clue how sorry I am. I hate doing that to you, and I wish that I never did it in the first place, but I can't go back and change it even though I wish that I could."

She nodded her head, but I needed her to say what was on her mind. I wouldn't have asked her to be honest with me if I couldn't handle it. I had done some fucked-up shit, and she shouldn't even want to be with me, but here we were. I loved her more than anything in the world, but sometimes I just snapped, and I couldn't take it back. Once it was done, it was done in my eyes. And the only reason I was sorry was because she didn't deserve that shit. I knew I should have been taking my medication so that I could control it, but I didn't want that medication to control me. I wanted to be able to make my own decisions.

Once everybody was finished eating, I helped her clean up the kitchen before grabbing Montana out of her seat and following Junie up the stairs. When we got into her bedroom, I watched as Junie went into her bathroom to start the tub.

"Can you undress her for me?" she asked, and I started to do that. When her clothes were off, I sat her down and decided to let her mother take her Pull-Ups off.

Strolling out of the bedroom, I went into our bedroom and rolled a blunt before sitting on the edge of the bed and lighting it. I always had to smoke a blunt before going to bed, but a part of me wanted to fuck tonight. I really wanted Junie to give me my baby boy. When she finally came into the bedroom, she pulled the covers back and climbed in.

"Is she sleeping?"

"No, she's watching *Frozen*."

"Like always." I chuckled before lying back in bed, making sure I put my head in her lap like I used to when we first got together. I wanted to take things back to the way they used to be, but I didn't know if she was willing to do that with me. She wanted me to be different, and I did as well, but when I got angry, I couldn't control myself.

"Do you hate me?" I inquired, not even wanting the answer.

"No, I just want you to think before you act."

"I know you do, and I hate that I get so angry to the point where I put my hands on you. You don't know how much I wish that I could tell you why I'm the way I am, but I don't want sympathy from anybody. What I want is for you to know that I'm sorry and I will try."

"That's all I want. Also, if you could be a little less controlling, that would be amazing. I mean, I know that you want me in the house all the time, but sometimes I just want to go out and have fun with my sister and best friend. I don't want to be one of those women who stops messing with my family or friends because of who I'm with."

"I hear you, and I'm willing to chill when it comes to that. I know that you need some moments by yourself without Montana or me riding you. I'm just scared that you might want to leave me. Like you might find somebody else and decide that this is not for you anymore."

"Jace . . ." she started, but I handed her the blunt so that she wouldn't say what I knew she wanted to say. I wasn't stupid. Junie wanted to leave me, but I wasn't going to let that happen, not without a fight anyway. I deserved to be happy, and she made me happy, no matter the fights we had. I didn't want to be with anyone but her.

The day I was diagnosed with this bipolar disorder was the day my mother started treating me differently.

"Mrs. Mario, he's not sick. He's just bipolar, and you might have to give him a little more attention than others," I heard the doctor tell my mother.

"What do you mean? If he's not sick, then what is he? He's the only eleven-year-old I know who beat a girl unconscious and is now awaiting a court date that could get him locked up for years!" she shouted as if I weren't in the room listening to them talk about me.

"I know that this is hard, but what you need to have is faith in your son. You need to show him a love like no other, and you need to make sure he knows that he did nothing wrong. It wasn't him. It's like he has an alter ego that comes out to play. And by 'play,' I mean hurt people. You need to make sure he's happy at all times."

"Sir, with all due respect, don't tell me what I need to do. My son needs help, help that I can't afford, and I also can't afford for him to hurt anybody else. You're sitting up here saying to let him know that he didn't do anything wrong, but he did. I don't care if it was an alter ego or whatever the fuck you're saying. He still hurt somebody."

The doctor only nodded his head. "He's free to go. Here's a prescription for some medication that will help him out," he said, handing her the little piece of paper and sending us on our way.

I thought she was taking me home, but instead she took me to my father's and left me there. In her eyes, he was the only one fit to handle my outbursts and make sure I got the help I needed. If only she knew that wasn't the case. Yeah, he got me my medication, but he also liked to see me get mad. He was the reason I got into the game at 17 years old and became one of the ruthless young boys on his team. He sent me to do all his dirty work, and his exposing me to all that at such a young age had me believing I didn't need my medication anymore. He kept me on it but still had me doing things I knew were wrong.

Rising from Junie's lap, I climbed under the covers just as she handed me the blunt back. Once the blunt was finished, I put the roach in the ashtray that was sitting on the nightstand on my side of the bed and pulled her close to me. She laid her head on my chest, and I closed my eyes for a while, then reopened them when I felt her hand gliding up and down my hard dick.

"You trying to fuck?" I asked.

She sat up, then straddled my lap without a word. Looking into my eyes, she pulled her shirt off, showing me her perky breasts. I rose just enough to suck on them while she moved her hips in a circular motion, making my dick even harder. Knowing I was about to kill them guts, I raised her, watching as she pulled her shorts and panties off, and I did the same. I knew this was pushing it, having sex while Montana was up. However, at this point, I needed some of my lady, and the way she was licking her lips told me she wanted the same shit.

"I love you, Junie," I whispered in her ear.

"I love you too, Jace," she let me know.

And for the rest of the night, we made sweet love.

Chapter Eleven

Dreux

Where Did I Go Wrong?

Sitting at this table waiting for Max to arrive almost had me hyperventilating. I didn't know what he wanted to talk to me about, but one thing was for sure. I knew it couldn't be anything good. This man had been a pain in my ass since the day I gave birth to Savannah. We always argued, and he made it seem like I couldn't do nothing right when it came to my child. The last thing I wanted was to sit up here and argue with him about something that wasn't going to change. For the last few weeks, he had been bothering me to let her come stay with him until she started school, but I wasn't feeling it. I wanted my baby at home with me, not with him and his wife.

"Dreux," his deep voice said, making me look up. When I saw that he had his wife, Sheena, with him, I rolled my eyes. I thought that this was going to be a lunch between him and me only. Had I known he was bringing the help, I wouldn't have come.

"What is she doing here? When you said you wanted to talk to me, you didn't mention that she was gonna be with you."

"He don't have to tell you anything about me coming anywhere with him. That's the perks of being somebody's wife. Something you will never know about if you don't stop with the childish antics," she snapped, making me laugh.

"I don't have time for this. Just say what you came to say so I can shut it down and we can go about our day."

"My daughter wants to come live with me."

"She's not old enough to tell you what she wants, so miss me with that bullshit. My baby is very happy at home, so you can really go on with that. Are we finished here?"

"No. I'm sick of you treating me like I don't deserve to be a full-time father in my child's life. I'm tired of only getting her on the weekend, and you need to make something shake."

"Or what?"

"Or we're gonna end up in court."

"And nothing is going to happen. I still have the very text messages from the other day that show you threatening me. You don't have the upper hand. As a matter of fact, you don't have a hand at all. I'm sick of you trying to tell me what I'm going to do and what I'm not going to do, and I don't have time for it. I'm out," I said, standing up.

His grabbing my arm tightly stopped me.

"You're not going anywhere, and we're not finished. I love my child more than anything, and I used to feel the same way about you until you fucked me over. When I got locked up, you decided that you didn't want to be with me anymore, not the other way around, so you need to figure that shit out and leave it in the past. I'm just a man trying to be in his child's life, and instead of understanding and helping me out, you want to keep her away from me. Making me get her on the weekends only. That shit is not right."

"That's not the way it was before. You could have gotten her whenever you wanted to when you got out, but you tried to take my child away from me. On so many occasions, I gave you a pass and said, 'He's just trying to be a father.' But when you threaten me and try to take away a child I've been raising by myself for years, it becomes a different situation, Max. I don't have no ill feelings toward you, and I'm not trying to make parenting any harder on you than it already is, but my child is content with the way things are, and so am I."

Yeah, I had my baby at a young age, but it didn't mean I wasn't ready to be a parent. I put all my outside activities to the side if they didn't include her. I was all about my child. As hard as it was raising her alone, not once did I think about giving her away or letting my parents raise her. Everybody thought I wasn't going to be mother material, and I busted my ass to prove every last person wrong. I had one person to worry about besides myself, and that was my daughter, so Max and his wife could kiss my ass.

"I know that, and I'm not trying to do that again. I know that the courts would never give me custody of Savannah because you're a good mother, but you should also stop trying to keep her away from me."

"Me keeping her away from you would require energy, and I have none of that for you anymore. I just want you to be in her life the same way you want to be in it without all the extra drama, your wife included. This woman has been texting my phone daily saying little slick shit like y'all not bringing my baby back home to me, and that turns me into a bitch."

When I said that, he looked at her and shook his head. "We're not doing anything, and Savannah is not hers to worry about. This is between you and me because only we two were in the room when you got pregnant. I'm sorry about that. Maybe I should have left her ass at home."

"Don't do me like that. I was only saying what you wanted to say, but you were too scared. If you wanted to leave me at home, you should have!" Sheena spat, getting up from the table and walking out.

Instead of getting up and following her, he reached over the table and put his hand on mine. "I'm sorry. I just want to be there for my child, and I want us to be in a better space."

I didn't believe a word he was saying. He forgot that I used to be around him when he used that bullshit-ass line on other people, so it was not going to work here.

"Max, I know you're on bullshit, so tell me what you really want so we can both get out of here. I don't have time for this."

"You're always saying you don't have time for something, but you need to make time for me. We need to get back to the place we were once. Friends. I don't want anything from you other than to know that I would be able to get my child whenever I want to without having to argue with you."

"Max . . ." I was about to say something, but then I shut my mouth. It didn't matter what I told him. He was going to still be up here with the same shit. It was best for me to not say anything and leave it alone.

Getting up from the seat, I grabbed my clutch and headed for the door without another word. As I walked through the parking lot to my car, Sheena's door opened. She stepped out of the car and made her way over to me.

"I know what you're trying to do. You want Max back, but I'm here to tell you that I will fight for my husband."

I just looked at her before laughing. "Girl, don't nobody want Max but you. I don't have time for his lying and cheating ways. I've moved on, so you can stop thinking that. Girl, you crazy."

I laughed hysterically before climbing into my car and shutting the door on Sheena and the scowl she was wearing. Knowing I hit a nerve, I pulled away from her with a smile on my face. The last person I wanted was Max's ass. That man couldn't sniff my pussy if he were the last man on earth. And the fact that Sheena thought she somehow won a prize had me even more tickled.

Pulling my car into the driveway of my five-bedroom, three-and-a-half-bath home, I got out of the car and went inside. Savannah and her nanny were sitting on the floor coloring when I walked in.

"Hey, how was your day, baby girl?" I asked my daughter.

"Good. We watched movies, played outside, and colored," Savannah said with a smile on her face.

I could tell she loved her nanny, and I loved her as well. My little sister, Victoria, was a blessing like no other. She was here for me when I had no one else to watch my baby. She was even staying with us so I didn't have to worry about dropping Savannah off anywhere.

"Whew, now I can get ready for my date," my sister said, getting up and heading for the stairs with me right behind her.

"Who are you going on a date with?"

"This guy I been talking to for a while. I like him. He might be the one."

"I know you're on cloud nine, but you need to be careful, Tori. You never know what these niggas really be feeling on the inside. And I saw those bruises you had on your neck and stuff."

"That was nothing. We were playing, but I got his ass as well." Victoria smiled and kissed me on the cheek.

Watching as she went into her bedroom, I walked the little distance to mine and went inside. Sitting on the edge of the bed, I took my shoes off and lay back on the bed at the same time Savannah was walking in.

"Mommy?"

"Yes, baby?"

"Can we watch some movies together?" she inquired.

"We sure can. Let me take a shower and go put some food on. You can pick the movies and meet me in the living room," I told her before hugging her tightly and shaking her in my arms.

Chapter Twelve

Deion

Ask for More

After meeting and chopping it up with Dreux a few times, I felt like it was time to take her on an official date. But when she hit me and cancelled, I almost felt like she was avoiding me. Now I was sitting in the private room in Lady Rouge, and I wasn't even paying attention to the dancer taking her clothes off in front of me. I wanted so badly to tell her to just put them back on, but she was into it, so I just let her continue doing her. It was when she tried to sit in my lap that I almost had a heart attack.

"Ay, nah, that's not about to go down up in here. Just dance," I told her. She let out a frustrated sigh before plopping down on the seat next to me.

"You're not into it, so what's the point?"

"My bad. I just have a lot on my mind. It's not you."

"I've heard that so many times that it's not even funny," she joked, making me laugh. "Oh, snap! I got a laugh out of you." She smiled.

"You cool people. What's your name?"

"Wynter."

"Nice to meet you. I'm Deion. Can I ask what a woman as beautiful as you is doing working in the strip club?"

"Money, which I need lots of. I have a case looming over my head, and in order for me to get it dealt with, I have to make money to pay a lawyer, and those people are not cheap."

When she said that, I nodded my head. She wasn't lying, so it helped that she was talking openly right now. "Good thing I'm a lawyer. What's the case for?"

"Assault."

Backing up, I looked at her from her head to her feet. There was no way this small-ass woman was able to hurt somebody, not in my eyes anyway. "What kind of assault?"

"Wait, did you just say you was a lawyer?"

"I did. I graduated from law school five years ago, and I've been doing it ever since."

"I wouldn't have guessed."

"I don't look like a regular lawyer?" I asked. She shook her head, letting me know the obvious. That was something I always heard, but I only wore suits and loafers when I needed to be in court. Other than that, you would catch me in my Jordans, jeans, and a long-sleeved shirt or something to that effect. I never tried to make it seem like I was something I wasn't, but I went to school for this shit for a long time, so I wanted to make sure I put that shit to work. Plus, it helped that I was one of the only black men who didn't sell out to the white people. I wasn't in this business to put black men away, but to help them. I didn't care how much evidence the DA's office said they had. If they couldn't convince me that my client was guilty, then I made it hard for them to convince the jury, which was how all my cases went. There was not a case that I lost, and I planned on keeping it that way.

"Okay, well, I got into a fight with my ex-boyfriend. Somebody called the cops for them to take him to jail, but when they got there, two white female officers arrested me instead. I was abused all the way to the jailhouse, and then they wouldn't let me make any phone calls, which caused me to be locked up for three weeks. It was a horrible experience."

I wanted to talk more about this, so I swiftly reached into my pocket and pulled out my business card. This was nothing more than trying to help her out. I knew what it was like to have all this trouble and nobody to help you fix it.

"I'm here to help, not make this shit any harder on you. We can work out a payment plan, and I will handle this case for you. This is my card, so hit me when you're off so that we can meet up and talk about it," I told her before handing her the card and getting up. Setting a couple of stacks on the table in the room, I walked out and left her to get dressed.

Making my way to the other side of the club, I spotted Korey sitting in his office and quickly made my way up there to see when Wynter's day off was. I had to know when I should be expecting her phone call. I didn't like to wait, and if she knew better and wanted me to beat this case, then she needed to call me sooner rather than later. The faster we got to work, the faster I could get this shit squared away and she wouldn't have to worry about it.

"Ay, what's up?" I asked, stepping into the office without knocking.

"Shit, thinking about Draya. She's officially giving me another chance, and I don't want to fuck this shit up at all."

"You just have to know what you want and what she expects of you and do that. It's not that hard, so don't read too much into it. All I can say is if you don't want to settle down with her, then don't waste her time, bro. You know how I am—love your woman, don't hurt her. You did some fucked-up shit to Draya when you had her, and now you have to fight to win back her trust. Don't be out here fucking that shit up. You wanted your family back, and now you have it, so make sure you keep it, nigga. I need to know when one of your workers is off."

"Who? I thought you were feeling Dreux."

"I am. This is strictly business, bro."

"Uh-huh. What's her name?"

"Wynter."

"Ahhh, she's off tomorrow. I try to give them two days off a week, but she has to come in for a meeting in the morning so we can square away some business for the entire team to know that I'm not one to be fucked with."

"A'ight. Well, handle your business like the business-man you are. I'm gonna get out of here. I have so much going on."

"I feel you. Hopefully we can get together this Friday like we always do."

"I'll let you know," I said, dapping him up, then heading out of the office and the building. I needed to head home and get some rest before it got too late. I had a long day ahead of me at the office, and I had to make sure I was at my best. These people were trying everything to make me quit, so I had to go ten times harder.

Getting into my car, I started it up and backed out of the parking lot. The entire ride to the house, I turned the music down so that I could think for a while. It'd been a minute since I'd been able to do this, so I wanted to take advantage of it before I made it to the house and saw Breann. Pulling up to the house not long after, I got out and went inside. She was sitting on the sofa with her homegirl, which made me sigh.

"When are you leaving?"

"Soon. Don't worry about it. I know you're ready for me to go so that you can bring your new bitch over here," she said.

"First of all, I don't have a bitch. And secondly, if I did, it wouldn't be any of your business now, would it? I told you to worry about yourself and you getting out of my house. I shouldn't have to come home after the day I've had and see your friends sitting on my couch."

"Why is that such a big deal? You act like she's in here eating your food or like I don't buy food in this bitch. You need to chill the fuck out before you make me say something I'll regret."

"I'll see you later, girl. I'm going to get going."

When she got up, I headed back to the door and pulled it open for her to leave. Once she was on the other side of the door, she turned to say something, but I slammed the door in her face before she could.

"Why would you do that?" Breann asked.

"Because I can. I pay the bills in this bitch."

"I don't know what the fuck your problem is, but tell that bitch to give you some pussy so you can get your panties out of the wad they're in, nigga!" she snapped, getting up and heading for the stairs.

I was right behind her, but instead of arguing with her any further, I went into my bedroom and shut the door.

Lying back on the bed, I put my hands over my face and covered it before sitting back up. Going into the restroom, I started the shower and stripped out of my clothes. Stepping inside, I made sure I turned my back to the door and let the water fall down on me. That shit was feeling so good until I heard the door slide open. Before I could turn around to tell Breann to get her ass out of here, she had her arms wrapped around me and was stroking my dick up and down.

"Chill out, man. Get out."

As good as the shit was feeling, I knew it wouldn't be a good idea to fuck her, and that was not what I was finna do. All it was going to do was put me in an even more fucked-up position with her. She already felt like she was entitled to me and what I did, so fucking her would only make her feel like we were getting back together, and that wasn't happening.

"Just a little taste. I swear I won't tell anybody."

"Nah, nope, hell nah. I don't want to take it there with you because then you're going to feel like we're getting back together, and that's not happening. I want you to get out of my shower and my restroom," I said, pushing her hands off my dick.

"You're such an asshole!" she snapped.

I heard the shower door slam, and I shook my head. I didn't know why she was trying to push herself on me when I had made it perfectly clear that I didn't want to be with her anymore, nor would I ever fuck her. When she had me, she didn't want to do right by me. Now she thought that was finna change, and it wasn't.

After I showered, I got out and wrapped a towel around my waist before going into my bedroom. Seeing that she left the door wide open, I closed it and commenced getting dressed. Once I was finished, I pulled my phone off the nightstand and shot Dreux a text telling her that I hoped she'd let me take her and her daughter to lunch tomorrow. Surprisingly, she hit me back telling me that was a bet.

Nodding my head, I smiled, then rolled a blunt and smoked before getting into bed and closing my eyes. Dreux didn't understand that I was trying to be in her presence. And the fact that she tried to put off on me what Korey and Jace were doing to their women made me feel a way. I wanted her to see that I was nothing like them niggas, although they were both my homeboys. I knew for a fact that them niggas were crazy and didn't appreciate a good woman.

Chapter Thirteen

Draya

Can't Raise a Man

I couldn't believe that I was really giving Korey another chance. Not after all the shit I talked about this man. I couldn't help the fact that I was in love when it came to him. You ever just meet a man you know would do anything for you? That was how I felt about Korey. Don't get me wrong, he got on my nerves, and he knew how to be persistent. That was my reason for giving him another chance, but I was so serious when I said he had no more chances to fuck up. The first moment I started feeling like he was playing with me and my emotions, he was gone, and that was a promise. I didn't have time to be going back and forth with this man.

A part of me knew I could have another man if I wanted one, but I didn't. Korey wasn't my first boyfriend, but he was the one who won my heart and had had it ever since. I knew what I was getting myself into when I got with him. Even my mother was rooting for Korey and me to get back together.

"I'm just saying I know in my heart that you and Korey belong together. He's a good father and treats you amazingly."

"It doesn't take away the fact that he played you like a fool. I don't understand why you and your sister can't just leave them niggas alone and focus on being parents and bettering yourselves. She's around here lying for her nigga, and you around here taking one back who did you dirty. I wish I had sons because I would have them send a message to both Jace and Korey!" my father snapped.

I knew he wasn't going to be happy. My father never did like Korey. He felt like I was ruining my life by being with him, and I wanted to show him that I could have a man like Korey and still pursue my dreams, and I did. He didn't want me to be a baby momma. Shit, he actually wanted me and Korey to get married the day I found out I was pregnant, but I had to let him know that we weren't ready for that step in our relationship. I didn't know if we ever would be.

"Daddy."

"I'm just saying if you keep taking him back after him fucking up, he's going to think that he can keep getting away with it, and that's not what you need to settle for. You need a man who will be faithful to you all the time and not make up excuses when they cheat."

"Oh, Barry, let's not act like you weren't a cheater back in our day. You used to do me dirty as well, but I loved your dirty-dick ass. Shit, I still do."

"But I stopped cheating on you a long time ago. What you don't want is for somebody to sit up there and do you wrong your whole relationship, then marry him and still have to put up with that. I learned from the mistakes I made with your mother and promised myself that if I had daughters, I would never want them to put up with a man like I was, and that's exactly what y'all doing."

I truly understood where he was coming from, and I loved my father for it, but he had to understand that Junie and I were going to do what we wanted to do at the end of the day. We were grown, and I believed we both knew what we wanted. I couldn't speak for the shit that Junie put up with because I wasn't in their household, but I did know that Jace was way different from Korey. He was not controlling, and he didn't tell me what I could and couldn't wear on a daily basis. If Jace could have made my sister wear turtlenecks and jeans for the rest of her life, he would have.

"Daddy, I know how you feel about Korey, but if you could just sit down with him and get to know the man he is today, I don't know . . . I feel like things are going to be okay for us this time. He keeps promising that he doesn't want to do me wrong, and I want to give him another chance."

"I hope it's not because of KJ. You can't be out here hurting yourself all because you want to give KJ a two-parent home. You have to be happy with yourself before you can focus on a relationship, and I'm sorry, I just don't think you are, Draya. I want you to be happy, I swear, but this man is not good enough for you. I know that you're going to do what you want to do at the end of the day, but you need to take your time and think about this shit before you end up over here crying yet again because he did you wrong," he told me, making me nod my head. I knew that it was a long shot trying to get him to see things from my perspective, but at least he was keeping it real with me, which some parents didn't do enough.

My father had never been the type to sugarcoat things. He would tell it how it was because that was who he was, and people loved him for it. Shit, I loved him for it, but I really just wished that he would get to know Korey before deciding not to like him. I guessed this was what I got for coming to my parents with all my issues.

Sighing, I got up, hugged him and my mother, then grabbed KJ and walked toward the door.

"Leave the baby," he hollered from the living room, and I did just that.

My mother grabbed KJ and looked at me. "Just give him time."

Nodding my head, I turned and walked out of the house. Getting into my car, I put it in reverse and backed out of the driveway. I knew it was a long shot trying to get him to have a conversation with Korey, but I felt like if we were going to work things out, then everybody needed to be on the same track about it. I didn't have anything against my father voicing his opinion at all, but the least he could have said was to give him time and he'd think about it. I never wanted to put my father in a fucked-up position and make the promise he made to Korey come true. When Korey and I first got together, my father told him that he would kill him if he ever hurt me, and he did, so I knew that was why he was feeling a way. He probably felt like Korey was playing with him and had no respect, and that was why he didn't want to sit down with him. *Oh, well. I tried.*

Pulling up at the restaurant where I was meeting Junie, I got out and went inside. "Table for two if she's not already here."

"Name?"

"Huh?"

"Your name?" the hostess asked.

"Oh, I'm sorry. Draya."

"Yeah, a woman came in here not too long ago and told me to bring you straight to the table," she said with a smile.

Following her to the table that was almost all the way in the back, I sat across from Junie.

"Hey, sis," I said.

"Hey, how did things go with Daddy and Momma?"

"Girl, now you know Momma has always been a fan of Korey no matter what he did, but that father of yours just wouldn't let up. He don't want me to be with him or nothing."

"Tell me about it. He was all over me about leaving Jace."

"Well, I agree with him on that one. You need to leave that nigga alone. It's almost like he has some kind of spell over you with the way you're always doing what he tells you."

"I don't always do what he tells me. I just have respect for that man," she replied, making me nod my head. I wasn't about to sit up here and argue with her. I knew what I saw, and Jace wasn't worthy of my sister. She should have left him alone. I just didn't know why she stayed, and I hated that. One thing my daddy was right about was that he didn't raise no fools.

"I'm just saying sometimes it comes off a little like you're his slave and not his woman," I scoffed.

I knew she was mad at me for what I was saying, but she needed to realize I wasn't saying these things to hurt her feelings but to let her know that she didn't have to put up with that shit. My sister was gorgeous, and I was sure, just like me, she could have any man she looked at, but she was so stuck up Jace's ass that it made it hard for her to think straight. I didn't know what kind of dick he was putting down on her, but I never wanted that in my life.

"Junie, you know what I mean."

"I know what you said, and I wish people would mind their business when it comes to me and that man. I would leave if that's what I want, but it's not."

"Okay, well, that's all you have to say," I said, looking at the menu to figure out what I wanted to eat.

I wasn't about to sit up here and keep giving her advice, especially when I knew firsthand that he wasn't right for her. If she wanted to be with him, then that was on her and not me. I loved my sister and would always be here for her no matter what, but when she did get enough of the shit he put her through, I hoped she wouldn't go back. I wanted her to prosper in life and never make it seem like she had to put up with that kind of disrespect.

Shit, the advice I was trying to give her maybe I should have taken for myself and left Korey where he was, but the love I had for this man was too strong. It was almost like he was holding my heart hostage and wouldn't give it back. Each time I came face-to-face with him, heard his name, or thought about him, my heart started beating fast to the point where I thought I might have a heart attack. It was all love, and that was all it had always been, despite everything that he put me through. If he was telling me he learned his lesson and would never do anything to jeopardize his family, then I should give him another chance, right? Maybe I didn't know what I wanted. Maybe I needed to take a step back and just see how this went before making plans for him to sit down and talk with my father.

"Are you really serious about giving Korey another shot?" she asked, breaking the silence that had grown.

"I want to, but I'm nervous. I don't know what to think half the time. It's only been a day, and I keep thinking that he might cheat on me again," I pouted.

"Girl, fix your face. You know that man loves you, and I think he learned his lesson. I don't think you're ever going to have to worry about that happening again. And if it does, we'll just jump his ass."

"I'ma shoot his ass. Fuck jumping him." *I'm not about to get my heart broken by this man again and let him get away with it.* But again, I was thinking too far into it.

Chapter Fourteen

Korey Sr.

Pullin' Me Back

The next morning, I woke up and went straight into the restroom so that I could handle my personal hygiene. After I finished, I walked out and dressed in some black slacks, a cream-colored dress shirt, some black dress socks, and some black Versace loafers. Grabbing my brush, I made sure my waves were looking good as well as my goatee before heading out of the bedroom and the house.

The entire ride to Lady Rouge, I was in deep thought about what I needed to take place today. I needed everyone to be on my side and listen to what I was saying in order to save their jobs and my business. The last thing I wanted was for my shit to go under because of all the violence. Kasey may not have been pressing charges or suing the company, but who was to say that somebody else wouldn't if this shit happened again? *I'm not about to let my name be in jeopardy or be in court all because the veteran dancers can't and won't accept the new ones who come through that door.*

About twenty minutes of eleven, I was pulling up at the club and saw that a few of the dancers' cars, as well as Laila's, were in the parking lot. Getting out of the car, I strolled up to the door and pulled it open. All eyes were on me, and the room grew quiet.

"You know, for me to have to come in three days in a row, there has to be something serious going on. I don't ever step foot in here unless it's to enjoy myself, which is why most of you don't even know I'm the one who runs this show. Laila handles any and all things I need done so that I don't have to come in here. The recent assault that took place is one of the most disgusting things I've ever had in my club since opening it up," I said, stepping directly in front of the room.

Everybody just looked at me, but my eyes were trained on Minnie, the one who had been around here causing all the drama among the workers, old and new. She was a veteran and had been working for me for a long time, so she knew what I would and wouldn't tolerate. She knew drama and fighting were two of the things I didn't tolerate. There was enough money flowing through here for everybody to make some, but the old dancers were being stingy and wanted to make the new dancers feel like they didn't belong. I'd been working on setting up a new club so that I could separate some of the dancers and make it where they didn't have to worry about the drama, and that was exactly what I was finna let be known today.

"Can I say something?" Minnie asked, and I motioned for her to come to the front of the room. When she did, she stood next to me and cleared her throat. Out of the side of my eye, I could see Kasey walk in and roll her eyes.

"Okay, I know that I haven't set a good example as one of the veteran dancers here, and I'm sorry. I don't know what came over me, and I'm sorry for my actions, Korey. It's just Kasey was talking so much shit that I couldn't take it anymore. I know that I shouldn't have hit her with that bottle, but like I said, I let my emotions get the better of me, and I couldn't control my anger."

"And that's the precise issue. You hit her with a bottle, and you know that I don't do that kind of shit. This is a business at the end of the day, one that is keeping your pockets and mine laced. I opened this up when I decided to get out of the game, and I'm not about to let you or anybody else make me feel like I have to go back out there just to make sure my family eats. Who else was involved in this scuffle?"

"Uh, Minnie, Dulce, and Gucci," Laila answered.

"Okay, for all of you, I'm putting y'all on suspension. Y'all all are the reason that one of my dancers and a favorite was laid up in the hospital last night."

"That's bullshit! How do we get suspended and Kasey don't when she was the one who started it?" Dulce asked.

"I didn't start shit. I clearly stated the truth, and your girl got mad. Y'all jumped me, and she hit me with a bottle. Not once did I lift my hands to put them on her." Kasey stuck up for herself.

"You a fucking liar!" Minnie yelled, and once again, all the girls tried to jump on her.

"Jump if y'all want to. I will shoot," Kasey voiced, holding a gun in her hand. Looking at her, I could tell she was dead-ass serious, and I couldn't blame her. I would probably be the same way if I had just gotten jumped and hit with a bottle the night before. Shit, I would have started spraying and laying all their asses down.

"A'ight, calm the fuck down! Dulce and Gucci, get the fuck out of my building before I fire y'all asses!" I yelled, almost losing my cool, but containing it to the best of my abilities. "You two, follow me," I added, looking from Minnie to Kasey.

Moving to the side, I allowed Minnie to walk in front of me while Kasey walked behind me. I didn't care what the fuck I had to do, but I knew I had to get them two to hash out their issues before somebody wound up dead and the cops were running in my shit. I did not fuck with them, so I needed this shit dead A-fucking-SAP.

When we got into the office, I slammed the door shut and turned around. Both Minnie and Kasey were eyeing each other with so much hate in their eyes, I couldn't do nothing but shake my head. "Korey, what do you want from us?" Minnie finally asked, breaking the long stare between her and Kasey.

"What I want is for you to stop trying to act like you're such a hard ass. Do you remember when you first started working here? You're a veteran over these new girls, but once upon a time, you used to be new as well. Let's not act like your shit don't stink or like I didn't have to pull in some of my dancers because you were complaining that they were fucking with you. You need to think before you open your mouth and say anything to me."

"I know, and I'm sorry, but it's not like I started that situation last night. I just ended it," she nonchalantly said.

"The issue is Dulce and Gucci. If you didn't have them two next to you, hyping you the fuck up all the time, you wouldn't have to worry about even being in here. You do know I could fire you and won't give two fucks about it. You, above all, know I don't put up with violence in my fucking club, so the fact that you would even resort to that shows me just how much respect you have for me and Laila—the two motherfuckers who got you to the point you're in where you don't have to do much to make all the money you do. I'm sick of y'all acting like I didn't do nothing, like I'm not the reason this club is a hit."

"So what are you going to say to her?" she asked.

"Don't worry about me!" Kasey shot back.

"Stop. I think that you two could hash this shit out if you didn't have motherfuckers in y'all ears trying to tell y'all what y'all shouldn't be taking. That shit is going to get both of you fired. Do you know Kasey had the control to get you fired and she didn't?"

"Why not?"

"Because I know you have two kids you have to feed, and I'm not a hater. I would never do that to anybody," Kasey told her.

"Thank you. I'm sorry for hitting you with that bottle. I took it too far, and that's not who I am. I think I let all the attention I'm used to getting go to my head. I got jealous when I saw that you were getting treated the same as I'm used to. I shouldn't have entertained the argument and kept minding my business. You're a cool girl, and I hope that in the future you will be able to forgive me."

"I do forgive you. Just don't let it happen again, because next time, I'm not going to be so nice about it." Kasey chuckled, and Minnie nodded her head in agreement.

"Okay, now that that's out of the way, I have a proposition for both of you, and I want to know if you'll be interested. I'm opening another club, and I need some of my heavy hitters in there to make it pop. I think that you two will be a good addition to my club, and maybe y'all can team up and actually show the newbies what it's like to get money."

"I'm down," Minnie answered.

"Me too." Kasey smirked.

Standing up, I stuck my hand out so they could shake it, and then they hugged one another. I was happy I was able to defuse a problem and not make a bigger one.

I grabbed my phone and car keys, and we all walked out of the office. I left the club and headed to meet Draya at my mother's house. I didn't know what was going on, but my mother wanted us to talk about what was going on. I didn't really feel like I had to explain that to anybody, but I was going just to get everybody off my back.

I pulled my car into the driveway of her home and got out of the car. Going up to the door, I put my key in and opened the door. Stepping all the way into the house, I made my way to the living room where I heard talking going on. I was shocked to see Draya, her mother, and her father, who was wearing a scowl on his face. I knew there was about to be some bullshit. This man didn't like me, and now I was sure he didn't like me at all. I just wanted to assure him that I had learned my lesson and I wanted to be there for his daughter and my son. I didn't want us to be separated, and I didn't want things to be where she and I couldn't coexist if things didn't go the way we both wanted them to. I loved her, and that was all he needed to know. Her mother, on the other hand, had always cut for me. Even when I cheated on Draya, she was calling my phone, telling me that I needed to get Draya back, and how she felt like we were meant to be.

"What's up, Ma?" I asked, kissing her on the cheek and sitting next to Draya. "How are y'all doing?"

"I'm good. Come give me a hug. I miss seeing you," her mother said, getting up.

After hugging her, I sat back down. Her father never said anything, so I had a feeling that he was about to go off about what happened between me and Draya the first time.

Chapter Fifteen

Junie

Unlove You

"Work! Yeah, work them legs out, ladies!" My trainer cheered all of us women on while we ran in place.

This was the end of the workout, and I couldn't believe that I actually lasted this long. I hadn't worked out in so long that I didn't know what it felt like to actually be back in the gym.

"Come on, kiddies, keep up with your mommies," she encouraged the children. Montana was running all over the room. "And time," she added, and we all stopped.

Sitting on the floor, I lay back to catch my breath when Montana sat next to me. "I want ice cream," she said.

"Okay, let Mommy get up," I told her before sitting up and wiping my forehead.

Letting my hair down, I put it back up in a messy bun and made a mental note of washing my shit when I made it back home. Standing up, I grabbed my gym bag, her backpack, and her hand, and then we walked out of the gym. When we got to the car, I buckled her in her car seat before climbing into the driver's seat and pulling out of the parking lot. I made my way to the ice cream parlor. She got an ice cream cone, and I got a shake. We sat in the parking lot and ate our ice cream while she watched cartoons. Once we both finished, I cleaned her up before making my way to the house. As soon as we pulled up, we got out of the car and went inside.

Jace was sitting on the couch with a blunt in his hand and a beer to his side—a sign to just leave him alone.

"Come on so I can give you a bath and get you ready to go to Momo and Papa's," I told Montana, then grabbed her hand and led her up the stairs, not even noticing Jace behind me.

"Let me talk to you."

"Jace, I don't have time. I need to get Montana bathed and ready to go," I said in a respectful way.

"You think I give a fuck? Why didn't you tell me Ace stopped by here?"

"I forgot. I'm sorry."

Wham! He punched me right in the eye, making me push Montana in her room and shut the door while she was kicking and screaming for me. This was something I never wanted my daughter to see. I never wanted her to think that this was something she had to put up with. Wham! He hit me again while cornering me against a wall.

"I missed out on a lot of money because of you not telling me, and I think you did that shit on purpose."

"I swear, I didn't," I cried, now holding my bloody mouth.

"What the fuck ever!" he snapped. And the moment he turned his back, I ran into the room with Montana, locked the door, and hid in her bathroom with that door locked as well. The sound of him banging on her bedroom door had her screaming and me crying while holding my baby as tight as I could. I knew she was scared. Shit, I was too.

"It's okay, baby, be quiet please," I pleaded with her before grabbing some tissue and holding my nose up.

Not long after, I heard the front door slam, but I still didn't move. I wasn't sure if he was gone, and I didn't want to be caught coming out of here only for him to put his hands on me again. Never had I ever thought that he would put his hands on me in front of our child. The way his eyes were made me think he was on something that had him higher than weed.

Montana came over to me and laid her head on my chest. We stayed in that same place until she went to sleep, and then I got up and put her into her bed. Sitting on the floor, I started to cry when a soft tap on the door startled me.

"Please, Jace, leave me alone," I pleaded.

"This is Ace," a deep voice answered, making me get up and go to the door. Putting my hand on the knob, I was about to turn it, but I was too scared.

"How am I supposed to know you're not lying?"

"I'm not. Here," he said, sliding a mirror under the door to let me see that it was him. After I finally pulled the door open, his face had shock written on it when he saw me.

"What the fuck happened to you?"

"Nothing, I got into a little fight," I lied like always.

"Come on and let me get you to the hospital," he suggested.

I was about to protest, but the stern look told me that he wasn't taking no for an answer. Nodding my head, I went to the bed to grab Montana, but he stopped me.

"I got her," he added, picking her up and leading me out the door.

When we got downstairs and out of the house, he opened the passenger door for me and sat Montana in my lap. "Unlock your door so I can get her car seat."

I did so, and he grabbed it and strapped her in. When he finally got into the driver's seat, he took off toward the hospital.

"Ohhhh." I grimaced in pain. My nose felt like it was hanging off my face, which let me know that it was more than likely broken.

His car finally pulled into the parking lot of the hospital, and I got out. He grabbed Montana, and together we went inside. As soon as I came face-to-face with one of the nurses, she led me straight to the back where they did X-rays and stopped the bleeding. I also had a patch over my eye because it was shut. Not even thirty minutes later, the nurse came back with a doctor.

"Your nose is broken, and your eye is going to need some time to heal. Right now, it's swollen shut, and we don't want to do surgery on it and damage it any more than it might already be. Your lip is also split down the middle. Can you tell me what happened?"

"I got into a fight. It's no biggie."

"It's a biggie. Unless you were fighting a heavyweight woman champion, only a man could make these types of bruises."

"How can you be so sure?" Ace asked.

"Because if we're looking at the way her eye was hit, you would have to be really strong or hit somebody really hard to close their eyes. It doesn't take as much weight and strength for a man to do this because he's stronger already. Now, for a woman, it would take a lot of strength behind that swing."

Ace looked at me, but I was sticking to my story. "She was way bigger than me," I lied again.

I didn't know why I was still sticking up for this man when it was obvious that he didn't care about me. For him to hit me in front of my daughter told me that. The hate I had for Jace's ass was growing more and more each time he put his hands on me. I knew that I had to get away from him before he killed me.

"Okay, well, we're gonna have to do surgery to get your nose back right. I know you probably don't want to do that, but we have no choice. It's too severely damaged to just let you walk out of here."

"Do you have anybody you want me to call to come up here and sit with your daughter?" Ace asked.

I could tell by the look on his face that he knew I was lying, but he didn't want to say anything. I felt like shit for sitting up here lying to him and this doctor, but neither of them would be able to save me from Jace, and that was just what it was. I had to make sure I did whatever I could to make sure my child was safe and that I still had a life to live. I didn't want to be one of those baby mommas who had to move and change my and my child's names just so Jace wouldn't be able find us.

"I'll call my mother," I said, pulling my phone out and calling her.

The phone rang twice before she picked up. "Hey, June."

"Ma, I need you to come up to the hospital and sit with Montana or pick her up. I have to have surgery on my nose. Don't ask."

"You know damn well I'm going to ask. What the fuck happened to your nose?"

"I got into a fight. It's nothing."

"Nah, it's something. I'm on my way," she said and hung up the phone.

I didn't even have time to tell her not to tell Daddy. He was the one who was going to know that I was lying and call me out on it. I didn't need that right now. The only thing I was worried about was my daughter being somewhere safe tonight and each day after. I knew that I had to leave this man in order for me to keep my life. It didn't matter how much I thought I loved him. That shit was out the window. The minute he hit me in front of our child was the end for me. I guessed that was all I needed to make me choose my life over him.

After we had been waiting quietly for a while, Ace said to me, "I don't know what happened, but you need to stop fighting and just walk away. You're too beautiful to be letting anybody put hands on you the way this 'girl' did."

"Thank you for being there for me."

"I'll always be here for you. Hit my line if you need anything," he said, grabbing my phone and putting his number in it.

Nodding my head, I watched as he walked out of the room at the same time my mother and father stepped inside. *I knew she was going to tell him.*

"Junie, what the fuck happened to your face?" my father asked, examining my face.

"Some girl. It happened so fast," I lied again.

Montana woke up and looked at my momma and father before speaking. "Daddy hit Mommy," she cried, reaching for my father, who picked her up.

"You're lying for this nigga? How long has this shit been going on?"

"Montana doesn't—" Before I could finish my sentence, he looked at me.

"Stop lying for him. It's time for you to live your life on your own. You don't need that nigga when you have me and your mother, and you have a beautiful little girl. Do you think this is something that she should see at her age?" he asked, and I shook my head.

"I know it's time for me to leave him."

"You're right about that, and you can come back home."

"I think I'm going to go stay with Draya for a few days. I just need to get my mind right. It's time for her to know what's been going on as well," I told them, and they both nodded their heads before hugging and kissing me.

I knew my mother was hurt just by the tears that were dropping from her eyes. I was so embarrassed that I didn't know what to say. I had sat up here and lied about him putting his hands on me again. And it wasn't fair to me or my daughter for me to keep taking up for this nigga when he didn't care that he was killing me.

Chapter Sixteen

Jace

Heart Attack

I didn't know what came over me earlier. It was as if I took out on Junie all the anger I was feeling toward Victoria and everything else that had gone wrong. She didn't deserve that shit, and I felt bad. So bad to the point where I couldn't even go home and look her in her face. That shit was out of line.

"Boss, did you hear me?" Kassidy, one of my many workers, asked.

I'd been chilling at the trap since leaving the house but wasn't doing nothing much. Shit, I was barely paying attention to what was going on. The only thing on my mind was Junie and Montana. I vowed to never lay hands on Junie in front of her, and all that went out the window.

"What did you say?" I inquired, finally looking up.

"I said this is one of the busiest days here. Are you sure you want to be here?"

"I'm about to go in a minute," I replied just as Ace's car pulled into the parking lot. *Just the man I want to see.* I needed to figure out why he thought it was okay to show up at my house out of the blue but not call to tell me he was there or on his way. I felt like both he and Junie were hiding something from me, and I planned on getting to the bottom of it. When he got out of the car, he walked straight toward me like he had something he needed to get off his chest.

"What's up, bro?"

"Don't 'What's up, bro?' me. You out of line for putting your hands on that girl the way you did. I just came back from taking her to the hospital." He grimaced, ice-grilling me like he wanted an issue. It ain't like she was his girl, so I was not understanding why he was so worried about what went on in my household between me and what belonged to me.

"I don't know who you think you're pumping your chest out to, but you got me fucked up. I don't have time for this shit. And you don't need to be going by my house and helping her do nothing. It ain't yo' fucking business!" I spat.

I knew a lot of the workers were probably trying to figure out what was going on, so instead of standing there, I moved and headed for my car.

"You know what? I'm sick of niggas like you, bro. You have a good-ass woman at home. I don't even know her, but I know if she's putting up with you and your shit, then she gotta be thorough. You ain't shit. Your little girl was the one who told her parents you put your hands on her momma, and that's fucking sad. You don't deserve neither one of them!" he snapped.

I was trying to count in my head so I didn't turn around and knock this nigga out. "What you said to me?"

"I said you a fuck nigga."

Turning to face him, I got as close as I could to his face before speaking. "When you get a girl and keep one, then you can tell me what you think about me. Until then, mind your fucking business. What goes on between me and mine don't have shit to do with you. Stay the fuck away from my girl, nigga."

"You do know I don't have to do shit you say, right? I don't work for you. I work with you, so you can't do shit to me. You may have these other niggas in here fooled, but you're a punk-ass nigga. If you will put your hands on a woman, then you should have no issue with fighting me, right? I would body yo' ass, Jace, and I put that on everything."

"I'm not about to do this with you, my nigga. You putting on a show, and I don't know why. It ain't like these niggas gon' respect you no more than they respect me."

"Do it look like I give a fuck about respect from these niggas? This is business, and I treat it as such. You need to do the same thing, bitch nigga."

I couldn't do nothing but chuckle at this nigga. I knew he was trying to get a rise out of me, and I wasn't about to let him until those next words left his mouth.

"I'ma take yo' girl, dawg."

As soon as those words left his mouth, I lost it. I swung at him, and we went at it a few times before the other workers broke it up.

"Stay the fuck away from my girl and my daughter, or I will kill you, and I put that on you, nigga," I pointed out before getting into my car and pulling off.

This nigga really had no idea who he was fucking with. Yeah, we worked together, but all of that went out the window with the way he just disrespected me.

The entire drive to the house was a long one. I was in no rush to get there, just in case Junie was there or she had the cops there waiting for me. My phone vibrating made me pull it out of my pocket. Looking at it, I shook my head when I saw that it was Victoria calling me. I didn't know why I fucked her ass. Now I couldn't get rid of her, and since she was planning on keeping this baby, it was making it even harder.

"Yo?" I picked up, knowing that if I didn't, she would just keep calling.

"I have a doctor's appointment at three, and I want you to come with me."

"I can't. I have other shit going on at home."

"I'm sorry. That wasn't supposed to sound like a question. You need to come to the appointment with me. I didn't get pregnant on my own."

"Victoria, you got me fucked up. I don't know who you think you talking to like that, but I didn't tell you to keep that fucking baby. You wanted to keep it, thinking it was going to keep me in your life, but guess what—I don't want to be with you!" I snapped and hung up on her.

When I finally arrived at the house, I braced myself when I saw Junie's car sitting in the driveway. I didn't know what I was going to say, but I did know I was about to beg and plead so that she wouldn't leave me. *It's a shame that I even have to do this. Maybe I just need to let her go, but without her, I'm nothing.*

Getting out of the car, I strolled up to the door and unlocked it. Stepping inside, I looked around before making my way around to see if she and Montana were home. Going up the stairs, I saw a letter on the bed and walked closer to it. Picking it up, I read the letter.

Dear Jace,
I think it's best if you and I sever ties. I can't keep living like this. If you go in the closet, you will see that my sister came to get everything I had over there. You can keep the car and the other shit you tried to buy me for beating my ass, but I'm done. Don't try to contact me. I need time to think about my next move.

Love, Junie

Sitting on the edge of the bed, I just thought about how everything I had done finally had her fed up. The cheating, lying, and beatings . . . I wasn't a good nigga for her. I would never want my daughter to put up with something like this ever. I had to do the right thing if I wanted to at least be able to get her back in my presence.

Getting up, I went into the restroom and straight to the medicine cabinet. Pulling it open, I grabbed the bottle of lithium that the doctor prescribed me the last time I went in for my annual session with the therapist.

I thought I didn't need these, but I did more than anything. I really hated the nigga I had become, and I wanted to end this shit. I wanted to be a better man, especially if I wanted to have my child in my life at least. Me not taking my medication was a good way for Junie to get custody, which was why I hid this shit from her in the first place. The last thing I wanted was for her to think I was a weak-ass nigga for having to take mood pills to keep me calm. I loved that woman more than anything, and I wanted to make sure I was right, not only for her, but for myself as well. I couldn't continue like this, and that letter . . . shit, her leaving was enough to make me want to get my shit together. All the way together.

Clutching the pills in my hand, I walked out and sat on the side of the bed. Rolling a blunt, I called her phone and listened to it ring to voicemail before calling again. I knew she saw that I was calling. I just wanted to make sure she and my child were good. Once I was finished with the blunt, I put it to my mouth and lit it. Taking a long drag from it, I held the smoke in before exhaling and leaning my head back.

I was getting comfortable until the sound of someone banging on the door and ringing the doorbell at the same time got my attention. "Man, fuck." I grimaced, getting up and going down the stairs with the blunt still in my mouth.

"Open the door, motherfucker! I know you're in there. I'm about to beat your ass," Draya's voice said.

Not being a scary nigga, I opened the door and looked at her. She and Dreux were standing there with bats in their hands, dressed in all black like they were about to kill somebody.

"I don't have time for this shit, Draya," I said, turning around and letting them in.

"And my sister had time to get her nose fucking broken by you?" she asked, stepping in front of me and pointing the bat at me. It was so close that the tip of it was touching my nose. "Just say something ignorant and watch I bust you in your shit."

Not saying anything, I removed the bat from in front of my face, and then I spoke. "If you were gonna do that, you would have. You don't want no smoke, and I don't have time for your shit. Tell Junie she needs to be home before it gets dark."

"Are you fucking delusional? She's not coming back," Dreux said, standing on the side of me with a mug on her face.

I swore today must have been Piss Jace Off Day. And if these bitches weren't like sisters to me, I would have most definitely slapped the fuck out of both of them. I just didn't want to hear Korey's mouth about hitting his girl, so I put my hands up and paced backward.

"She'll be back. I know Junie. She loves me."

"Nah, nigga. That love went out the window the day you decided to lay hands on her. My sister deserves so much better than you, and you're lucky. I know if I kill yo' ass, it would hurt her and my niece, or yo' shit would be beat in!" she snapped, making her way toward the front door with Dreux right behind her.

"Yeah, you bitches better get out." I chuckled.

Before I knew it, they jumped on my ass, and everything went black for ya boy.

Chapter Seventeen

Dreux

Talk That Talk

Me and Deion were on our official second date, and I had to admit, it felt so good to be around a man who wasn't threatened by me and the money that I made. We were having a good conversation, and he was giving me advice on business from a lawyer's standpoint.

"I would have to say you need to put everything in writing at this point, even for your workers. You don't want nor do you need anybody getting over on you. I'm sure you're good at what you do, and had I known you early on, I surely would have hired you to decorate my house. I know that it's hard being a woman and having a business of your own, but in order to see money, you need to hold your customers to the same standard they hold you. If they get over on you, take their asses to court, because at the end of the day, you're putting in the work and they're waiting until after to say they don't like something. Ask their input, and if they don't give it to you, give them examples of what you're feeling for their house to see if they want it," he said.

I was hearing everything he was saying, but my mind was on something else. His lips and the way he kept licking them had a bitch's hormones rising. I never had a man of his stature in front of me, and I loved being in his presence. Just the two times we'd met up, I knew that he was somebody I could have in my life as a lover or friend. He was my type of nigga.

"I hear what you're saying, and that's exactly what I'm going to start doing. I'm sick of people getting over on me, and now it's about to be strictly business from here on out. I don't want to be friends with any of them, and I don't want them to think they could get over on me, not even a little bit. I've been cautious about who I do business with because some of these white people do the most. I love all my loyal customers, but I need to start treating them exactly like that."

"Exactly. And if you ever need a lawyer for anything, you know I have your back."

"I thought that lawyers had a specific area they worked in," I said, now wanting to know more about him and his job.

"They do, but me, I like to help out no matter how. I will drop everything to help somebody out when and if they need it. I let them know up front that they can't get over on me and that I need half my money up front."

"And what if they have no money to pay half up front?"

"Then I work out a payment plan that works for both of us. I'm thinking about going independent after this year. My company is a biased one, and because I'm not white and don't do white people shit, they want me out of there. They have tried everything to get me fired, but nothing has stuck. They don't like the fact that a black nigga is out here helping other blacks get off for things I know they didn't do. Instead of being for the people, they're for the money, and I don't have time for that shit anymore. I have a few more cases I'm taking this year, and I'm done after that."

"With the mind frame you have, I know you'll be able to go far on your own, and then you'll have law firms begging to have you come work for them."

"And I'ma tell them all the same thing. I'm good." He chuckled. "I've been enjoying myself with you, and I hate that the night has to come to an end. I hope that we can do this again," he added, grabbing the check from the waiter. We had been sitting there fifteen minutes only talking, and these people were ready for us to go.

"I hope so as well."

Once he slid the bill in the check presenter, he handed it back to the waiter, and we got up and headed for the exit. I saw Max coming in.

"Well, funny running into you here. Is this a date?" he asked, making me roll my eyes.

"Deion, Max. Max, this is Deion." I introduced them, and they just looked at one another.

"What I want to know is where is my child while you're out on a date with a nigga!" he snapped.

"She's fine, and you don't need to be worrying about her. Worry about your wife and the kids she can't have, so she's trying to get you to take mine away from me."

"You do know I could have snatched Savannah and left town. You would have never found us, but I'm trying to do things the right way."

"Max, please go to hell. One thing I know you're not dumb enough to do is kidnap my child."

"But is it really considered kidnapping when she's my child?"

"Yes, it is actually. It doesn't matter if she's your child or not. If you take her from her custodial parent, it's kidnapping," Deion said, making me look up at him.

"Mind your business. This don't have shit to do with you!" Max snapped, stepping up.

"I am minding my business, and she's it."

As much as I loved seeing Deion put Max in his place, I knew it was time to go. They were making a scene, and everybody was now looking. The last thing I wanted was for us to get put out of this restaurant and told that we couldn't come back.

"Let's go," I said.

"Yeah, y'all go before I have to do something I may regret."

"You need to check yourself and my credentials. Don't let this suit fool you." Deion smirked before grabbing my hand and leading me out of the restaurant and to his car.

When we got there, he pulled the door open for me, and I sat in the leather seat, closing my eyes. His seats were so warm I could have gone to sleep right there. When he finally got in, he looked over at me.

"You good?" he asked.

"I'm fine. I just didn't want you to be going back and forth with him. That's the shit he gets off on. If he thinks he can piss you off, he's happy with himself at the end of the day," I explained to him. If he was going to be in my life, he needed to know that Max got off on things like that and that it was best to just ignore him. *Shame the devil, and do not give him your energy,* I told myself when he started with me. I had let this man get over on me too many times, steal my energy, and make me feel some way. Then I had to get myself together while he moved on and enjoyed his life.

"I know. I don't know what came over me, but one thing I can't stand is disrespect. You're gonna have to get used to that while you're with me. And he's disrespectful as hell. I understand that's your daughter's father, but if he had come up on me one more time, I was going to lay his ass down."

His deep voice held a serious tone, and that shit was sexy as fuck to me. He was like a respectful-ass nigga, which was something I wasn't used to, not one sticking up for me anyway. Max was a very well-respected man in the streets, so whenever I got with a dude and he found out who my baby father was, they would stop talking to me out of the blue. No phone call, text, or nothing, just leave me wondering. For so long he had run my life. I couldn't step out of the house without him texting me to let me know he knew where I was and that I needed to go home. He didn't let me do anything when we were together. Me getting pregnant for him just topped it all off. He wanted me to marry him and some more shit, but I declined. I couldn't put up with his controlling ways, and that was why I knew what kind of shit Junie was putting up with. She may not have told us out of her own mouth that she was getting beat on, but I knew she was. That was always the next option for a controlling nigga when he felt like he was losing his grip on you. He would use his hands to make a woman fear him, and that was exactly what Jace was doing to my girl.

I still didn't divulge what took place at Jace's house today to Deion because I was sure, when he saw Jace, he was going to tell both him and Korey about it. I didn't feel bad about it at all. He deserved every bit of that ass whooping. *Now he knows what it feels like to get your ass beat and not be able to do anything about it.* Those bats were like his hands today. He got to witness firsthand what it was like to be weak.

When Deion pulled into the driveway of my home, we sat there for a while until I turned in his direction. "I had a good time." I smiled.

"Me as well. Come on, I'll walk you to the door," he offered, and we both got out.

When he came around to my side, he put his hand on the small of my back as we walked. Putting my key in the door, I unlocked it and pushed it open before turning back toward him.

"Be careful, and text me when you make it home."

"I got you," he replied, leaning down and kissing me on the lips.

When he backed away, I walked into the house with a smile on my face, then shut and locked the door.

"Come tell me all about it," my sister said from the living room sofa, and I did. I gave her all the details, even about Max showing up. She was smiling from ear to ear when I told her how Deion put him in his place.

"How was your and Savannah's night?"

"Good. You know she's always good for her nanny. I need some advice, though."

"What's going on?"

"Okay, you know I've been seeing this guy, right? Well, he has a girl at home. I don't know the issues going on in their home, but I'm pregnant. He wanted me to get an abortion, but I decided to keep it. It don't seem like he has any interest in wanting to be in the baby's life, but he keeps telling me that he will take care of it. I love him, and I want to be with him, but I don't know if that's something he wants."

"First of all, I don't know what you were thinking fucking with a man in a relationship anyway. You know Momma didn't raise us like that. Secondly, if that man isn't showing any interest, it's because the girl didn't know about you or the baby, or he just genuinely don't want to have a baby with you. I don't know, but you need to talk to that man. What's his name? Just in case I have to pull up on him, I can ask questions," I joked, and we both shared a laugh. She knew how I was, and I wouldn't be no different behind her and my niece or nephew.

"His name is Jace."

Chapter Eighteen

Deion

She Knows

When I made it home last night after bringing Dreux home, I had to take a cold shower. Feeling her lips on mine had my dick so hard that I knew if I didn't let her go, I would have wanted to get inside of her. I wasn't trying to take it there with her right now. Now I was up and getting ready to go so that I could make it to court on time. I had a good case set up for getting Wynter off for the shit they were trying to give her two years in jail for. She was harassed and abused by the cops the night they arrested her. The city prosecutors were out of their minds if they thought I was about to let this shit go. That just wasn't about to happen.

The sound of my phone ringing made me pick it up when I saw that it was my boss, Carl. "Hello?"

"Hey, I was just looking over the case file for this girl Wynter. Are you sure you want to put your name on the line for this girl? She has been in a lot of trouble in the short time since she turned eighteen, and this is no different."

"Yeah, I'm sure. At the end of the day, she needs to receive justice for what the cops did to her. The least they can do is let her off for something she didn't even do."

"And how do you know she didn't do it?"

"Because she's my client, and I have confidence in her. I know that she wouldn't lie to me."

He scoffed. I knew that my law firm wasn't going to get behind me, and that was why I told them that I was taking the case. I didn't ask. They knew I wasn't the type who needed to ask permission for anything. Not when I knew that this would be a win for me, and that was all I cared about. I needed to make sure that my client got justice for the things she went through.

"I have to go. Thank you for the luck," I said and hung up the phone on him before he could respond. I didn't have time for nobody to knock me off my square, and that was exactly what he was trying to do.

Grabbing my briefcase, I walked out of the house and got into my car. Starting it up, I backed out of the driveway and sped all the way to the courthouse. I didn't have time to waste. I liked to be there a little early so that my client and I could go over her testimony. They would try to call her to the stand, so I wanted her to be prepared.

After I parked, I got out of the car and made my way to the front of the building, where I saw Wynter sitting.

"Good morning." She smiled.

"Good morning. Walk with me?" I asked, and she got up and followed me into the building.

As soon as we got to a conference room, I turned around and looked her dead in the eyes. I needed to know, for myself and no one else, if she had something else that she wasn't telling me or something that could derail this whole day. I didn't like going into court without knowing all the facts just in case the opposing lawyer tried to pull something out of their hat that I didn't know about.

"What's up?" she questioned.

"Is everything I need to know in here? I don't want no surprises. I need to make sure that you and I are on the same team and that nothing can catch us off guard."

"I swear to you everything you need to know is in that file. I may have a rap sheet, but I'm not that bad. I just don't want to go to jail for something I didn't do and had nothing to do with. It's not fair."

"I feel you, okay? Now, it's gonna be tough in there. I know that this isn't a trial or anything, but you need to treat it like it is. Whatever questions the judge or the other lawyer asks, you need to be prepared to answer truthfully, because if you lie, you might fuck me and you out of this case. And they can take you to jail without even getting your side of things." I kept it real with her, which was something I always did. I never allowed my clients to walk into the courtroom without letting them know what could go wrong. They needed to understand that things could take a turn for the worse if they decided to get up on that stand and lie.

Looking into her eyes, I nodded my head, and we walked into the courtroom since we were one of the first cases up.

Two hours later, we were walking out of there winners, and she was free.

"Celebratory drinks?" she asked.

"I'm with it. I'll follow you in my car," I told her, and we both walked out of the courthouse. Getting into my car, I took my phone out and texted Dreux to make sure she was okay and to see how her day was going. When she hit me back, she said she was at work but had a lunch break coming up in the next hour. I made sure to let her know that I would be coming to bring her lunch. There was something about being in her presence that made me feel good. And the fact that I could be myself around her was the best thing in the world. Usually, I would have to hide my brain, but she didn't make me feel like that. Instead, she embraced it and me.

Pulling into the parking lot of the Chill Grill, I got out and followed Wynter inside, making sure my eyes didn't travel down to her ass. Some of us men didn't like to look at a woman's ass, but it was normal for us. At the same time, with the fact that I was really feeling Dreux, I felt like even if I looked, that would be cheating on her, and we weren't even together at the moment.

As soon as we sat at the bar, my phone started to ring. Looking at it, I saw that it was Breann and quickly declined the phone call. I didn't know why she was calling me. One thing about being broken up that she didn't understand was that she didn't have to call me to see where I was or what I was doing. Shit, we didn't even have a friendship.

The phone rang, and it was her yet again, so I sent her back to voicemail before putting my phone on silent and looking at the menu for whatever drink I wanted when the bartender walked up on us.

"What can I get for y'all?"

"I want a Hennessy and Coke on ice," Wynter replied.

"Uh, I'll take a club soda," I told her, and she walked away.

"You don't want a drink after that?"

"Nah, I don't drink when I drive. It's dangerous."

"One won't hurt you, and I can make sure you make it home." She smirked and licked her full lips at the same time.

"Oh, that's sweet of you, but I'm kind of seeing someone." I shot her down easily.

"Oops, I wish I had known that before developing a crush on you. I don't know what it is, but I can never get the men I want. They're either married or in a relationship. I just want one man who's about me so that I don't have to go out looking for somebody."

"Maybe you should stop looking. If God wants you to have a man, he will come to you and treat you like you've never been treated before. I can understand just wanting somebody, but that's how some women end up in fucked-up situations. You're a good woman, I can tell, so just hold off. I know that your Prince Charming will be coming after you in no time."

"Thank you. You're so sweet. I've never met a man like you before, and it's crazy. I swear if you weren't in a relationship, I would get you." She smiled at me, letting me know she was serious.

Wynter was cool, but she wasn't my type. She and I wouldn't be able to mesh well because she reminded me so much of Breann. They had the same qualities. I didn't mean that in a bad way, but they were both just looking for the next man to take care of them. That was where I fucked up with Breann. I saw her situation, and because I wanted to be with her, I got her out of it, and she started staying with me. We weren't even together for that long before I moved her in, and she started trying to run my life and what I was doing.

"So when was your last relationship, and what was it like?"

"It was horrible. He put his hands on me and made me feel like I wasn't worth shit. I don't know why, but I stayed with him, thinking that he loved me. Then one day, I just left. No goodbyes, no explanation. I just packed up my things, walked out of that house, and never looked back."

"I'm happy that you got yourself out of that fucked-up situation. No woman should ever have to put up with a man treating her like she's less than a queen. You deserve so much better, and I have a feeling that you'll get it soon enough," I let her know, and she nodded her head.

"Thank you. I guess for now I will just keep working and making my money. Thank you again for helping me out with that situation. Had it not been for you, I would probably be locked up for two years."

"Yes, I wasn't about to let that happen. I told you I don't lose cases. Everybody knows that when I step in that courtroom, I'm coming with all facts. I'm not half stepping, because people like that want to see black men and women down."

"That's the truth."

This case was the eye-opener I needed to know that I needed to leave the law firm and do my own thing for a while. I just needed to be able to show them that I didn't need a law firm behind me to handle my business. To be honest, I was the reason the firm got put on the map anyway. Before me, nobody was winning cases. They were getting paid thousands to millions of dollars just for their clients to end up in jail. I made that and more and still kept my clients from going to jail.

"I'd better go. Good luck." I smiled at her before getting up and walking out of the bar.

Getting back into my car, I pulled out of the parking lot and headed to get Dreux and myself something to eat before heading to her job. She was probably swamped like she said, so I wanted to at least show my face to let her know how serious I was about getting to know her and being there for her. I didn't care if we ever made it official. At least I would get to be in her presence as whatever. She was my type of woman, and I knew without a doubt that she and I would always be in each other's lives.

Chapter Nineteen

Korey Sr.

Posed to Be in Love

Wrapping my arms around Draya, I slid my dick deep inside of her while she whined and moaned in my ear. I was on the verge of cumming, and she had already let her juices off on my dick. We both had been in heaven for the last hour, and I didn't want this to end. I was taking my time making love to her body, and that was the way I wanted it to be. I wanted her to know that I hadn't been giving nobody her dick since the day she called off our engagement. She was the only woman I wanted to be deep inside of the way I was.

"Mm, shit," I groaned in her ear.

Raising her head, she kissed my lips while sliding her tongue in. I sucked on it while gripping her ass cheeks and pulling them apart. Pounding my dick deeper inside of her, I closed my eyes and sucked on her tongue until my seeds slid off into the condom that I was wearing.

Sliding off me, she lay on her back, and I got up and went into the restroom. Pulling the condom off my dick, I flushed it down the toilet before walking back out and getting back into bed with her. As soon as my head hit the pillow, she put her head on my chest, and I wrapped my arm around her waist. It was four o'clock in the morning, and I was tired and ready to go to sleep, but the sound of my phone going off got my attention. Sitting up in the bed, I picked it up and saw that it was Laila.

"Hello?"

Draya got off me and threw herself down on her side of the bed on her back. I could see her rolling her eyes. I didn't do nothing but shake my head.

"We have a problem," Laila started.

"What is it?"

"They have some dudes in here causing a ruckus, and the bodyguards won't stop them."

"What you mean? It's their fucking job. Laila, I don't have time for this. You need to get them out of my shit before they tear it up!" I snapped and hung up the phone. She knew better than to be calling me about something like that. I made a mental note to talk to Bo and Brennan because they had me fucked up. Laila shouldn't have had to call me about anything like that, not when it was their job to handle shit like that.

"What happened? Time for you to go home to your bitch?" Draya asked.

"Draya, chill the fuck out with that shit. That was the manager of my strip club. Don't do that. I don't understand how you want to be with me if you don't even trust me to answer my phone. It doesn't matter how late it is. When she calls I have to answer because that's how I make my money. I don't tell you who you can answer the phone for at three and four o'clock in the morning, so don't do that shit to me."

"I'm not getting phone calls at those times. My phone is off when my baby is home, and when he's not, I only have it to where your mother can call me, so miss me with that bullshit. You know what? Good night!" she snapped and rolled over on her side.

She knew I didn't like when she did shit like that. She knew I had a business to run, one that stayed open later than most strip clubs, so I needed to know when shit was going down or when motherfuckers were disrespecting my shit. Letting out a frustrated sigh, I lay back in bed and stared up at the ceiling. I didn't know what else to do. No matter what, she wasn't going to trust me the same way I trusted her. She would never do anything to hurt what we had, and I was trying my hardest to show her that this time I was serious about us. I didn't want to keep living in the past, but it seemed like that was all she knew how to do. She didn't want to forgive me, but she kept saying she was not holding it against me anymore. *I need her to make up her mind because this ain't it.* I didn't need her to remind me of the fuckups I made before we got engaged because that was not what I was here for. What I was here for was to work hard to win her trust back. I was communicating with her more. I never left her out of shit, and I hadn't even been to the club with my niggas since the night I saw her because the last thing I needed her to think was that was something I needed to live. I didn't like going out anyway. When I did, I got drunk and ended up in the bed with some random bitch, and that shit was scary. So I'd rather stay in the house with my kid and her. She needed to understand that if that was the life I still wanted, I wouldn't have tried so hard to get her back.

Draya was the only woman I wanted to be with. She was the one I knew would carry my last name. At the end of the day, I just needed her to understand that shit, and then we would be happy. It was going to take a while for her to get used to the fact that her man owned one of the biggest strip clubs out here, but I needed her to trust that I would never take advantage of that and cheat on her with another woman, because that was not where I was anymore. I was really a changed man and just wanted her to see me that way, not the way she was used to seeing me.

Hearing light snores coming from her side of the bed gave me the okay to ease out of the bed and head downstairs. I needed to smoke if I wanted to get some sleep tonight. She was still hurting from the shit that happened between us, and I understood that she wanted clarity and didn't want to worry about me cheating on her, but I'd given it to her. *I guess this is the shit I have to deal with since I'm the one who actually fucked up the relationship.*

Strolling through the living room, I saw Junie moving around in the kitchen, and I walked straight in there.

"You good, sis?" I asked. I still couldn't believe this nigga Jace had been putting his hands on this girl the whole time. Shit, what was even more shocking was that she had actually stayed with him. The old Junie would have left Jace the first time he did that shit. I guessed because she had a child with him, she thought that he would change.

"I'm okay. What about you? I'm surprised you're even able to walk around after all that just went on in that room," she joked and laughed.

"Shitttt, you know how it goes down. You want to smoke?"

"Uh-uh, I don't know what you've been doing with your mouth."

"Nothing. We didn't even get that far. She just wanted some thug lovin'," I cracked, and we both laughed.

Heading out the door that led to the patio, I sat down and put the pre-rolled blunt to my mouth. Lighting it, I took a long pull from it and held the smoke in before exhaling that bullshit that just happened. In order for me to actually be able to make this shit work, I knew that I was going to have to take all the shit that she dished out to me.

"What's wrong?" Junie asked when I handed her the blunt. I guessed she could see I had something on my mind.

"Your sister constantly throwing it up in my face what I did. I hate that shit, but I know I have to put up with it because of the things I put her through."

"You don't have to put up with it, but you do need to understand where she's coming from. Now, don't get me wrong. I know that I'm the last person who should be giving advice with my latest situation, but I know that she loves you, and you know that. She's just having a hard time adjusting to having you back in her life. She wants to get all that hurt off her chest, but she doesn't know how to just sit down and talk about it. She likes to throw jabs, and that's something you have to get used to. Either talk to her about it or don't, but I can tell you right now if you two don't sit down and have a serious conversation, things are not going to get better for either of you. She's going to doubt everything that you do when you're not with her, which will then result in the blame game. Then you'll both be miserable, and it'll be like you're working things out for nothing."

"I hear you and I'm with it. I know that you had a situation with Jace, but you give the best advice, and I'm happy that you're talking to me. I plan on having a conversation with her to let her know that if she can't trust me, then we can't do this. I don't want her to be unhappy and unsure of what we have going on. I know what I want, and it's her, so I need her to be sure. How are you doing, though?" I questioned, tired of talking about Draya and me.

I needed to see what was up with her so I could figure out how I wanted to bring this shit to Jace. I wanted this nigga to know that he was out of line for putting his hands on that girl, and a part of me wanted to bust his ass as well.

"I'm fine. I know that Jace is your friend, but I can't be with him anymore. I'm so scared for my life. He hit me in front of our child, something he swore that he would never do. I don't know what's up with him, but I can't put up with it anymore. It's been this way for a while, and I kept my mouth shut because I didn't want anybody to know what was going on in my household. Now that everybody does, I know that my family is going to be watching me like a hawk to make sure I stay away from him."

"Do you even want to be in his presence again?"

"Not really, but I know in order for him to understand where I am, I'm going to have to have a conversation with him in person. That letter didn't do it, because he is still calling my phone. Shit, he has been blowing my shit up to the point where I had to change the number, and then he got that number. It's aggravating, and I hate that I have to keep Montana away from him because I don't know what he would do. I don't know the mind frame that man is in anymore. He goes from zero to one hundred real quick, and all hell breaks loose."

"One thing I know you don't have to worry about is him putting his hands on Montana or doing anything to hurt her. He loves his daughter. I want to whoop his ass so bad for what he did, but Draya's and Dreux's asses already did that." I chuckled, trying to make light of the situation.

"Yes, they did." She laughed as well. "I'ma head up before Tana wakes up," she added, getting up and handing me the blunt back.

"Good night, sis."

Chapter Twenty

Draya

Speechless

When I woke up the next morning, I turned to the side of the bed where Korey was supposed to be lying and saw that he was gone. Rolling my eyes, I was about to get out of the bed when my door opened, and Junie was standing there with KJ in her arms.

"So you just gon' sleep all day while li'l man acting a fool?" she asked.

"Girl, it's like eight o'clock in the morning. I'm tired."

"Nobody told you to be in here fucking all night. Yeah, I heard y'all nasty asses," she said with a goofy smile on her face.

"Girlllllllll, that shit was needed. My bad. We'll try to be silent next time," I told her. I honestly was not trying to be loud. I forgot that she and my niece were in the room next door, and I was high as hell, so I didn't care.

Finally climbing out of the bed, I grabbed KJ from her and laid him in his swing that was in my room. I went into the restroom and handled my personal hygiene.

"Do you want me to take Tana with KJ to Mom and Pop's?"

"Yeah. I just don't want them to see me like this any-more. If you had seen the hurt on their faces when Montana told them that Jace had put his hands on me, your heart would have broken. I know mine did."

"Of course it hurt them. No parent wants to ever have to get a phone call saying their child is in the hospital, no matter how old the kids are. That shit hurts, and Pops knew something was going on. He just didn't have enough evidence. Now that he does, he might try to kill Jace."

"I know, and that's something I don't want to happen. I know what he did to me was wrong, but he's still Montana's father. She loves that man, and he loves her. Just because we're not together anymore doesn't mean I want him dead."

"I'm happy you said that because I was going to kill him the night I went to his house with Dreux. I beat his ass so good that he was begging for me to stop."

"Thank you for that, but I never want you to put your-self in that position to possibly go to jail for defending me that way."

"Miss me with that. I'm going to always defend you no matter what. He was way out of line. He wasn't going to get that beating until he called both me and Dreux some hoes. All bets were off then. He had us both fucked up, so we took everything that he had done to you out on his ass. And I promised him that if he ever tried to jump crazy with you again, that would be a bullet in his ass instead of my bat."

She shook her head but said nothing. My sister loved Jace's dirty drawers, but she needed to understand that if a man could put his hands on you, that meant he didn't love you. He loved the control he had over you. We all knew something was going on, but none of us had the proof that we needed to do what we all knew was going to have to be done.

Once I was finished handling my personal hygiene, I walked out, and she was gone. Getting dressed in an off-the-shoulder sundress, I slid some sandals on my feet, then brushed my hair up into a ponytail. Grabbing KJ, I took him into his room, laid him on the changing table, and cleaned him up before dressing him in a white tee, Levi's overalls, and some white Air Force Ones. Brushing his hair down, I sat him down on the floor and let him walk around the room while I got his bag together. After I finished, I picked him back up and carried him down the stairs.

"I'm ready!" I yelled. Montana walked over to the door with her overnight bag, dressed in the cutest dress that matched the one that Junie was wearing.

"I'll be back to get you so we can go to the spa and just spend some sister time together today. I might invite Dreux as well."

"Okay, I'll be waiting," she said as we walked out of the house.

Once I had the kids settled and strapped in, I started the car and backed out of the driveway. The entire ride to my mother and father's house was silent. I had a lot on my mind, especially thinking about what happened between Korey and me. I knew that if I wanted to make this work, I needed to get how I was feeling off my chest. I had been holding this shit in for a long time, and it was time to let it go. The only way I could do that was by letting this man know how much he hurt me. I tried to act like a hard ass, but I was really soft on the inside and felt like when I needed him the most, he was fucking around on me.

Last night when his phone rang, it just reminded me of all the times he would get a call, leave the house in the middle of the night, and not come back until the next morning. It just didn't sit right with my spirit. And when

I woke up this morning and he wasn't there, it made me feel like he was back up to his old ways. I hated feeling that way. I wanted to trust him, but it was hard.

Pulling into the parking lot of my parents' home, I parked and cut the engine to the car before getting out, grabbing KJ, and letting Montana out since the doors had the child lock on. Walking the little distance to their front door, I was about to put my key inside when it opened.

"I was sitting in the living room waiting for you." My mother smiled, taking KJ from me and kissing him on the cheek, then doing the same to Montana. They had these kids so spoiled, but I loved the fact that if Junie and I couldn't depend on nobody, we both knew we had parents who would ride for us no matter what.

"That's their problem now and why they think they can do no wrong."

"Girl, whatever. Come in. Why didn't Junie ride with you?"

"She didn't want you or Daddy to keep seeing her like that. She knows that y'all are hurting to see her hurt, and she wants to ease that pain."

"She won't be able to. I just hope she stays away from Jace's ass. I don't know why she didn't want to move in over here."

"She will, but you have to give her time. She wants her space to get herself together. And let's be honest. You and Daddy will batter her until she decides to be done with him for good. Me, I just talk to her. I know that she's done with him, but in a situation like that, you can't be too sure."

"I hear you. I just want to be there for my baby during this time," my mother said just as my father strolled into the living room.

He hugged me and kissed me on the forehead before looking at my mother. "What are y'all talking about?"

"Jace and Junie."

"Oh, I'm going to catch up with his ass soon, and when I do, his ass is mine."

"Daddy, calm down. Not in front of Montana," I whispered.

He looked behind him to see her standing there with her head down. Leaning down, he picked her up and held her tight. "I love you, Mo," he said, calling her by the nickname he had given her.

"That's my cue. I'll be back to get them tomorrow," I let them both know before kissing my mother, father, Montana, and KJ, then leaving the house.

On the way back to my place, I pulled out my phone and texted Dreux about the spa date and gave her the address. I was about to set my phone down when it started to ring. Looking at it, I saw that it was her and answered.

"Hey, boo."

"Hey, do you mind if I bring Victoria?"

"You don't have to ask. She's like our little sister, so of course you can bring her," I let her know.

"Okay. Let me know when you make it there, and I'll pull up."

"Got you."

We hung up the phone, and I pulled into the driveway of my home. Not even getting out, I blew the horn and waited for Junie to emerge. When she did, she had tears rolling down her face, and I got worried. If Jace had popped up at my house on some bullshit, I was gonna hurt him for real.

"What's wrong?" I inquired as soon as her ass touched the passenger seat.

"Nothing. I was just in there thinking about all the shit I went through with Jace and the fact that I'm one of the victims who actually survived getting beat on. I know that the tables could easily turn. I could be dead if he don't want to see me with anyone, but I'm happy to be out, you know? I hate that I had to keep you and Dreux—shit, even Momma and Daddy—in the dark about what was going on all because I was scared of what he might do to me if I told. I have never put up with anything like that before, and I don't ever want to experience that shit again."

"Well, then you need to make sure you stay away from him. It's time, sis. I'm happy that you got out of that situation too," I said, driving away from the house and heading to the spa.

An hour later, I was relaxed, and my face felt good. My nails and feet were done, and now I was sitting in a sauna with my girls.

"Victoria, how are you?" I asked.

"Going through it with my baby daddy. Can I ask y'all advice?"

"Sure."

"Yeah, of course. You know we're here for you," Junie chimed, but Dreux said nothing.

"Okay, so I love my baby father, but he's in a relation-ship. He keeps saying that he didn't want me to have this baby, but the baby is cooking, and now I'm scared that he might dip. On top of that, he has a major issue with putting his hands on me."

"Oh, no, ma'am. What you not gon' put up with is a man putting his hands on you. You need to leave his ass in the dust and take care of your child."

"Yeah, I agree. I just got out of a bad situation myself, and all I can say is if he puts his hands on you once, he will do it again and again. You shouldn't want that to be you. You're so young and have a whole life ahead of you, so don't give no man that much control over you. I did, and now I have to figure out life without him. I thought he was the love of my life, but he loved the control he had when it came to me. He knew I was scared of him, so he used that to his advantage each time that he could. You just need to focus on your and this baby's future. Leave that man where he is."

I was proud of my sister. She was using what happened to her and giving somebody younger than all of us that advice. *I hope that Victoria actually takes the advice and runs with it instead of getting it and deciding to keep fucking with that nigga. Nothing good can come from being with a man like that.*

Chapter Twenty-one

Jace

Losing My Mind

When I finally got up this morning, I made sure I popped my pills and handled my personal hygiene. Looking in the mirror, I couldn't believe that Draya and Dreux had me looking like I got in a fight and lost in the worst way possible. I wasn't about to hit either of them, and I deserved that ass beating. They made me feel the way I was sure Junie felt each time I put my hands on her, and that wasn't a good feeling. Not being able to defend myself the way I wanted to was crazy. When I finally got myself together, I got dressed and made my way out of the bedroom with a pair of shades on.

Walking out of the house, I texted Junie to let her know that we needed to talk. She read the message but never responded. I wanted to see if I could talk her into coming back home and at least try to give me a chance to make up for all the mistakes I had made. I knew that was far-fetched, and with the way I left her the last time, I wouldn't text me back either if I were her. I couldn't let it be known to myself enough how much that changed the way she and my daughter would look at me forever. I felt so bad about doing what I did, and the worst part was knowing that I lost the woman of my dreams because I couldn't control my anger.

Not only was I in the midst of dealing with all that, but I also had to deal with Victoria having my baby soon, and I wanted to be there for that baby as well.

Pulling up to the trap house, I shook my head when I saw Korey and Deion standing out there. I just knew they had come to put me in my place, and truly I didn't have time for it. The only person I wanted to talk to was Junie. It was time I let her know about the bipolar disorder, but it was not for her to forgive me. It was for her to understand that I never wanted to put my hands on her the way I did. That shit was beyond me, and now I knew it was a mistake for me to stop taking the medication altogether. Losing her and Montana was enough to make me want to get back on it and go see the therapist I had on speed dial but never used.

Before I could even get out of the car, they were both at my car door. I got out and eyed both of them before removing my shades. I made it my business to let both of them know what happened between me, Draya, and Dreux so they could know I didn't do anything to either of them. Deion was feeling Dreux, and Korey was in the midst of making things work with Draya. I also looked at both women like sisters, so I knew it was bound to happen sooner or later.

"Damn, they did a number on you," Deion joked before chuckling.

"Shit, I still feel the pain in my legs and back from each swing they took at me with those damn bats."

"I could have told you that was coming. You know Draya don't play about Junie. What I want to know is what you were thinking."

"I don't know what came over me, but I want to talk to her. I just want her to know how sorry I am, and I don't want her to keep my child away from me. I fucked up, and I need to explain to her why I did what I did," I said.

I wanted both these niggas to know that I didn't do it on purpose, but I also wasn't ready for them to know about my bipolar disorder. The reason I kept it a secret from them was that I didn't want them to think that I was incompetent of doing what I was doing. I wanted to be seen as this man with much respect who could handle just about everything, but deep down, I was ready to snap. I was already being viewed as the worst of the worst with the way I was treating not only Junie but all the women in my life, including Victoria. She was carrying my second child, and I was treating her like shit or like we didn't have nothing in the beginning of us fucking around.

"I don't know what to tell you about you and Junie having a conversation, but if you truly just want to make peace and let her go on about her life without guilt-tripping her, text her," Korey replied, making me look at him. I had to make sure he was serious before responding.

"I'm not texting her."

I deserved to be able to see her face to let her know what I needed to let her know, and I was sure she would be able to actually understand if she could see the proof with the medicine I was taking. I didn't want her to think that I was just telling her this to try to get her back. I did want her back, but I also knew that wasn't possible with what I did. I also wanted her to tell me to my face that she was done with me.

"You don't deserve nothing. You need to let her go, bro," Deion said. I could tell that he was trying to be real with me like always, but I didn't want to hear that.

"Man, watch out. I have work to do. I'll catch y'all later," I said, sidestepping both of them and heading up the driveway to the house.

As soon as I was in, I shut the door behind me and went straight to the back so that I could count up the money we made yesterday. I didn't even want to be here today, but I knew if I didn't come in, Ace would think he got to me, and that was the last thing I ever wanted a nigga to think.

The feeling of my phone vibrating in my pocket told me somebody was texting me. Pulling it out, I saw that it was Junie telling me to meet her at Draya's house. Texting her back, I asked if Draya was going to be there, and she told me yes, but if I wanted to talk, this was my only chance.

Letting out a breath, I strolled right back out the front door and got into my car. The entire ride to her house had me on edge. I didn't know if maybe I was about to walk into an ambush or what. I knew for a fact that her father was probably looking for me. He let it be known when he found out I was dating his daughter that if I hurt her in any way, he was going to kill me. But I didn't think nothing prepared him for the way I was actually hurting her.

When I finally pulled into the driveway of the house, Draya and Junie were sitting on the porch smoking and drinking. Getting out, I saw that Draya had that bat sitting next to her, and I decided to be on my best behavior.

"Hey, thank you for allowing me to come talk to you. I know I'm the last person you want to see, but I just felt like it was time for me to come clean about why I was so enraged all the time."

"Okay."

She wouldn't even look at me, and that hurt me even more.

"When I was young, I was diagnosed with bipolar disorder. I know that's the last thing you expected to hear from me, and I'm sorry I didn't tell you this before we got into a relationship. I just didn't want you to think something was broken inside of me. I never imagined putting my hands on you, but you were the reason I stopped taking the medication. I didn't think I needed it anymore."

"But you did need to take that medicine. I was wondering how you would go from zero to a hundred in seconds. It was like you had two different personalities, but I didn't know why," she said.

I could hear the hurt in her voice, hurt from me keeping it from her all these years, and hurt from the fact that I let it affect both of us to the point of no return. I knew that was what she was feeling because I was feeling the same way.

"Hurting you made me hurt, and I'm sorry for that. I know you will never be able to forgive me, but I felt like the least I could do was apologize for the way I treated you. Also, I would like it if you wouldn't keep Montana away from me. I love her with everything in me the same way I love you. She's literally the best thing to ever happen to me."

"Jace, I want you to know that I do forgive you. I've been around here beating myself up for doing that because my heart feels like you don't deserve that. I never want to make things hard for you, and I will never take Montana away from you. Although she saw what happened, it doesn't change the way she feels about you. I even talked to Draya about that, and she said that I would be hurting my child by taking her away from you, and that's something I don't ever want to do."

"So what about us?"

"What about us? I don't know about that part just yet. I know that I can't deal with you putting your hands on me, no matter the bipolar disorder. You had the chance to keep taking your medication, and you decided not to because you felt like, with me by your side, you didn't need it, but you did. You let me down by putting your hands on me. I let myself down for putting up with it for too long, and I will never do that to myself again. I'm not selling myself short for no man, and that includes you. I've seen too many crime shows where women who get beat on by their significant others come up missing when they don't want to put up with it anymore, and I don't want that to be me."

"I would never kill you."

"Jace, you don't know that," Draya chimed in. "Bipolar doesn't let you know when you're going too far. You can kill and not realize what you've done until it's too late. You need to get yourself together, and Junie needs to be her own woman. I know that this don't have anything to do with me because it's not my relationship, but she is my sister. And as much as I know she loves you, she has to let you go, and you need to do the same. I know that's not something either of you want to hear, but that's what it is."

"Yeah, she's right," Junie agreed, and I nodded my head.

"Well, thank you for taking time out of your day to hear me out, Junie. I love you," I told her before turning and walking back to my car.

Chapter Twenty-two

Junie

I'm Leaving

After that conversation with Jace, I had so much on my mind. I didn't know he had all that going on, but it made sense. When he would snap on me about the littlest shit, I just thought that maybe he had a lot going on and that I wasn't doing nothing but making things worse.

"I love him, Draya." I kept it real with her.

"So you're willing to go back? What if he doesn't change? What if he's just telling you this to make you want to come back? You really need to think about this. I'm not for it at all if that's you're thinking," she said.

This entire time we had been talking, I never said anything about going back. I was just getting the way I felt about him off my chest. I needed to. I hadn't been able to talk to anybody about the way I was feeling. Everybody thought that I was trying to give myself a reason for going back to him, but that wasn't the truth. I was really just looking to get the way I was feeling off my chest so that I didn't have to have these thoughts anymore.

"I'm not saying I want to go back to him. Draya, what I'm trying to do is make it to where I get the way I was feeling off my chest, but of course you want to make it about something else. What I need is for you and everybody to know that this isn't going to be easy. I want everybody to know that I'm going through a lot, and I just want to make sense of this shit."

"I know what you want to do, and I'm here for you always. But I want you to remember that you're going through the motions of knowing that you don't have him anymore. You have given up your house and everything. It's going to make you want to go back because of the love you have for this man, and that's not what I want you to do. I want you to know that you have me, Momma, Daddy, and Dreux behind you one hundred percent. We will do whatever we can to make sure you and Montana get back on your feet and back in that happy place you deserve to be in."

"Thank you."

I didn't know what else to say. It was like she had everything figured out, and she was right about everything she had said. I needed to focus on me and my daughter, not Jace. Whatever he had going on still wasn't a valid reason for him to put his hands on me. He could have kept taking his medicine, and I kept it real about that part. That was the way I felt. I felt like if he wanted to keep taking it, he would have, but he didn't want to. He just didn't think it would get this bad, to the point where he lost both me and his daughter. As far as keeping Montana away from him, I would never do that because I knew how much he loved her. He treated her like a princess, but I also didn't want my daughter to grow up and remember this moment about her father. I wanted her to remember him as the man who did whatever he could to make sure she was a happy little girl.

"I hope that you know that you have me. I'm sorry for spazzing off on you like that. If you want to talk to me about anything pertaining to Jace, I'm here to listen.

I just want to make sure that you understand where I'm coming from first. He's not welcome in this house anymore, and I want you to know that he will never be around me. That nigga has to understand what he did wasn't cool, and I want him to know that."

"I think he knows it. He knows that he isn't going to get me back, and that's what I need for him to get through his head. I want him to know that I don't have to put up with that kind of shit, and I can actually be with any man I want to. I'm so happy to be out of that situation. Now I can live my life better for me and for my daughter without having to worry about hearing his mouth or what he thinks about it."

I stopped going to college and quit my job to make Jace feel secure. It didn't make me happy, but the fact that he was happy was enough for me. I didn't know how I didn't see at first that he didn't mean me any good to make me quit my job, but I didn't. I stayed with him because I loved him, and that love wasn't going anywhere anytime soon. He just went from meaning the world to me to not being in my life at all. I wanted us both to focus on ourselves. Jace and I were not meant to be at the end of that. He needed to be alone for a while. I didn't want him texting my phone, trying to get my attention, or trying to make me feel bad about leaving him. I did what I had to do for me, and I wanted everybody to understand that. I didn't have to be with him or put up with the way he was treating me all because I had a baby for him. And I hoped other women understood that as well.

We as women had to realize our worth and know that these men were nothing without us. Jace was going to be miserable. I could see it in his face, and I didn't want that for him. I wanted to grow old and be with him for the rest of my life, but that was not the way shit went down. I had to live with it the same as he did.

Draya got up and went up the stairs, and I sat down, putting my head in my hands. I just closed my eyes and shook my head. I didn't know how I was going to make it through life without having Jace next to me. Yes, life with him was hell, but I didn't want to have to start over with a new man.

My phone ringing snapped me out of my thoughts. I grabbed it and saw that it was Ace. I didn't know how he got my number or what he wanted. I was appreciative of the way he was there for me, but I wanted him to know that we couldn't continue what we were doing, whatever it was. "Hello?"

"Hey, I hope you don't mind, but your girl Dreux gave me your number. I was calling to see how you were doing."

"I'm fine. It's gonna take some healing, but I think everything will be fine."

"Good. I don't know why I'm so worried about you. It's not like I will ever have a chance with you."

"First of all, why would you think that you didn't have a chance with me?"

"Because you're Jace's girl," he responded.

"I'm not his girl anymore, although I've been thinking about giving him another chance. He finally told me what was wrong with him, and I can't help but feel bad for him."

"Just because you're feeling bad about it doesn't mean you have to give him another chance. That man has done things to you that you shouldn't be putting up with anyway. You're beautiful, and you and your daughter deserve to be treated like queens. You shouldn't want her to think that is a way of living life," he let me know.

I nodded my head as if he could see me. "I know. I don't know what I'm thinking. I'm just scared of starting over with a new man. I don't even know if I'm dating material. I feel like I may be broken."

"You're not broken. You just haven't met the man who will make you happy or a priority. You need to know that you deserve the best, and I'm sorry, but Jace is not that for you."

"And how do you know that?"

"Listen, I want to be your friend, but I know that if you give me the chance to prove to you that I can treat you the way you deserve to be treated, you don't have to worry about Jace or anything," he told me.

I was all for giving him a chance as a friend, but that was it. I didn't see actually getting into another relationship anytime soon. "I think you would do fine as my friend, but I don't know when I would be ready for a new relationship."

"That's fine with me as long as you'll let me take you out to lunch or dinner . . . as a friend, of course," he suggested, making me smile.

I always had men who tried to get with me, but I couldn't see myself without Jace, and now I didn't have a choice but to move on. I had to make the right decisions for myself and my child. The one thing I didn't want to be was in another fucked-up situation with a new dude, so it was imperative for me to just be his friend before anything else.

"As soon as my nose heals, I'll go out. Until then, I think it's best for me to just stay in the house. If you want to come to my sister's house and chill with me, I would like that."

"I'm down with it. How long will you be staying with your sister?"

"At least for another week or so. I'm in the process of looking for a new house. I just have to make sure it's everything that my daughter and I need. She's the only one I need to focus on right now."

"I can feel you on that, and I might be able to help on the house thing. Let me hit you right back though. It's going to be about an hour."

"Okay," I said, and he hung up before I could ask more questions.

Ace was a cool dude, and he seemed like he would make a good friend and lover possibly, but that was the last thing on my mind. Right now, I just wanted to make sure he had my best interest in mind. I didn't need a man in my face just plotting to get me back with him and start cheating and lying to me. Jace had ruined that for me. He had me feeling like I would never find the love that I needed. Shit, he drained me of that. All I tried to do was make it work with him, and he didn't appreciate it. He took it all from me while making me hate him instead of feeling love from him.

I never wanted to go through the things I went through with him with anybody else. I really just wanted to be single for as long as God allowed me to. I was one of those women who thought the way he treated me was because he loved me, but it wasn't. It was because he wanted to control me, and I was dumb behind him.

Getting up, I rolled a blunt and went out on the back porch so that I could smoke and get my mind right. I didn't know what else needed to be said between Jace and me after "I'm leaving."

Chapter Twenty-three

Dreux

Fed Up

I was waiting at the restaurant for Max. It was time for us to sit down once again because he was back on his stupid shit. As soon as he saw Deion and me, he started acting stupid again. He made it seem like I was trying to make him feel some way, but that was far from it. He wasn't that important for me to do all that. We were literally just Savannah's parents, and that was it. I had some other shit on my mind, so the last thing I wanted was to be having this conversation with him all over again. I just wished he would stop acting like he deserved anything from me, because he didn't.

"Well, hello. I didn't think you were going to show," he said with a smug look on his face.

"You don't know me. I don't know how many times I have to tell you that. I'm not that little girl I used to be, and you can't stand that. You want me to be something you're used to instead of seeing me as the grown woman I am today. You have tried time and time again to take my child away from me, and now I let her go with you for the night and you don't want to give her back to me."

"I know what I'm doing, and it's for the best. She shouldn't be around a man she doesn't know."

"Well, first of all, she hasn't been around Deion like that. And secondly, if she had been, it's none of your business. You act like I told you the same thing about your wife with her fucked-up attitude. So now we can handle this the right way or the court way. I'm not about to do this with you any longer," I told him just as Deion walked up with some papers in his hands.

"You gon' do whatever I tell you to do because I have the upper hand."

When he said that, I smiled.

"Nah, you don't have the upper hand in nothing. You're going to give her child back, or these two nice officers are going to arrest you and your wife for kidnapping when they get to your house," he let him know, then moved to the side just as the cops were walking up.

Now, I didn't fuck with cops, but I was willing to do whatever I had to do to get my child back. I didn't want her to be in this position. No child should ever have to witness their parents going at it. It didn't matter how many times I tried to work things out with Max so we didn't have to worry about the bickering and fighting. He always did something to make me regret it. I didn't have anything against him wanting to be in our daughter's life, but when you've been putting up with it for so long, you start thinking that some people are just not worth your energy, and that was where I was with him.

"Max, I just want my child back. That's it," I pleaded with him.

He said nothing, just got on his phone and called somebody. "Bring her in," he said and hung up the phone. Standing up from my seat, I got myself ready for when his wife walked in with my child because I was about to beat the brakes off her ass.

"She's not worth it. I know you want to do it, but let her and him make it. With this, you will be granted full custody without him getting any visitation rights."

Nodding my head, I knew he was right, but when she walked in with Savannah and my daughter started crying, I rushed her, knocking her to the ground.

"Bitch, you want to be in this shit with Max, and now you can go down with him. I'm sick of you and him playing with me. Have your own fucking kids!" I snapped before the cops pulled me off her.

I just knew they were going to arrest me, but instead they walked me back to Deion and Savannah, and I hugged my child as tight as I could. She meant the world to me, and the fact that Max was really plotting on taking her away from me was all I needed to take his ass to court. *I'm not about to play this game with him anymore. He's now out of our child's life, and he has no one but himself to blame.*

"Stay here. I want to say something to your father," I told her before walking over to where Max and his wife were standing.

"As of now, you will never see Savannah again. I've tried time after time to make this work with you, and you've just been playing me a little too close for comfort. I can't do this with you anymore, so you'll be receiving court papers in the mail soon." And with that, I walked away from him, grabbed my daughter by the hand, and we walked out of the restaurant.

Getting into the car, I pulled out of the parking lot, and Deion was right behind me. I had some other shit on my mind that I needed to work out, like how the hell

I was going to tell my best friends that my sister was pregnant by Jace. *This shit is beyond me.* I hated being put in this position. It was not fair or fun. I thought by keeping the secret that I was doing her a favor as her big sister, but it was becoming too much for me. I shouldn't have even asked her who the father was. She could have kept that shit to herself. I didn't know when I was going to tell them, but I knew sooner or later I was going to have to come out with it. I didn't want to be around them knowing this secret. Then when they found out I'd known, they'd hate me.

When I made it back to the house, I got out of the car, and we went inside.

"Vannah!" Victoria yelled as she ran to her and hugged her. She had been just as beat up about this situation as I had. And I had to admit, just seeing the way she loved on my daughter told me that she was going to be a helluva good parent. *I just hope that she leaves Jace alone before she becomes his next victim, because behind her, I will actually kill him.*

I was about to shut the front door when Deion knocked on it. Pulling it open, I hugged him as tight as I could. "Thank you so much. I didn't think you were going to get my text message."

"Of course I got it, and I made sure I brought reinforcements with me just in case he tried to make a scene."

I couldn't take it anymore and kissed his lips. They were so soft, just as I imagined. Putting his hands on the small of my back, he squeezed it, and we kept kissing passionately. The spark I felt with that kiss was something I hadn't felt in a long time, and I knew that Deion was meant to be right here with me. *I just hope that it actually works out. I don't want to be hurt anymore.*

"Come on, we need to talk," I said, grabbing his hand and leading him upstairs to my bedroom. As soon as we got in there, he sat on the edge of the bed. I grabbed a pre-rolled blunt and put it to my mouth. Lighting it, I took a long drag from it, then sat in my plush chair that was in front of my vanity mirror.

"What are you hoping to come from this?"

"Shit, I want to be with you. Simple as that. I haven't met a woman like you before, but I have to tell you something," he said. "Now, I don't want you to be mad at me for not telling you this before. Nothing has happened between me and this girl since we broke up, but she has been staying with me until she gets her house in order," he added, making me frown.

"Who?"

"My ex, Breann. We don't sleep in the same bed. Shit, I don't even hold a conversation with her. I keep telling her that I want her to get out, but her house isn't ready."

"Hotel her ass quick. I'm not about to start nothing with you and you still got the next bitch staying with you, so if you want me, then you need to show me. She needs to be gone."

He should have known I wasn't going to get mad at him for that, but I didn't want her in his presence. *She doesn't deserve to be around him at all, especially not when he's with me. It's me or her, plain and simple. I like him, and I know he likes me, so he just has to show me how serious he is about me. I'm not holding anything back from him or this relationship, so I want him to do the same thing. Everything needs to be fifty-fifty as far as this relationship goes because, even with my busy schedule, I will still be making sure I handle my business as his woman.*

"Okay, I will handle that as soon as I get back home. Until then, I was wondering if I could chill here with you and Savannah for the rest of the day."

"Of course."

Blowing smoke out of my mouth, I went to hand it to him, but he pulled me down on him instead. Kissing my lips, he parted them with his tongue, and I sucked on it while grinding my pussy on him. I hadn't had dick in a long time. *I want to make this worth it if I'm going to get it.* I wanted him to knock the dust off this pussy.

Whap! He slapped my ass and grabbed a hold of it while kissing my lips some more. I had to back up before we had sex. As bad as I wanted it, the last thing I needed was for him to think that I was an easy fuck. I had morals and held myself to high standards, so he was going to have to work for this shit. *On top of that, I have to make sure he's all for me before I actually open up and give him a piece of me.*

Sitting up on the bed, I hit the blunt once again before passing it back to him. "Are you going to spend the night with me?" I asked.

"If you want me to."

"I do, but I want you to want to spend the night with me."

"Oh, I do." He smirked, then leaned over and kissed me on the lips before continuing. "Just let me go put this girl out of my house. I don't want to do anything to make my lady mad."

"Your lady?"

"I mean, that's what you are, so ain't no need to sugarcoat it. I been wanting to take it there with you, but I didn't know how you were going to feel about it."

"I feel good about it. Now hurry back," I told him just as he headed for the door.

When he walked out, I went into the restroom, ran some bathwater, then dropped some bath bombs in it. I lay in the tub relaxing when my phone started to ring. Picking it up off the floor, I saw that it was Draya and answered.

"Hello?"

"I don't appreciate you acting like me and Junie did something to you. Now, do you want to tell me why you've been acting so stank?"

"Come to the house, and we can talk," I said and hung up the phone. I guessed there was no better time to tell them than now.

Part 2

Chapter Twenty-four

Junie

Back 2 Life

I was finally able to live my life without having to worry about Jace and his attitude and hand problem. These last three months had been nothing short of amazing, and I wanted to keep this same luck. I was able to tell Jace to stop calling and texting me if it didn't have anything to do with our daughter, and he actually complied. I was not used to that, but I wanted to keep it that way. I wasn't missing him as much as I was when I first had to leave him. I had to keep living my life. I would never let a man trap me into thinking that he put his hands on me because he loved me. I didn't even know what made me feel like Jace loved me when he did it.

Having my own place was the best feeling in the world. I got to come home and actually relax, especially when my mother and father had Montana.

"So how's everything?" Ace asked. "Do you like the house?"

"Yes, I love it. Thank you so much for putting me in contact with your real estate agent and interior decorator and also for paying for everything, although I specifically told you that you didn't have to do that."

"I know, but I like helping you out," his deep voice said.

Looking up at him, I was about to respond when the door to the office opened, and Jace walked in. "What's up? What's this about?"

"Nothing. Let me go get Montana," I said, making my way to the back where she was in my office coloring and snacking. Having a job was so new for me the first time around, but once I got used to it, I was on it. Not a day went by that I didn't have a new client coming in and thanking me for making their house feel like a home. It made me happy that I was finally in a place where I was doing what I loved to do as well as making others' homes feel like that: a home.

When we got back to the front, Jace and Ace were staring each other down with mugs on their faces, and I just knew something was said. "So you fucking with this nigga?" Jace questioned, making me cock my head to the side.

"If I am, it's not your business. Have fun with your daddy. I'll see you tomorrow," I told Montana, leaning down and kissing her on the cheek. Jace had a lot of nerve to be asking if I was fucking with Ace like that had anything to do with him. What he needed to realize was that we were coparenting, and that was it.

When they walked out of the building, I turned my attention to Ace. "What did you say to him?" I asked.

"Nothing. He asked me what was going on, and I said I was just checking up on you. That's it. You know I'm not the type to talk about my business, especially to a nigga like that. I don't have anything for Jace, and he's even more pissed because I told the plug he needed to find somewhere else for me to work. After all, it's not working for me anymore."

I had no choice but to believe him, because what reason did he have to lie? Nothing was going on between

Ace and me. We were just friends. He understood why and so did I, and that was all that mattered. Everybody wanted me to make it official with him, but I wasn't ready for another relationship. I wanted to just live my life and be happy like I'd been.

"Well, do what you have to do to make you happy. I don't have anything against you working with him. I just don't want him to know anything that's going on in my life."

"Is Jace in the past for real?"

"Yeah, why?"

"I'm just trying to figure out why you haven't given me a chance. I know you're saying you don't want to get into a relationship, but damn, I'm here, and I want to be here for as long as you let me."

This was the problem with having male friends. They always wanted to take things to the next level when I wasn't ready. "I like you, Ace. I do. I'm just not prepared. I do want to give you a chance, but I have to make sure I'm ready for all that comes with giving a man like you a chance. I don't want to be giving you half of me while you're giving me all of you. That's not fair to you. I think I'm okay with being your friend right now. That way, I don't have to worry about hurting you in the process."

I just really wanted him to understand that we were good as friends and there was no point in us switching things up. It didn't have anything to do with Jace. He was living his life, and as far as I knew, he was now living with Dreux's sister and they were this happy family, so he was the least of my worries. If she wanted to put herself in that position, then that was on her.

"I hear you, but at least let me take you out tonight."

"Can't. Plans with the girls."

"A'ight." He put his hands up in the air as if he surrendered.

I never wanted to have this conversation with him. I really wished that he would have just gone with the flow. It was not like we had sex or anything. I didn't even kiss this man. All we did was chill, and he'd been letting me vent to him about everything that went on with Jace and me. He was like my best friend, and although I knew that I wanted more from him, I also knew that I had to be realistic about it.

Neither of us wanted to be hurt in the end. Ace was an excellent dude. He had taken a liking to Montana, and she did to him. I was fascinated with him. I didn't want him to think I was taking him for granted, though. "I don't want you to think I'm taking your friendship for granted, Ace. You mean a lot to me as a friend, and I don't want to lose that, and I know if we get into a relationship and it doesn't work out, I will lose that."

"You don't have to worry about that. I'm waiting for you, ma. I think we have a lot in common, and I know that I won't come by another woman like you."

"What you mean by that?"

"I mean, you're amazing with your daughter and mine. You never make her feel differently because she's my child. You have me fascinated with you to the point where you're all I think about. I haven't felt the way I feel about you for another woman in a long time. I don't want to rush things either. I just wanted to know if Jace was the reason why you weren't trying to go there with me."

"No, he's not," I told him again.

"Good. I'll see you later on, I'm sure." He smiled and hugged me.

I kissed him on the cheek, and we stared at one another for a while before he walked out of the building. Going to the door, I watched as he got into his car and backed out of the parking lot while waving at me. Smiling, I turned and went back to my office. Sitting down in my chair, I started in on the paperwork I had left from a job I did yesterday when my phone started to ring. Looking at it, I saw that it was Draya and quickly picked up. "Hello?"

"Hey, boo, how are you?" she asked.

"Good. Montana just went with Jace, and that was awkward."

"Why?"

"Ace was here."

"What's going on with you and him? That man likes you. I don't know why you don't just give him a chance."

"Because I don't want to hurt him. He's a perfect guy, Draya. He deserves all of me, but when I'm ready, and right now, I'm just not ready for all that. I need him to wait. I have to get myself together. I don't want to lose myself in another man, so I need to take my time and actually figure out what I want."

"I understand exactly what you're saying, and if he waits for you, then that should show you how much he likes you. I know that Jace did a number on you, but you don't want to feel like he's still running you by you not getting into another relationship. Meanwhile, he has Victoria around your child."

"I know. I still can't believe that Dreux knew that her sister was pregnant with Jace's child and waited to tell us."

"Yeah, have you talked to her about it yet?"

"No, I don't know what to say to her. I just want us to work together. I feel like we have to rebuild that trust that was lost, so right now I just want to handle my business. I'll talk to her about it soon, though," I let her know.

"Like today soon. Stop procrastinating. You need to start telling people how you feel, Junie."

"I hear you, momma. I'll talk to her when she comes back. Talk to you later on," I said and hung up the phone before she could respond.

Chapter Twenty-five

Draya

Cater 2 You

Being part owner of Lady Rouge changed my life in a big way. I was always at work, and if I wasn't, then I was home with my son and man. He didn't like the fact that I had wanted to work with him, but I figured it would help him get some of the stress off him. He had been coming home later and later since Laila had quit, so it was time for me to step up and help my man the way any fiancée would. He didn't even want to give me a chance. His ass thought I was trying to dance in this bitch, and I had to let it be known that I was not even that type to take my clothes off for money. All I wanted to do was help him out with the women. They were used to Laila, but now they needed to get used to me.

"Minnie, I'm not about to sit up here and go back and forth with you. You got the right one. I don't work for you. You work for my man and me. If this is the way he let you talk to him or anybody, then I don't understand why you still have a job."

"Okay, and? I have my job because I'm the one who brings him in the most money."

"No, that's not true. Kasey is his top-dollar bitch here. You barely see what you were making at the other club, and maybe it's because all you do is complain and think you're better than the rest of the dancers. Let me bring you back down to two inches, sweetie. You're not better than none of the other girls who dance."

"Whatever."

"The idea I have is to make sure you and all the girls see more money than y'all have ever seen. Do you know how many men love a good costume night? I swear y'all females swear y'all know everything, and y'all don't."

A knock on the door got my attention, making me look up when Korey walked in. I smiled and got up from my desk. Walking around, I kissed him on the lips, and he held me tightly while sliding his tongue in my mouth. Moving back, I put my hand on his chest.

"What's going on in here?" he asked.

"Your girl wants us to start having a costume night. She doesn't understand that some of us are used to the way things were at the old club, and it seems like she's trying to come in and change things up. I don't like that. You need to put her in her place before I quit," Minnie told him before getting up and walking out of the office.

"I could snatch that little bitch up. This is your fault," I snapped at him.

"Wait, how did this become my fault? I just walked through the door."

"It's your fault because you got her thinking she can just talk to people any kind of way. No wonder Laila quit. I wouldn't be putting up with this shit. She has one time to come for me like she ain't got no sense, and I'm going to lay her ass out, then have her dragged out of here."

"What's this idea you were bringing to the table?" he asked, changing the subject.

"Okay, costume night. It's sure to lace their pockets and ours. You shouldn't want them to keep doing the same stale-ass shit. That shit gets old, and then the customers are going to want to go somewhere else. It's time to bring heat, because right now the only dancer making good money is Kasey, and that's because she switches it up."

"So she's the one who helped you come up with this idea?"

"Not the costume thing, but yeah, on the idea to change up the routines. They need to come harder. I mean, you do want to see money, don't you?"

"Hell yeah. With all the money I'm putting into this shit, you damn right."

"Well, you need to have my back and let them know that this is what it is, and there's nothing you can do about it. Your hands are tied or some shit. All I know is you need to have my back."

Nodding his head, he grabbed my hand and led me out of the office and downstairs, where all the dancers were sitting. As soon as we stepped in front of them, all the talking ceased, and Korey had their attention. Stepping back, he pulled me back to him. "As you all know, this is my fiancée, and she's part owner of this club, so y'all need to start respecting her and listening to what she's saying. She will never put y'all in a position that will have y'all not making any money. She ran her idea by me, and I think it's a good idea, so good that I'm going to be using it for the other club as well. It all comes down to if you want to make money or not. I'm not here to babysit anybody. Listen and learn," he let them know, and I nodded my head.

"I don't want y'all to think that I'm just coming in and switching things up to make this shit harder for y'all, because I'm not. If y'all would stop fighting me, then you would know that I'm here to help. I'm for y'all, so like my fiancé said, listen to me and y'all won't have to worry about what the next bitch is doing, because y'all can be making close to ten thousand a night with the shit I have set up," I let them know, and they all nodded their heads.

If they had gone along with it the first time, I wouldn't have even needed Korey here for this. I didn't want to have to run everything by him when I was the one running this club, and they needed to get that through their heads. The sooner the better. That way, we could have a clear understanding.

"How about we get out of here?"

"Do you think that's a good idea? I mean, I want to get everything ready for the night. I don't want the new manager for tonight to have much to do except watch things. I promise I'll come straight home when I'm finished."

"A'ight." He kissed me on the lips and made his way out of the building.

Making my way back up to the office, I shut the door behind me and sat down. I needed a break. I was tired, and I just wanted to get the rest of this shit done so that I could go home. The one thing I wanted Korey to know was that the way to not have a lot of work to do the next day was to get it all done in that day.

Sitting up straight, I grabbed the books and finished going through them and made sure the music and everything was together for the night manager. Once that was finished, I got up and walked out of the office, shutting and locking the office door behind me. Not saying anything to the girls, I walked out of the building and got into my car.

The entire ride to the house was long. It felt like I was driving more than usual. Finally pulling up, I was about to get out when my phone started to ring. Looking at it, I saw that it was Dreux, and I hit the decline button before getting out. I wasn't ignoring her. I just felt like the way she went about everything left a bad taste in my mouth. I also felt like we didn't have anything to talk about. She withheld that information from Junie, the one who was in an actual relationship with Jace.

Getting out of the car, I went inside, and Korey was sitting on the sofa with a sleeping KJ on his chest. Moving closer to both of them, I leaned down and kissed my son on the cheek, then Korey on the lips. "I guess I'll start the food."

"You don't have to cook if you don't want to. I can order something. I know you're probably tired."

"Are you sure you don't mind? I know that you love it when I cook."

"Yes, I'm sure, babe. Go ahead and take your shower, and I'll order some Chinese or pizza."

"Ooh, Chinese, please."

Making my way up the stairs, I went into our bedroom and turned the shower on before stripping and getting in. Standing close to the water, I let it hit my body in all the right places, then bathed and got out. After drying off, I threw my robe on with nothing underneath and walked out. Korey had the food sitting on the coffee table in front of him, so I started to eat.

"How was your day?" I asked.

"Good. I wish you had left with me, but I understand you wanting to get everything together."

"I'm happy you understand it, but I want to spend more time with you. I know these last three months have been busy, and never have I imagined being that busy."

Honestly, I never thought that owning a strip club was all that work. It was like Laila didn't do much to say she was the manager. I had to go in and change everything up. I had to make sure the books were straight and the girls were good. I had to make sure they had everything for their nights in the club.

"Do you think you need an assistant?"

"Yes, if I want to get out of there sooner than four o'clock in the evening. I want to be out of the club before it gets too late. I don't want to be spending all this time away from my son or you. I didn't think it took all of this to run a business."

"Okay, we'll start interviewing for assistants tomorrow, because I can use one too. We have to start making time to plan the wedding. I don't want to be engaged for the next five years."

I nodded my head. I could understand where he was coming from, but he had to know that I wasn't trying to get married sooner than we had to. The last thing I wanted was to be out here married and unhappy. I wanted to make sure this was something we both wanted for real before we actually took that step.

"Are you ready to be married to me? I mean, like faithful to only me for the rest of your life?" I asked, and he looked at me with a smirk on his face, then pulled me to him. He kissed me on the lips. I wrapped my arms around his neck, and we shared a long, passionate kiss before he answered.

"Hell, yes, I am already. There's not another woman I want to be with. It's you and me," he said, making me smile.

I loved Korey with everything in me, and the fact that he was sitting up here telling me that there wasn't another woman he wanted to be with, I loved that. He had me feeling so secure to say that before we weren't even together, and when we did get together, shit was rocky. I was still hurting about the shit that he put me through, and I couldn't get past it, but now that we were here, I wanted us to maintain this shit forever.

Chapter Twenty-six

Dreux

Reflection

These last three months I'd spent with Deion had been nothing short of amazing. This man had shown me the most respect, given me all his attention, and he never made me feel like I had something to prove to anybody. He never flirted with another female in my face, and when he was in the club and women tried to holla at him, he was quick to put them in their place, which was something I loved about him. I could only hope that things remained the same so I didn't have to worry about us ever not being together. He had helped me get custody of my daughter, and now I didn't have to worry about seeing Max and his wife ever again. I hated this for my daughter, but at the end of the day, I had to do what I had to do in order to protect both her and myself.

She asked about her father all the time, and there was nothing I could do about it. I knew she was missing her father, but I couldn't risk him seeing her and her not coming back home to me. She didn't fully understand what was going on, and I had to live with that. Be careful who you have children with because it can put you in fucked-up positions.

With her being 8 years old, all she wanted to know was when she could go with her father, when he was going to come to see her, and some more shit, and I didn't know how to explain to my 8-year-old that she couldn't see her father.

"Mommy?" her little voice asked, making me look up.

"Yes, ma'am."

"I want to see my daddy. I miss him."

Putting my head down, I shook it. "Come here, boo," I said, and she came over to me. Moving back in my chair, I sat her on my lap. "Your father can't see you right now. I hate this for you, but Daddy tried to take you away from Mommy, and I had to make sure he didn't."

"I want my daddy," she replied with tears in her eyes.

That made me feel even worse. "Okay, let me figure something out," I told her, and she nodded her head, then got up and walked out of my home office. Sitting back in the seat, I rubbed my hands down my face and sighed. Picking up my phone, I called Deion, who picked up on the second ring.

"What's up, babe?"

"Vannah is asking for her father, and I don't know what to do. I want her to see him just to ease her mind, but I'm also scared that he might not bring her back."

"Hit him up and tell him to meet you at Chuck E. Cheese or Dave & Buster's."

"Will you come with us?"

"Of course. You know I won't let you go into a situation with him and his wife alone. I got you. Hit me with the time."

"Okay."

"Are you sure you're okay?"

"No, I'm not. I have a child asking for her father because she doesn't understand what he did, and I hate that I have to do this to her. She loves her father, and I feel like I probably ruined their relationship," I explained. I didn't feel good about this shit at all and slowly was regretting taking him to court for full custody. *I don't want to be around him or his wife, but for the sake of my child, I'll do it.* "Let me call you back." I hung up the phone.

Blowing out a very frustrated sigh, I hit the call button on Max's name and put the phone to my ear. The wait for him to answer had me anxious and scared as hell.

"Hello?" his deep voice said.

"Um, hey. I know I'm the last person you probably thought you would hear from, but Savannah misses you, and I'm pretty sure you miss her as well."

"I do. She's my princess."

"How about we meet at Dave & Buster's?"

"Are you bringing that boyfriend of yours?"

"Are you bringing your wife?" I countered.

"Nah, that didn't work out. I left her after the whole court thing. What time do you want to meet?"

"Um, give me about two hours. I just have some things to finish taking care of, and then we'll be on our way."

"A'ight, bet," he said, and we hung up the phone.

I didn't waste time texting Deion and letting him know that he didn't have to come. The only reason I wanted him to come was that I thought Max would be bringing his wife, but to hear that they weren't even together had me wanting to ask questions. Maybe if he wasn't with her, we would be able to work out something for the sake of Savannah, because I didn't like to see my baby suffering like this. I knew for a fact that her father was like her ace boon coon.

Once I finished what I had to do, I got up and walked out of the office. Making my way upstairs, I stopped at Savannah's room, and she was laid across the bed with her earbuds in. "Hey, get dressed. I'm taking you to see your father," I told her, and her face lit up.

Jumping off the bed, she came over to me and hugged me tight. "Thank you so much, Mommy. I love you." I could tell she was smiling the entire time she was talking. "You don't have to thank me, momma," I told her before letting her go. Going into my bedroom, I changed my clothes and sat in front of my vanity so that I could put my hair up into a bun on top of my head.

Once I was finished, I got up, and we both walked out of the house.

The entire drive to Dave & Buster's had me nervous. I had the jitters. I didn't know what was going to happen, but I knew what should have happened, and if he didn't come in there with his head on right and his attitude in check, then this shit wasn't going to work. I needed us to figure this out for the sake of Savannah, because seeing her hurting and asking for her daddy was something I never thought I would have to deal with. I knew how much she loved him, but I thought that she would understand why I did what I did. But she didn't, and that made sense. She was still a child, of course. She didn't know all the things that went on behind closed doors.

"Are you excited to be seeing your father?" I asked, looking at her through the rearview mirror.

"Yes, ma'am. I miss him so much." She smiled while looking out the window.

When she said that, I couldn't do anything but smile. My daughter was the spitting image of her father. She had his hair, his eyes, his mocha skin color, and she stood tall just like him. If you saw me, him, and her in a room together, you would think I had nothing to do with the making of that baby or she got all those features because I disliked his ass for half my pregnancy, if not all. He got on my nerves so bad that I couldn't and didn't even want to be in the same room as him.

Finally pulling my car into the parking lot, I didn't see his car and wanted so badly to call Draya or Junie for some advice, but I knew neither of them was fucking with me like that. I still felt bad that I waited to tell them both about Victoria and Jace, but I also wanted them to understand why I kept it a secret when I first found out. I didn't want either of them to think I had anything to do with any of that.

"Mommy, come on," Savannah urged, pulling at my Balenciaga jacket.

"Okay, let's go," I told her before looking in the mirror and making sure I looked good. Getting out of the car, we went inside and looked around until I saw Max sitting at one of the tables with a pizza, wings, and cups for drinks. I grabbed hold of Savannah's hand, and we made our way over to him. I didn't think she needed to hold my hand as badly as I needed to hold hers. I wanted to be comfortable around him alone, and she was the only one who could give me the comfort I needed.

"Daddy!" she yelled as soon as we got closer to his table. Letting my hand go, she ran to him and hugged him. He kissed her on the forehead and her cheeks.

"I've missed you, little one," he told her, and that warmed my heart.

Seeing Max right now had me feeling different about him. I had a feeling that the only reason he was acting the way he was acting was because of who he was married to.

"What's up, Dreux? Thank you for letting her come see me. I know that this must be hard for you, considering all the things I put you through. I don't want you to think that I'm ever going to do that to you again. I will never do that to you or her again," he apologized in so many words, and all I could do was nod my head. I didn't have much to say at this point. I was just doing what I thought was good for my daughter.

Sitting down at the table, I looked around, then pulled my iPad out to try to get some work done for a house I had to decorate tomorrow. I didn't want to be at the home all day, so I figured if I sent the wife some 3D videos of what I wanted to do, then she would okay it, and I was right. As soon as I sent her the videos, she hit me back and told me that was exactly what she wanted.

Nodding my head, I was about to do another video when Savannah walked over and closed it on me. "Can you play some games with Daddy and me?"

"Sure," I said and got up.

Putting my iPad back into my purse, I followed her around, and we played some games until she got to a ball pit. Then I stood back and watched her and her father play and throw balls at one another. When they got done, they both made their way back to me. "Mommy, can I spend the night with Daddy?"

I looked at him. He put his hands up as if he didn't put her up to that, but I knew him.

"Um, I guess. If it's okay with your father."

"Daddy said it's fine, but he wanted to make sure you were okay with it," she answered for him, and all I could do was nod my head. I wasn't going to be the bad parent and say no, not when I knew she really missed her dad and wanted to spend time with him. It wasn't like anybody could scold me about her going to spend the night with her father.

"You sure? I don't want you to think that I'm making her ask. She asked me, and I told her to ask you."

"It's fine. I know how much she misses you. You can bring her back home tomorrow," I told him while looking in his eyes to let him know I was serious about him bringing her back home tomorrow.

"I will have her back at about five or six."

"Promise?"

"I promise, Dreux." He smiled.

"Okay, well, I'm going to head home," I said, getting up from the table and leaving.

Chapter Twenty-seven

Jace

Don't Judge Me

I'd been taking my medication for the last three months, and it felt like I wasn't getting anywhere with it. The only thing it accomplished was making me feel weird as hell. Granted, I wasn't putting my hands on no woman, but the feeling of me wanting to put my hands on Victoria had me thinking that this shit wasn't working at all.

"Give me some money so that I can go shopping for dinner tonight. Don't you want me to look good?" she asked with her hand out like always. She didn't know just how much she was pissing me the fuck off with that shit.

She acted like I was made of money or some shit, like that shit grew on trees or something. She didn't want to get a job. Shit, she didn't cook or clean. All she did was sit around and talk shit all fucking day.

"No, you don't need anything new to wear. Go put on something that you haven't worn in that fucking closet," I snapped at her. I'd been trying to keep it together so that she wouldn't be around here crying like a baby, but she was pissing me off day after day. Now I saw what niggas were talking about when they said we always traded the woman who didn't put us through a lot for bitches who made us wish we could die on the spot. I never thought that I would admit it, but I was missing Junie more with each day that passed.

Seeing her the other day with Ace had me hot. I wanted to fuck that nigga up and knock off that smirk that he wore each time we were around each other. I just couldn't be around here letting it be known that I was jealous that he was around her. I could understand her being friends with him, but I knew that nigga, and he was looking for something more with her, and I wasn't feeling that.

"I bet if I were Junie, you would give her money with no questions."

Here she went with this shit, always bringing Junie up, and I hated that. She was acting like Junie was living with us or something, I kept telling her to keep her name out of her mouth, but it was like she loved for me to snap at her about that shit. I didn't understand how she was jealous of Junie when she was in the house with me, which was precisely what she'd been wanting for the longest. It just wasn't what she thought it was going to be. I tried to tell her I was not that nigga who was about to be around here letting her do what she wanted to do. The only reason her ass was here was that she and Dreux got into it, and Dreux put her out of her house.

If it weren't for that shit, she would have been at her sister's house, but Dreux was right. I got her pregnant, so she was my responsibility.

"Can you stop bringing her up when you don't get what you want? I told you I don't like that shit, and instead of you listening and doing what I asked of you, you still on that childish shit, and I don't like that. You act like we don't still have to be around them. I don't even want to go to this dinner shit now. You got it," I told her before getting up and walking out of the bedroom.

I didn't know why she was always fucking with me about Junie. She acted like she wasn't just in her face smiling and asking for advice. Not only did I fuck up by getting her pregnant, but I also fucked up the relationship they had with Dreux. I felt bad because they had all been cool for a while, so it didn't feel good to know that their relationship was somewhat ruined because of me and what I did.

"Yeah, let that be the reason. You just don't want to take me out. I'm so close to having this baby, and then I'm out of here."

"And I hope you're leaving my child with me when you get out of here. I'm not about to play with you about my child. You still on that wanting to be young shit, and I don't have time for this shit with you."

"Whatever, Jace," she said and walked right by me.

She didn't know how bad I could have broken her fucking neck after the way she spoke to me, but instead, I let her pass without making a scene. I didn't want to be in jail behind fucking this girl up. She would have called the police on my black ass in no time for me putting my hands on her, and she fought back all the time.

"You lucky I'm changing."

"Mm-hmm."

When she walked out of the room, she slammed the door behind her, and instead of going after her like I usually did, I sat on the couch and put a pre-rolled blunt to my mouth and lit it. Taking a long drag from it, I held the smoke in, then blew it out. I had to make sure I got high, really high, just to deal with her. I didn't know what I was thinking fucking with and getting her ass pregnant, but it was too late for me to have those questions. I wished her stupid ass had gotten that abortion when I told her to, but nah, she thought that having a baby by me was going to keep me. Little did she know I wasn't going for it.

I didn't let Junie having Montana stop me from doing me, and I'm not about to let her having my son do that either. I would always make sure she was good, but we didn't need to be together for us to make sure our son was good. Shit, I was still surprised that Junie was letting me get Montana even with Victoria staying here, but that told me that she was really over it. Plus, we all knew I wouldn't let nothing happen to my child. Victoria wasn't a bad person either. She was good with kids, and she loved my daughter like she was her own.

Once I was finished with the blunt and calmed down, I went into the closet and pulled out things for us to wear. Making sure we dressed similarly, I grabbed her heels and my loafers and went into the restroom. Shutting the shower behind me, I started the shower and stripped out of my clothes. Stepping inside, I turned my back to the water and let it run all over me before grabbing my towel and Axe shower gel, and I started to bathe. I wasn't trying to be in there for an hour, so I rinsed, showered again, then stepped out.

Wrapping a towel around my waist, I walked out of the restroom, and she was now sitting on the edge of the bed.

"Come on, go shower and get dressed so that we can go," I told her, and she stood up without a word. Looking at her, I grabbed her arm, making her look up at me. "I'm sorry for snapping at you, but you have to understand that when you bring up Junie, that shit makes me feel some way. I don't like that shit. I'm trying to leave her in the past, and when you bring her up, that makes me think about her. It's like you don't want to be here, and you want to cause issues so that you can go. If you want to, just let me know, and I'll set you up in your own place, and we can just coparent. I don't like living under this stress. I'm already on this medicine, and I want it to keep working. I don't want to feel like I'm taking this shit for nothing."

"Jace, maybe I did move in with you too fast. I don't want us to be fighting all the time, especially when the baby gets here. I want us to be able to be around each other without getting into it. I know I'm wrong for bringing up Junie every time I get mad, but I was the side piece for so long that now that I have you, I know that if you did her the way you did her, you might do me the same way."

"You don't know that, because you won't even give me a chance to make shit work between us. You want to keep bringing up my past and what I did back then. I don't want to think about that shit because I know I did some fucked-up shit to Junie. You have to understand I'm trying to be a better version of myself, so I need you to work with me. As far as you getting your place, I think that would be a good idea for now," I told her, and she nodded her head.

It seemed like that was the only thing we had agreed on since her moving in here. She wanted me to change my house decor up, and I told her that wasn't happening. I liked the way Junie did it, and I wanted to keep it that way. We both had a ways to go before we were ready for a serious relationship. I knew I was pushing it by having her move in a month after Junie left, but I thought that it was a good idea for me to keep an eye on her since she was carrying my seed, but that shit was dead now. She needed her own place, especially with her being young, and I needed my space because this shit wasn't working and hadn't been since she moved in.

When she went into the restroom, she came right back out. "I don't want to go to the dinner. You can go. I'm going to stay at home."

"You sure?"

"Yeah, I think it's a good idea. I don't want to be around Junie knowing I was sleeping with her man behind her back and, to make matters worse, I got pregnant. I know she will never say anything to me again, and I don't want to make things harder for my sister. She's already trying to mend those relationships all because she was protecting me and my secret."

I nodded my head when she said that. I knew what she was saying, but we couldn't worry about that. We had to let them work that out for themselves. It wasn't like Dreux had known for long about her sister and me. She had just found out, and instead of ratting her sister out, she kept her secret for as long as she could. But when that shit started eating away at her conscience, she told Vicky that she had to tell them both what was up. Nobody expected them to stop fucking with her the way they did. I especially thought they would have understood why she kept the secret, but I guessed that didn't earn you points with females who were supposed to be your friends.

I finished getting dressed, kissed her on the forehead, and left the house. I had to be the one to make things right between Junie and Dreux. I wanted them to know the truth, and that was that I didn't even know Victoria was Dreux's little sister until she was already pregnant.

Getting into my car, I started it up and backed out of the driveway. I wasn't in no rush to get to the restaurant, so I smoked a blunt all the way there just to get my mind right before going to sit down with all these motherfuckers.

Chapter Twenty-eight

Korey Sr.

All of Me

Dinner was hella awkward with having Jace around. Nobody was saying anything to one another. "Jace, why are you here?" Draya finally asked.

"I wanted to come out just to set things straight between y'all and Dreux," he answered.

"You can't set anything straight. That's her job, and she hasn't said anything to either of us."

"Yes, I have. I called both of you, and neither of you would answer the phone, and when I tried to talk to Junie at the office, she ignored me," Dreux said, and this was the most they said anything to one another the whole dinner.

"Can y'all just work this out? I mean, it's not that hard. She only kept that secret because that was her sister. I know y'all both would do the same thing for one another," I said. I was tired of them not talking, but they were always bringing it up when they were around the house. Draya had asked me for my advice, and now I was giving it to her. At first, I was staying out of that shit because I didn't want to be in the middle of it, but this shit was getting ridiculous now.

Neither Draya nor Junie said anything because they both knew I was telling the truth. They both just needed to be real. They weren't mad that she kept that secret for her sister. They were mad that she knew it was Jace.

Dreux said, "I wanted to tell y'all, but I didn't want to ruin her confiding in me, but the moment I felt like I had to tell y'all, I told her that I couldn't keep it from y'all any longer. When I found out she was messing with Jace, I almost beat her ass. She knew what you had gone through with his ass and wanted to be with him. I don't know why, and I don't condone that shit. I just want her to get it together for the sake of my nephew."

"Dreux, I'm not mad that you knew about them. I'm mad that it took you so long to tell me. I mean, she sat in my face and got advice from my sister and me only to be fucking with my baby daddy," Junie said.

"And that's exactly why I was mad at her. I wanted to give Jace another beatdown, but it didn't pay. She was caught up in loving him, and there wasn't anything I could do about it. I tried to talk some sense into her, but she wasn't trying to hear that shit. She was deaf when it came to anything I had to say about Jace."

"And she's living with me for now. I have to find her a place soon because it's not working out. We both came to an agreement that she has to get her own place and we just need to coparent," Jace said.

"I think that's a good idea, bro. The last thing you need is to be in another relationship after what you put Junie through. I don't even see how you moved Victoria in with you. She wouldn't be staying with me at all." I kept it real with him. I didn't know why he did this shit in the first place. He made shit hard for both me and Deion. To have our women not talking meant there was always something slick being said on my side, and I didn't like that shit. They all needed to get their feelings out on the table and move the hell on.

"I don't know, but we both know now that this shit isn't going to work."

All the women got up from the table and made their way outside, leaving me, Jace, and Deion at the table. "You put us in a fucked-up position with this shit. Draya kept asking me if I knew about you and Victoria."

"But you didn't know. Nobody did. I kept that shit a secret from everybody who had a mouth to go tell. I knew that neither of you niggas would be able to keep it on the hush, so I kept it a secret, and I didn't even know Victoria was Dreux's sister until she was already pregnant."

"You need to get it together, my nigga. I don't like being in the middle of somebody else's bullshit," Deion told him, and I nodded my head in agreement before getting up and throwing enough money on the table to cover the entire dinner.

"I know, and I will. I just want to make sure I do what I have to do for my children, and a relationship isn't it anymore."

"Good. Keep it that way," I let him know before dapping him up and making my way out of the restaurant. I already had my own shit going on with trying to run my club, and I didn't want to have something else to worry about. They didn't know how much stress this had put on me. When Draya's ass didn't have Dreux to hang with, she was up my ass about everything that went on at the club.

When I got into the car, she was sitting there with her lip poked out.

"What's wrong with you?" I asked.

"Why you in there dapping him up like you cool with him? You need to leave him alone."

"I'm not leaving him alone. That's my boy. You know that. What we all need to do is mind our own business so that we can go about our lives."

Heading to the house, the ride was silent. I guessed she didn't have anything to say, and I had already said what I needed to say. Nobody was about to make me stop fucking with Jace because of the shit he did. She didn't have to worry about me doing no shit like that, and that was all she needed to be worried about.

When we finally made it home, she got out of the car and slammed the door behind her.

"Ay, you do not have to slam my damn car door like that. I don't know what the fuck your problem is, but you need to calm the hell down," I snapped at her, but she didn't say anything. Instead, she walked right into the house and closed the door on me.

Shaking my head, I opened the door and walked in. I didn't know what else to say to her. She was mad for no reason at all. She was acting like I was the one cheating, and I didn't like that shit.

Making my way up the stairs, I went into our bedroom and walked right in. "Draya, I don't know why you treating me like I'm the one cheating on you. It's not me, it's never going to be me, and you need to get that through your head. I know that you don't like the way shit went down with you and Dreux, and that's understandable, but what you need to understand is that you can't make me, as a grown-ass man, stop fucking with my nigga all because he cheated on his girl. You don't have to worry about that shit happening with us again, and that's all there is."

"I know, and I'm sorry. I just don't like that neither you nor Deion told him he was out of line."

"You don't know what we told him because it ain't nobody's business. If I'm gon' check that nigga, it's gon' be in private and not for everybody to know." I had to let her know that just because I didn't get on a nigga's ass in front of her didn't mean it didn't happen. I could have told him about himself, but what difference would that make? That nigga would still make his own decisions at the end of the day.

She said nothing.

As bad as I wanted to say something else, I kept my mouth shut and went into the restroom so that I could take a shower. I wasn't about to go back and forth with her about somebody else's business. I told her that had nothing to do with us, and she needed to get that through her head before she pissed me off. Slamming the door behind me, I started the shower and stripped out of my clothes.

Stepping into the shower, I made sure I let the water hit my body everywhere before grabbing my shower gel and showering. After doing that twice, I rinsed and got out, wrapping a towel around my waist. I went into the bedroom, and she was laid back in the bed with a blunt in her mouth. It was a good thing KJ was with her parents for the night, because I was tired and just needed to get some rest without him whining throughout the night like somebody was doing him something.

Sitting on the edge of the bed, she handed me the blunt, then started rubbing my back. "I'm sorry for jumping on you the way that I did. I guess this whole situation got me on edge. I don't know if I'm mad at you about you not telling him nothing or that that could have been us."

"That would have never been us. I know what I did in the past, and I never want to hurt you the way I did before. Seeing you cry all the time did something to my spirit and my heart, and I don't like that shit. I would rather have you over hoes any day, but you also have to understand that when my boys do something, you can't automatically go back to thinking about what I did. You said you forgave me, and that's what it needs to be."

"You're right, and you don't have to worry about me bringing it up again. I promise."

"Good. Now kiss me," I told her, and she did.

Lying back, I pulled her on top of me and rubbed her ass cheeks while sliding my tongue into her mouth. Not wanting to waste any time, I raised her dress up and ripped her thong right off her body. Undoing my towel, I grabbed my dick and slid it deep inside of her while she gripped the sheets and closed her eyes.

"Mm," she moaned out.

Hitting her with deep strokes, I made sure I massaged her ass cheeks to give her that feeling she loved so much. "Damn, you feel like heaven," I whispered in her ear.

"Don't stop." That was my cue to speed my strokes up. Bouncing her up and down as hard as I could, I focused on my nut and hers at the same time. I knew we both had built up frustrations with one another and it wouldn't take us no time to cum, and I was right. By the time I went to flip her over on her back, she was cumming all over my dick.

Raising her legs, I put them over my shoulders and went back to work on her pussy. She got hers, and now it was time for me to get mine. I didn't care what nobody said about niggas who nutted fast. If a bitch got some good pussy, he gon' nut up quicker than usual. That was how this was feeling, especially with the way her pussy was gripping my dick, and she was purring in my ear. Pushing myself deeper into her, I closed my eyes and let my seeds off into her golden spot.

Lying on the side of her, I held her until we both went to sleep.

Chapter Twenty-nine

Deion

Mesmerized by Her

After that disaster of a dinner, I just knew shit was going to be off between everybody. The other girls just didn't want to forgive Dreux for the minor mistake she made, as if they wouldn't have done the same exact thing if Victoria were their sister. I was trying to get my mind off it, so I was working on some cases I had in front of me. Some of this shit was literally open-and-shut cases, and it seemed like nobody wanted to take them but me. Looking at all the mail I had, I just knew I was going to be there all day long.

"Uh, Char, can you bring me some coffee? It's going to be a long-ass day."

"Yes, sir."

Grabbing the first stack of papers, I went through them, called the district attorney's office, and together we set a date to get these minor cases squared away. Then I handed my assistant the phone numbers and addresses of all the clients who needed to be in court at the end of the month. I wanted her to call and send the letters so they wouldn't have a reason to not show up for court. Taking a break, I decided to go over some of my mail when I came across a letter.

The stamped word "urgent" made me rip the letter open, but as I read, my heart sank. I didn't know what to think or what to say, so I called the person I knew I could confide in, and since it was about her, she was the only person I needed to see.

"Hey, baby," she said as soon as she answered.

"I need you to come to my office if you can. I know that you're probably busy, but I have something I want to show you."

"Okay, I'm on my way."

Hanging up the phone, I held the letter in my hand for a little while longer before setting it down and going over some more of the cases I had so that when she came, I could leave after giving her the letter. I wasn't about to keep the letter because it didn't have nothing to do with a case. The only thing they mentioned was her being kidnapped when she was a child and how they thought she was dead until they saw a picture of her. I didn't know why they would send that shit to me. I just wanted to give it to her so that she wouldn't think I was trying to keep it a secret, which was something I wouldn't do anyway. She told me to always be real with her, and I would never not be.

Lost in my thoughts, I didn't even hear my office door open until I looked up and saw Dreux standing there. "You okay?" she asked, coming over to me.

Nodding my head at my assistant for her to close the door behind her, I turned the entire chair around and pulled her in my lap. Rising, I kissed her on the lips and held her slim frame close to my body. "I'm good, baby. How about you? How was work? And you never hit me and told me what happened with you and Max."

"Nothing. I let Vannah go with him since she was practically begging me. He seems to be in a better place, and he's actually trying, so I have to give him that. What's up, though? I know you ain't call me up here just for that."

"No. Here. Somebody sent this here. I don't know if you know about it, but they asked me to give you the letter, and I want to make sure I do that. You can decide what you want to do with the letter from now on, but I just want to know if you want me to look more into it for you," I told her before handing her the letter.

She opened the letter and read it, and her eyes got watery. Closing it, she set it on the desk and looked into my eyes.

"Is this some sick joke?" she asked.

"Baby, I don't know. All I know is the letter was delivered to me, and of course I read it because it was mailed to me, but when I saw what it says, I called you first."

"This is crazy. My parents are my parents. Nobody kidnapped me. This is somebody trying to get something out of me, and they won't succeed. You don't have to do any further investigating. I don't even want to know if it is true. It's been too long for me to even want to go looking for answers. I'm happy where I'm at." She shrugged, but I could see in her eyes that she was unsure, but I wasn't going to make no moves without her knowledge.

I pulled her close to me, and she laid her head on my chest and started to sob. Rubbing my hand up and down her back, I tried consoling her, but the way she was crying confirmed she was confused about what was going on. If I were her, I would have wanted answers, but I couldn't make her want them. That was something she had to want for herself. It was her life and it concerned her, but I would have asked my parents about it first to see what they told me before just putting it off. "Do you want me to leave with you?" I asked.

"If you want to. I don't want to ruin your workday. I know how important it is for you to get everything together for the cases you may have coming up. I just need time to think about this and maybe talk to my mother and father to see what this is about."

I nodded my head, completely understanding. "I just want you to do what's best for you. If you don't want answers, then don't go looking for them, because who knows what you might find out on the way to those answers? Some parents won't tell you the truth anyway because they would think they did what they were supposed to do. You don't have to worry about anything, though. No matter what, I will be here for you, baby." I had to let her know that whatever she wanted to do, I would be there for her. She was my main priority, she and her daughter. I felt like they were my family, so I always made sure when I moved that I thought about both of them.

"Thank you. Right now I just want to go home. I might stop by Draya's and talk to her. I miss her."

"Okay. Call me when you make it where you're going. I can walk you out, though."

She got off my lap and made her way out of the office, and I was right behind her. When we got on the elevator, I pulled her close to me and held her. She said, "Thank you for telling me instead of investigating on your own."

"You don't have to thank me. I'm doing what any man would do. Dreux, I don't know if you know this, but I like you a lot, and I don't want to lose you, so I'm willing to do whatever I can do to keep you." I hadn't felt this way for a woman in a long time. She made me happy, and she made me feel like I could do anything I wanted to put my mind to. She never made me feel basic or treated me like a basic nigga. She treated me like a king and always told me the words I needed to hear to keep this shit going. She didn't know, but she was like my saving grace out in this world.

"I know, and I like you too. You're so sweet, and the way you treat me like a queen is the only thing I've been wanting from a man."

"And I will treat you that way until you tell me you don't want it anymore. I hope that don't come anytime soon." I smirked at her.

"You don't have to worry about that. I'm going to come over tonight since Vannah isn't home."

"Noted."

When the elevator doors finally opened, I grabbed her hand and led her out the door. I looked both ways, which was something I was used to doing from the time I spent in the streets before getting myself together.

"See you tonight," she let me know while I held her car door open for her so that she could get in.

Nodding my head, I leaned down and kissed her on the lips before shutting it and stepping back. I always had to watch her until her car disappeared just to make sure she was good before I went back into the house or the building.

After finally going back in, I didn't even stay long. I grabbed some of the cases I had for tomorrow and decided to head home early so that I could straighten up and cook before she came over. I never wanted her to have to worry about anything when she came to my house. That was her safe haven, somewhere she could come and relax. Somewhere she could just be naked in the mind and not have anything to worry about.

"I'll see you in the morning," I said to my assistant. "You don't have to stay once you finish making those calls and getting those letters together."

"Okay. Bye, boss," she replied without looking up.

Turning, I got on the elevator and rode it down. As soon as those doors opened, I speed walked out of there and got into my car. Starting it up, I pulled out of the parking lot and headed straight to the house. I had no stops to make because I had weed and cigars at home as well as wine and bottles of Ace of Spades and Patrón at the house. I had a lot on my mind, and I wanted to make sure I relaxed as soon as I got the food on and the house in tip-top shape, even though it wasn't that bad.

Finally pulling up to the house, I got into my car and headed for the door. Once I opened it, I went inside and set my briefcase in my office and started picking up some of the papers I had in the living room and on the sofa. I set them where they belonged. I vacuumed, then went into the kitchen and started the dishwasher and took out some steaks, shrimp, and baking potatoes.

Once I had the entire house cleaned, I unbuttoned my dress shirt and sat on the sofa so that I could roll my blunt. I needed it after this day, and it wasn't even a long day. Putting it to my mouth as soon as I had it sealed, I lit it and took a long drag from it and held the smoke in my lungs before blowing it out of my mouth and hitting it again. Leaning my head back, I turned the TV to ESPN and watched a game that was on while smoking.

Getting up, I made my way upstairs and decided to take a shower. While in there, I thought about Dreux and the way she felt when I was deep inside of her. Looking down, I saw my dick standing up, and I couldn't do nothing but shake my head. She had me sprung off her pussy game, and we only fucked a few times, and that was because we both needed it. Having sex with somebody who actually shared the same feelings you had for them was everything to me, and Dreux and I had some of the best sex I'd had in a long time. She made me not want to fuck with no other female, and I would always make sure I kept the promise I made to her the very first time we had sex and not give another woman what belonged to her. I was so serious about what I had with her that I would be hurt if she hurt me, which was why I was trying so hard to make sure she was always happy. I didn't want another fucked-up situation like I was in with Breann.

Chapter Thirty

Dreux

Girls Need Love

When I left Deion's office, I was confused and didn't really know what to think. I had told him not to investigate, but deep down, I knew I would have to get some kind of answers out of my parents about what this person was talking about. If I was kidnapped, I didn't know that, because they didn't treat me any differently. They treated me and Vicky the same way, and I loved them for that. I had nothing to worry about when I was young, and never did I think I was kidnapped or adopted, so for these people to wait this long to come forward and say I was kidnapped was a reach for me. I had no respect for people who would do that. This could be the sick joke of somebody who really wanted to get something from me.

Finally pulling up at Draya's house, I got out of the car and went to the door. Before I could knock, it opened, and both she and Junie were standing there. "Can I come in?" I asked, and Draya moved to the side, but Junie stayed out with her arms across her chest and a mug on her face.

Stepping into the house, I thought she was gonna swing, so I looked at her. I didn't care how bad I felt for knowing about my sister messing with Jace. If she had put her hands on me, we were gonna have to rock in this bitch.

She looked at me, then smiled and hugged me. "Come here, ho. You know I can never be mad at you for too long, and I actually think I was mad at you for no reason. I had a talk with Ace, and he told me I was tripping. I shouldn't be mad at you for keeping the loyalty to your sister, and when you said that me and Draya would have done the same thing for one another, you were right. I'm sorry I made you think you had to choose me over your sister, because I never want you to think that."

"It's cool. I'm really sorry I didn't tell you sooner. I wanted to, but I didn't want you to be mad at me or think I set them up on some slick snake shit. I wanted to see if she was going to tell you, and that's the only reason she came to the spa with me that day. I also got on her ass because she was sitting there getting advice from you and Draya."

"Oh, I would have given her the same advice if I had known she was messing with Jace. I wish she had saved herself, but if that's what she wants, then that's on her at the end of the day."

"Exactly."

"So tea us, bitch. How did she end up staying with Jace anyway?" Draya asked.

"We got into it. She was all in my face bucking and shit while defending that nigga, so I put her ass the fuck out."

"Damn, that's fucked up."

"No, y'all want to see something that's fucked up?" I asked, pulling the letter out of my purse and handing it to Draya.

By the time they were finished reading, they both had tears in their eyes. Getting up, they came over to me and wrapped their arms around me. I know they felt my pain, but I wasn't about to shed any more tears until I got the answers. I needed to get them from the only two people who could give them to me. I didn't want it to seem like I was taking this stranger's words over theirs, so the only thing I could do was let them tell me what they needed to tell me first, then decide depending on what they said.

"I'm so sorry. What you gon' do about this?" Junie asked.

"Nothing until I talk to my parents. They're the only two who can give me the answers I'm looking for, and if I feel like they're lying to me, then I'll let Deion do his investigating and we can get the truth."

"This shit is crazy, sis. You know we're here if you need us. I know that this is a lot, so I'm happy we squared away the tension. I didn't know what to do without talking to you, but I can admit I talked so much shit," Draya told me.

"I know. I did as well. I will never keep anything from you bitches again. Y'all are my best friends, and without y'all, I have nobody else besides Deion and my baby."

"Speaking of Savannah, where is she?"

I was hoping she wouldn't ask me that because I knew they would think I was a dumb bitch for letting my baby go with Max after what he did, but she needed her father. "She's with Max."

If looks could kill, I would have been dead, because both these bitches had their faces turned up and were rolling their eyes.

"I know," I said before they could go in like I knew they wanted to.

"Yeah, what the fuck were you thinking after everything he put you through? I wouldn't have let her go anywhere with him," Draya went off.

"I know, but she was literally crying for her father. She told me she needed her father, y'all. That shit hurt me, and I felt like I was hurting her by keeping her away from him. She loves her father, and no matter what, I can't keep her away from him."

Junie put her two cents in. "I feel you on that, but damn, he put you through a lot. I don't know if I would be able to put myself back in that position with him."

"Trust me, I'm nervous, but I know he won't do anything to ruin what little chance he has left. He told me that he left his wife. He felt like he was letting her have more say-so than she should have, and he was sorry about it. I still have my eye on him, but as long as my baby is happy, that's all that matters to me right now. She's all I have, and I want her to be happy because if she's not, then I'm not happy either."

They both nodded their heads when I said that, knowing I was telling the truth. No mother could tell me she would willingly keep her children away from their father if she knew that the father was a good one deep down in her heart. I just felt bitter doing that to Savannah, and anybody who knew me knew that my daughter meant the world to me.

"You're right. I mean, if he's willing to actually work this shit out for the sake of being in his child's life and really wanting to do better, then I say do what you have to do. But the moment he hurts you again, I'm going to be on his doorstep with my bat in my hand," Draya said, making me smile.

This was why I loved her ass. She was always ready to ride for me the same way I would do for her and the same way I did for Junie. These girls were like my sisters, so I always had to make sure we were good. I didn't know if this situation was going to ruin our friendships, so while I had the chance to make things right, I knew I had to, because not talking to them every day hurt my soul.

Looking at my Rolex, I saw that I still had a little time left before having to make my way to my man. "Where the weed at, bitches?" I asked, and Draya chuckled before getting up and going into the kitchen. When she came back, she had a blunt in her mouth and two more in her hand. Setting them down, she passed me the blunt, and I hit it.

"So what have I been missing?" I asked.

"Nothing really. Me and Korey are trying to figure out this whole thing with me actually working. He can't handle the fact that I'm always at the club and that I don't want to leave earlier than I have to. KJ is at my parents' house when I'm working, so I don't have him to worry about. I just want to do what I can to make sure these clubs make the money they're supposed to be making."

"I feel you on that. I don't think Korey can't handle you working. I think he didn't think you would actually want to do it. He probably felt like once you saw how much work he put into running those clubs and dealing with those women, you wouldn't want to be there anymore. Just keep your head up and keep doing your job, but make sure you balance your work life and home life."

"Yeah, the last thing I want is for him to feel the need to step out on this engagement because I'm working so much. I made a schedule so that I could be home before it gets dark. I don't want to slack on my motherly and fiancée duties," she responded, and I nodded my head before looking at Junie. I wanted to know what was going on between her and Ace.

"Me? Oh, just working. You know that."

"Nah. You and Ace?"

"Oh, he wants more than I'm willing to offer right now. You know with everything I went through with Jace, he ruined me. He made me not want to get into a relationship for a long time. I just want to make sure

Ace's intentions are pure before I actually fuck with him. I know how much he can't stand Jace, so I don't want to be a pawn in his game just to fuck with that man. I want Jace out of my life for good, but with Montana, who loves her father to death, it is hard. I would never keep her away from him, but he doesn't know his boundaries."

"You need to let him know what they are. He shouldn't be asking you anything that don't have to do with y'all daughter, and he don't have the right to be getting mad about what you do either. Now, as far as Ace goes, you might want to keep him on the friend level until he actually proves to you that he's not using you or just trying to fuck. You don't want to jump out of a bad situation and into a worse one," I told her. I was just trying to give them both the best advice I could because I knew how hard this shit was.

After we finished the second blunt, I got up and made my way to the door. Pulling it open, I hugged both of them, then walked out, got into my car, and left.

Chapter Thirty-one

Draya

Loyalty

After Junie left, I got up and took a shower while waiting for Korey to come home with KJ. I was happy that he and my father actually got to a place where he didn't threaten that man if he came to pick up his son. Korey had finally proven himself to my father, and now he was trying to pressure both of us into getting married, which we were going to do. I wanted to plan the wedding, but I had so much other stuff going on that it wasn't going to be easy, and I didn't want to have to do everything by myself.

After the advice Dreux gave me, I was going to need to sit down and have a conversation with him just to see what he wanted from me. I thought that he loved having me work at the club, but I was starting to feel like he was only tolerating me because he thought that I would think he was spending too much time at the club, which I used to. I saw how much work it took to handle a club, and I liked it. I loved feeling like I was needed, and although I had a rough time with the girls at first, they were finally starting to understand that I was there for them and not trying to stop their money flow. I told them all they had to do was put their faith in me and I was going to make sure they saw a lot of money.

I kept my word.

The club I ran was actually seeing more money than it saw before I took over. I made sure everything was taken care of, and the girls actually took my advice about changing up their dancing so they didn't keep doing the same watered-down-ass dances they had been doing.

When I got out of the shower, I wrapped a towel around my breasts and went into the bedroom to see KJ and Korey laid back in the bed, watching TV. "Why didn't you say anything when you came in?" I asked, walking over to him and kissing him on the lips.

"Tired," he said, looking into my eyes, and I could tell that he was.

Nodding my head, I got dressed, then grabbed KJ from the bed and took him to his nursery. Laying him back on his changing table, I took his clothes off, then picked him up and went into the restroom so that I could get his bath out of the way before feeding him. My son didn't have a hard time getting to sleep, and he slept all night some nights. It was very rare that he woke up whining.

Once I had the water running, I took his diaper off and gave him a bath. Getting him out, I wrapped his little robe around his body and took him into his room. Laying him in his crib, I went to his dresser and grabbed his pajamas and socks. After he was dressed, I took him downstairs with me and sat him in his swing in the kitchen while I started to cook. I was making fried chicken, mashed potatoes, and Velveeta Shells & Cheese, which were my favorite.

As soon as I had the chicken, mashed potatoes, and water for the shells going, I sat in front of KJ and played with him. His laugh was so intoxicating that I knew he was going to have females in love with him just off that. He looked just like his father from head to toe. He was Korey's twin. I used to hate that, but I loved it now. *My son is going to break some hearts, but one thing he will learn is how to treat a woman.*

"I love you, baby boy," I told him, and he giggled.

Getting up, I went to the stove and finished the food, then fixed him a little plate and fed him. Once he was finished, he was rubbing his eyes and whining, which told me he was sleepy. Getting up, I grabbed a wet napkin and cleaned his face before picking him up and taking him upstairs. Laying him in his crib, I put his TV to cartoons and cracked the door when I walked out. Going back downstairs, I fixed myself and Korey plates before taking them up.

"How was work?" I asked, trying to make light conversation as we ate.

"Good. Them bitches was getting on my nerves. I need to find a manager to replace Laila before they run me crazy."

"If you need some help, let me know. I missed you today."

"Oh, yeah? How much?" he asked with a smile on his face.

"A lot." I winked before reaching over and grabbing his dick.

I looked into his eyes, and he nodded his head, which let me know that I could get some of that good dick.

As soon as I finished eating, I got up and took the plates downstairs, then cleaned the kitchen before going back up. When I got back into the bedroom, he was up and in the shower, so I got under the covers and looked at the camera we had in our room to check on KJ. He was sleeping so peacefully.

"My son asleep?" Korey inquired, emerging from the bathroom with nothing on but a towel wrapped around him that held nothing from my imagination.

"You know it."

He dropped the towel and made his way to the bed, and I knew shit was about to be up from here. When he climbed on the bed, he pulled the covers back and climbed right in between my legs. Kissing my lips, he wrapped one of his arms behind my neck and held me close to him while our tongues danced for a little while. Using his legs, he opened my legs a little wider for him. "Open up for me," he whispered in my ear.

Doing as he told me, I pulled my legs open as wide as they would go, and he grabbed his dick and sat it right on my clit. Rubbing it up and down on it slowly, he looked into my eyes, then came down and kissed me again, but this time he slid his dick in me. He made sure he fed it to me a little at a time like always.

"Ooh," I let out when he got all the way in. Using my hips, I adjusted myself so that it wouldn't hurt when he stroked me. As soon as I was right, he started giving me long, hard strokes while gripping my hair in a closed fist. "Yessss," I moaned out.

Putting my arms around his back, I dug my nails in his skin while he pumped his long, thick dick in and out of me at a medium rate. One thing I could say was this man knew how to fuck me just the way a woman would want to be fucked. Arching my back, I closed my eyes and bit down on my bottom lip at the same time he attacked my G-spot with his pole.

"That shit feels good, don't it?" he asked, and I nodded my head, not being able to form the words I knew he wanted to hear. He came down and put his head in the crook of my neck while picking my legs up and drilling me nonstop until my juices were flowing out of me and onto him and the sheets. This was the best thing about having Korey back in my life. I didn't have to worry about fucking nobody else and adding another body to my body count. He had that covered, and plus, this pussy had been his since the first time we fucked.

"Mm," I purred in his ear, and he stopped stroking me and lay still.

Putting all of my strength into my legs, I started to move my hips back and forward. He was tired, so I wanted to put in work as well because I did not want him to cum without making me cum at least two more times.

"Fuck." He grimaced, rising and pounding deep inside of me. I couldn't even keep up anymore because each time I tried to throw my pussy at him, he answered with two deathly strokes that made my knees go weak. He put his arms behind me and held me close while slowing his pumps down and making love to me instead of fucking me. It should have been a shame just how much this man knew what to do to make me cum repeatedly. He had me in a trance, and this was exactly why I couldn't get over him when I should have been over his ass.

"Shit, I'm about to nut," he groaned in my ear, and I could tell he was trying to hold back, but the movements I was doing were going to make it hard for him.

Pushing himself deeper inside of me, he let his seeds off inside me then lay on top of me for about five minutes.

"Babe, I can't breathe," I managed to get out, and he rolled off and lay on his side of the bed.

"My bad, bae."

Getting up, I went into the restroom and wet a warm towel before cleaning myself up and grabbing another one for him. When I walked out, he was laid out, snoring like a grizzly bear. Shaking my head, I got in the bed and wiped his dick off before covering him with the comforter and lying beside him. Resting my head on his back, I closed my eyes and joined my baby in a deep sleep.

The next morning, I woke up to the smell of breakfast being cooked. I rolled over in the bed. Looking at the clock, I saw that it was a little after nine, and I quickly jumped up, realizing I was late for work. I had a thing about being on time. That way, I could get out of there on time, and this was fucking with me. Getting up, I went into the restroom and handled my personal hygiene before dressing in some tights and a long-sleeved shirt and going downstairs.

When I walked into the kitchen, the sight before me was the sexiest shit I had ever seen. Korey was playing with KJ like I always did in the morning, and he was feeding him. "Good morning, my handsome men." I smiled and strolled over to them. Leaning down, I kissed KJ on the forehead, then Korey on the lips.

"Good morning, beautiful."

"Why didn't you wake me this morning? Now I'm late."

"You were tired, I mean snoring and shit, so I decided a little more sleep wouldn't hurt you. The club will always be there, Draya," he said, and the stern look on his face told me I needed to relax. He was right. I was drained, but I loved what I did, and in order for me to set an example about the girls coming in on time, or at all, I needed to be there early every day.

"Thank you for the extra sleep. I'm going to do my hair and head out. Do you want me to take him to my parents?"

"Nah, he can stay home with me today. I'm not going in," he let me know, and I nodded my head before kissing him again then grabbing some turkey bacon off the plate that was in front of him. "I fixed you a plate. Take it with you."

Going upstairs, I quickly threw my hair into a bun and put on some black-and-white Air Max shoes, then grabbed my car keys and clutch. Heading back down, I grabbed the plate, said my goodbyes, and made my way to the club.

Chapter Thirty-two

Korey Sr.

You're the One

When Draya left for the club, I looked at my son. "I guess it's you and me, li'l man," I told him, and he started smiling. He wasn't used to Daddy being around all the time, but it was exactly what I needed after being at work all the time. I never wanted my son to think I was always at work and we never spent any time together when he was a child, and I didn't want him to hold that shit against me either. My son was everything to me. He was the reason I breathed, the reason I went so hard, and I wanted him to know that when he got older.

Getting him out of his seat, I took him upstairs and wiped him down, changed his diaper, then got him dressed so that I could take him to see my mother. She had been calling me for the last two days, saying she missed her baby and how she wanted to see him, so it was a must I brought him by her house. I didn't know why Draya was utilizing only her mother and father when my mother would love nothing more than to watch her grandson. I didn't like the way that made her feel. It was almost as if Draya didn't want him around her.

After he was dressed, I grabbed his hand and led him to my bedroom, where I threw on some slacks, a gold and black Versace shirt, and some loafers to match. Brushing my hair, then his, I picked him up and carried him out of the house.

Once he was strapped in, I got in and started the car up. Backing up out of the driveway, I headed straight to my mother's house. I had to go by and check on Jace, so I was going to have to leave KJ at my mother's, which I was sure she wouldn't mind. Getting on the expressway, I made sure I didn't speed, and I kept checking on my son in the rearview mirror. I was always extra careful when he was in the car with me because anything could happen. I may have been on the legal side with my moneymaking, but the nigga within was pure gangsta, and I would put any nigga on their back for disrespect.

I pulled into my mother's driveway. She was sitting outside on the porch and didn't give us time to get out before making her way to the back door and pulling it open. "Dang, you could have at least let me park."

"Boy, give me my damn baby and you can go. I only want to see him anyway."

"Don't do me like that, Ma."

"It seems like you're letting Draya forget that I was the one here for both her and you when y'all was going through that minor separation. She's treating me like I did her something, and it's taking everything in me not to cuss her ass out," she snapped at me, which told me that she was in her feelings. She and Draya were close when we were first together, but when we broke up, she started to feel like my mother was covering for me a lot of times, but she kept it cordial with her just so I could get my son. I had to let her know that my mother would never cover for me. She loved Draya like she was her own daughter.

"Ma, I'm not letting her do nothing, but I will talk to her because she doesn't have no reason to be treating you the way she is. I don't want this to become us. Her father still can't stand me, and I don't want the two women who mean the world to me to not be on the same page."

"Well, you'd better talk to her before I do because I'm on the verge of saying fuck her and not fucking with her anymore."

"That's not necessary. I got it. You good watching KJ for me?" I asked, and she gave me a look that told me to leave.

Nodding my head, I got into my car and left the house. The entire ride to Jace's, I had a lot on my mind, like whether something happened to this nigga when he made it back to his house, because nobody had heard from him since then. Swinging my car into his driveway, I got out and walked up to the door and started banging on it like I was the cops, knowing that was going to get him to the door, and I was right.

When he pulled the door open, he had a mug on his face and a big-ass gash on the side of his face. "What the fuck happened to your face, my nigga?" I asked, getting pissed.

"Man, me and Vicky got into it, and she threw a fucking glass at my head. Her ass had to go last night. I don't know where the fuck she went, but she had to get the fuck out of here."

"So you put her and your unborn child out?"

"What else was I supposed to do?"

"I don't know. Maybe you should have left her here and gotten a room. Shit, you could have come stayed at my house for the night. Call her and make sure she and that baby are good, and then tell her to come the fuck home."

He nodded his head. Moving to the side, he let me in the house, and we went into the living room. I watched as he grabbed his phone and called her.

"Vicky, come home. Yeah, I know, but you need to come back home. Now." He hung up the phone.

I didn't know what was going on. This nigga was meeting his match if you asked me, but I wasn't going to tell him that. I just wanted him to know that he had to get his shit together. God put Vicky in his life for a reason.

"You need to start looking for a place for her soon. You can't be going through this."

"I know, but maybe it's my karma and payback for the way I did her and Junie. My hands didn't care. Shit, I was beating Vicky's ass, but she fought back."

"That's because yo' ass shouldn't have been putting your hands on her anyway."

"You don't think I know that shit? I hate that I was the way I was, but now I'm trying to do better, and it's not enough for her ass. Even after saying we weren't going to be together, I still tried to come home and make shit better, but she found herself thinking that I was trying to get back with Junie, and shit went left. I don't have time for that shit, and it took everything in me not to really choke the life out of her. I wanted to murk that bitch last night."

"I feel you, but you have to learn to walk away from certain shit. Like when you know she's starting, instead of engaging in that argument with her, just tell her she got it and leave the house. I don't know how you and she are going to coparent when she can't keep her hands to herself and neither can you. You know I don't condone a nigga putting his hand on a woman, so you really need to think before you do something like that. That shit can land you in jail for a long-ass time and away from your kids."

"I know, and that's why I think it's best if she moves out today. Vicky used to be everything. I mean, she didn't argue, and she didn't bitch up until she got pregnant. Then she started acting like I had to tell her everything that was going on in my life. It was like she didn't understand that she was a side piece."

"Yeah, but where you fucked up at is getting her pregnant. If you wanted her to be a side piece or to stay one, you shouldn't have been sloppy and fucking her raw. Now you're stuck with her for eighteen years, and let's not forget she's only nineteen years old, my nigga. You're going to have hell with her. Be grateful you don't have to go through that twice. Junie is grown, and she don't do all that."

"I fucked up by letting her go," he admitted to me, and I couldn't do nothing but agree with him. I wouldn't be his friend if I didn't tell him the truth and had him around here thinking he didn't do nothing wrong when it came to that girl, because he did.

"Yeah, you did. I still don't know what you were thinking when you put your hands on her the first or the last time. You bugged the fuck out. That girl loved the fuck out of you."

"And now I have to be silent about her moving on because I know she won't take me back. I fucked that all the way up."

"At least now you can try to focus on you and your children," I said just as the door opened and Vicky walked in. Her hair was all over her head, and she looked like she had been physically dragged. "You good, V?" I asked, and she nodded her head.

"I'm a little sore, but I'm good."

Deciding to leave them to handle their business, I got up and headed for the door. "A'ight, I'll holla at y'all later."

Walking out of the house, I got back into my car and decided to go by the club to check on Draya and make sure everything was good. She could handle herself, but those females could be ruthless when they wanted to. The last thing I needed was for my fiancée to be into it with the dancers like she was with Minnie. She was close to being out the door anyway because she had been on some slick shit.

When I got there, it was packed, so I got out and went inside. Stepping through the entrance, I looked around for my lady and saw her heading up to the office. I went up right behind her. "Bae, we need to talk."

"Okay, what's up? Where is KJ?"

"He's with my mother, who feels like you don't fool with her anymore, and she wants to know why."

"I love your mother, so why would she think I don't fuck with her anymore? I don't have nothing against her. She was my savior when me and you weren't together," she explained, and it sounded like there was just a bit of miscommunication on both of their ends.

"Maybe you need to call and talk to her, because she's trying to figure out why KJ only goes to your parents' house, and I'm trying to figure that out as well."

"Well, it's nothing like that. I just figure that sometimes she wants a break. She always has him, and we have to learn to split time between both families."

"Yeah, okay," I said, sitting down on the sofa and watching her work for a little while longer.

I had to admit, seeing her in her element made me happy. It was like she was a new person when she was here. She was all about her business. Seeing her go from spot to spot to check on the books while watching the cameras for the private dance area had me proud to call her my woman. Now all she had to do was put some of that energy into coming home and spending time with me and her son, and we would be all the way good.

Chapter Thirty-three

Junie

I Got a Thang for You

Ace and I finally went on the date he had been asking me on for weeks now. I felt like it wouldn't be a big deal to give him a chance since he was practically begging me to let him take me out. I knew he didn't want to be friends, and although I tried to make it seem like I didn't like him, right now the truth was that I did. He was so sweet to me, and he had never put pressure on me, so this was my decision.

"How was your day?" he asked.

"Good, and yours?"

"It was cool. I'm not gonna lie. I was happy when you called and let me know you were ready to let me take you out. I'm still not rushing you to be with me, but I just want you to know that I will always treat you like a queen."

That was one thing I didn't doubt about him. He treated both me and Montana like we were queens. He didn't have kids, so he tried his best to treat my daughter as if she were his own, and that was the one thing I would ask for if I was with a man.

"I know, and that I will always appreciate from you."

"Do you think it's a bad idea to explore feelings you're having because you know the person you're with went through some shit?"

"No, I don't think it's a bad idea. I just want time to heal properly before hopping in a relationship and hurting the person who's trying to show me that he cares."

"So you think you may hurt me? How?"

"I don't know. I may not be able to reciprocate the love you show me, and I know how that can make a person feel. I went through that before, and I don't want to put nobody else through it."

He nodded his head, I guessed to let me know he understood where I was coming from. He probably didn't care about that, though. He wanted to be with me, and part of me wanted to be with him as well. I just didn't want to be hurt again, and that was the only thing stopping me from going all the way with him. He was in the streets the same way Jace was, and I knew what came with messing with a man like that.

"Listen, you don't have to worry about me hurting you, and I know for a fact that no matter what you went through, you won't hurt nobody because that's not who you are as a person. You're kindhearted and you love people. That nigga just broke you down, but it won't be long before you're back to that person you used to be. When you do get her back, I want to be the one who spends all his moments with her."

He was the first person to ever know me without actually knowing me. I didn't know if he had a thing for reading people or what, but the person he described me as was the same person I used to be before Jace broke my spirit and left me with no hope. Before now, he was the only man I wanted to be with, and now I wanted to imagine being without him. I hated him so much that he could be on fire and I wouldn't spit on his ass.

"Thank you for that. I needed it after all I've been through."

"I know, and that's why I'm here. You don't ever have to worry about being in anything alone as long as I'm here. There's not a person who can keep me away from being there for you."

This was exactly why I liked spending time with him. He knew all the right things to say, and he knew that no matter what, it wasn't going to get him no pussy. He was my friend, and he might just be my lover if he kept playing his cards right, but I was not giving up no honey until we made it official.

For the rest of dinner, we talked and got to know one another a little bit more. I wanted to make sure he knew all there was to know about me. When we got up, he paid and grabbed my hand so that we could leave. Walking out of the restaurant, we went to my car, and he opened the door for me. "Thank you."

"You're welcome. Can I get a kiss?" he asked, and I nodded my head.

Leaning in, he kissed me on the lips, and I pulled him closer because the feeling of his soft lips on mine felt so good to me. I wrapped my arms around his neck. He slid his tongue into my mouth and moved it around, which had my knees going weak.

"Mm," I moaned out and put my hand on his chest to push him back a little bit.

"You like that?" He smirked, and I nodded my head and smiled at the same time.

"You make me want more, but I don't want to rush things and have you in my bed."

"I'm not rushing things either, baby girl. We have all the time in the world to do that. I just wanted to feel your lips."

"Okay, and now we both have to go home and look crazy," I joked while laughing, and he joined in.

"You can come to my house with me if you want to. I promise to be the perfect gentleman if you don't push me."

"Let's go," I said before sitting in my car and shutting the door.

The entire way to his house, I was doing a lot of thinking, and now that I knew how Ace's kisses felt, he made me want to go all the way with him. Pulling up to his house, I parked right next to his car, then got out. "You ready to see where I live?" he asked.

"Lord, I hope it's not a pigsty," I joked, and he laughed.

"Nah, I'm not nasty."

Grabbing my hand, he led me to the front door and opened it. Letting me step in before him, he closed the door and locked it. He led me to the living room. I sat on the sofa, and he took my shoes off, then started rubbing my feet, which was feeling so good.

"You have some pretty feet," he admired.

"Thank you."

"I have a question. Would you get back with Jace if you had the chance?"

"Hell no. You asked me that once, and I told you my answer then. It's not going to change. That nigga lost me for good. I've given him too many chances, and I don't have it in me to give him another one."

He nodded his head.

"Have you ever put your hands on a girl?"

This was a question that had been burning in my head, and because I felt like I knew Ace, I felt like he wouldn't lie to me. The look on his face asked me if I was out of my mind.

"Nah, my momma would put her foot up my ass if I even cuss at a woman. She doesn't play that, and I don't know how, but she finds out everything."

"Sounds like a good parent to me," I giggled.

"Sometimes she can be overbearing. She's the reason I can't keep a woman in my life. She's always saying it's because Momma knows best, but I think I know best as well."

"Eh, a lot of men think that, but then they bring home women they know their mother isn't going to like. A lot of men pick women based on their looks and not what they can bring to the table." I kept it real with him. He had to know that if I was going to be in his life, then he had to get used to hearing the truth and not necessarily the things he wanted me to say. "Friend or not, men pick women based on what she can do in the bedroom and not around the house or for him."

"And you know this how?"

I stood up and turned around. "I know I look good, but I work, cook, clean, take care of my man, and make sure he's always in the right mind for whatever business he's into."

"What do you think about being with another man in the streets?"

I had to think about my answer before replying. I didn't want to make him feel like I had no interest in being with another man in the streets. I just wanted to make sure this man didn't have that many issues like Jace's ass had.

"Uh, I mean, as long as he knows how to take care of me at home and not make me feel like I'm a second option when it comes to the streets, then I'll give another street man a chance, but I know that men won't do that."

"I do."

"You sure about that?"

He moved in a little closer and put his hand around me. Pulling me closer, he kissed my lips, and I was so into it that I climbed on top of him. "Mm," I moaned while grinding my pussy on his dick. I knew he felt it because the slacks he was wearing left nothing to my imagination. He stood up, and I wrapped my legs around him.

"Bedroom?"

I nodded my head, and he carried me up the stairs and went into the bedroom. He laid me back on the bed, climbing in between my legs. I was so into it that I had forgotten all about my not wanting to fuck him motto until he backed up and took his shirt off. "Ooh, tempting."

He sighed and sat down when I said that. "I knew you was gonna stop it before it went too far."

"I'm sorry. I just want to be official before I give up my goods. You know some men get it, then stop messing with you, and I just want to make sure we're in this together. I don't like looking stupid."

"And I don't know how many times I have to tell you that you don't have to worry about that with me. I'm not looking to make you look crazy, and you're the one who don't want to make things official with me. I'm all for it, and not just so I can fuck you. I really want to be with you," he explained to me, and I felt like now was the chance for me to give it to him for real.

"As long as you know I want you to always be honest with me, and the first time I feel like you're not being all the way real with me, I will be out of this shit."

He looked me in my eyes, then pulled me to him and kissed my lips. "You don't have to worry about that." The kiss got intense, and he pulled me back on top of him, and before I knew it, my shirt was being slipped off my body. My body was screaming for him to keep going, but he stopped after a while and laid me back on the bed. Getting off the bed, he went into the restroom, then came back out not even five minutes later and with nothing on but a towel. "Now, are you sure you want to do this with me? I don't want to make it seem like I'm trying to pressure you into giving up your goods."

"You're not. I really want it, and I need it as well." I smiled, then stood up and took off the rest of my clothes, ready to give Ace my all.

Chapter Thirty-four

Jace

I Miss You

I was sitting on the sofa really thinking about the shit Korey said when he was here. It just made so much sense, so today I was out looking for somewhere to stay for Victoria and our unborn child. I didn't like the feeling of putting her out because she put her hands on me, and I really felt like this was my karma. I was missing Junie so much. She may have gotten on my nerves sometimes, and I may not have deserved her for the things I did to her, but she took care of my home and made sure I had nothing to worry about. She was the reason I was ready to give this shit up with Vicky. I thought that she was mature, and that was the only reason I even fucked with her, but she was not mature at all.

Korey was also right about another thing: I was being sloppy with my cheating when she got pregnant. It was like I just didn't give a fuck about hurting Junie, and in the end, I didn't know just how much I was hurting myself.

"Do you like this one?" I asked Vicky for the third time today. It was almost as if, with all the houses I took her to, she found something minor to hate. Even when I thought she couldn't hate the house because it was too nice, she still frowned.

"This one is not that bad. I just want to look at it once more before I make a decision. Why are you rushing me to find a place anyway?" she asked, side-eyeing me.

"This is something we both agreed on, remember?"

"Yes, I remember, but I didn't think you would be trying to get me out this soon. I thought before the baby came, but I meant weeks."

"Nah, you need to be in your own place before the baby comes so you can get used to that shit. I know you're not ready to move, but we're toxic. We barely get along, and I don't have time to be fighting you off me each time you decide you want to jump."

I had been doing good by not actually putting my hands on Vicky in a fucked-up way, but she was still tempting me, and my therapist told me the best way to avoid going back to that old me was if I actually let Vicky's ass go and only focused on my child when she was gone. I didn't need to be fucking her or nothing else, and there was no need to give her false hope thinking she had a chance at getting me back. I tried the shit, and it didn't work out, which told me right now the last thing I needed to be worried about was a relationship. *I'm about to have two kids out here in the world, and it's time for me to act like it. I don't ever want Montana to think a man putting his hand on her is love, and I don't ever want my son to think it's okay to put his hands on a woman. It's a must I set a better example for my kids, and that means me getting the toxic out of me and from around me. I want to be able to watch my kids grow up, graduate high school and college, get married, and have kids of their own. In order for me to do that, I have to get out of the streets and set a leading example.*

"I'll take this house." Vicky finally spoke, snapping me out of my thoughts.

Nodding my head, I looked at the real estate agent to let her know she could finally sit down and do the paperwork.

Two hours later, we were walking out of the house, and Victoria had the keys to her brand-new house. The only thing left for me to do now was get her a better car, and she would be set. I would help her furnish the home and maintain the bills. I didn't want her to have too much on her plate, but I also wanted her to know that it wouldn't be a bad idea for her to get a job just to help out. I knew how some women thought, and the last thing I wanted was for her to think she wouldn't have to work. *If we're not together, I'm not about to be paying all the bills myself and taking care of you and the baby.* She was going to have to pull her own weight for the things she needed and wanted.

"Now I know you may think you don't have to work, but in order for you to take care of you and not depend on me, you're gonna need a job. I'll put money in your account and pay the bills as well as take care of my child, but it's not my job to take care of you," I let her know.

"I know that, and I understand. As soon as I have the baby, it's back to work and school for me. I have to do what's best for both me and my child. The last thing I want is for you to think I'm depending on you any more than I should. As long as you make sure the baby is good, then I'm good."

It felt good to have this conversation with her. Sometimes she made me wonder if we could really make things work, and maybe in the future we could, but right now I needed to keep striving to be a better man, so I had to let her go.

"Do you want to get back with Junie?" she asked, throwing me off guard.

I could have easily told her that if I had the chance, I would jump at it, but I didn't have that chance, so I answered, "Nah. This whole thing is the reason why I think it's best for us to separate. We're toxic together, and I just need time to be alone."

She nodded her head but said nothing, so I hoped that was the answer she was looking to hear, because it was the truth.

When we made it back to the house, she got out, and I backed out of the driveway once I was sure she was in safe. I had some moves to make if I really wanted to get out of the streets, and that meant me going to sit down and talk with my father. He always gave me the best advice.

The entire ride to his house my mind was racing. I was afraid of change. I loved for things to stay the same, but in order for me actually move forward in my life, I had to think like a grown-ass man and not a little-ass boy. I thought about a lot of the shit Deion and Korey had told me, but for some reason, I just didn't think I could be them. Those niggas knew they wouldn't be in the streets for a long-ass time, whereas this was all I ever knew. This was how I got money. This was how I made sure my kid was taken care of and my home was good. I never had to rob nobody because the streets kept me laced with the money. I needed to handle my business.

Pulling up to his house, I got out and went right inside using my key. Marvin Gaye was playing in the kitchen, so I made my way in there, and there he was, sitting at the bar, smoking and listening to his music.

"What's up, Pops?"

"Hey, look who finally decided to stop and see his old man." He smiled and gave me a hug.

My father and I were close at one point, but when I got older, I started thinking I knew everything and started doing my own thing. I was in and out of trouble from the ages of 16 to 18, and then I got myself together and finally started to move differently—the way he had been trying to get me to move, but I was too dumb to listen.

"What you in here doing? With the way that music was blasting, I would have thought you had a woman in here."

"Hell nah. You know all these old women do is bicker, and I'm too old to be with a youngster." He chuckled, dapping me up. "Now, don't get me wrong. They have tried," he added.

"I bet. I need some advice."

"Okay, but first I want to know how my daughter-in-law is doing, and my granddaughter."

"Me and Junie aren't together anymore. We've been broken up for almost four months now. And Montana's good, same ol' same ol'."

"Damn, what happened? Don't tell me you put your hands on her again."

When he said that, I just looked at him to let him know that was why. I didn't have it in me to say that shit, because all it did was remind me of the good woman I had and that I took her for granted when I should have been holding her close to me.

"Son, what have I told you about that shit? You can't let that bipolar disorder control you and your actions, because after a while that excuse gets old."

Nodding my head, I didn't say anything because he had been telling me this all my life, and I chose not to listen to it. I felt like if a woman loved me, then she would have tried to understand me and what I was going through, but now after all this time, I actually understood why he was telling me what he was telling me. I just wished I had gotten it sooner.

"I didn't tell her about the disorder until she was already gone. I know I should have told her about it the moment we got together, but I didn't want her to think of me as a monster, but she thinks that already. All we do now is talk about Montana. If it's not about her, then she acts like I don't exist."

"I told you when I found out the first time you put your hands on her that she was going to leave you alone and you would be feeling bad."

"On top of all that, I cheated on her and got the other girl pregnant, so I knew for a fact that once she found out about it, I could do nothing to get her back," I told him, and he just shook his head. I knew he was disappointed in me, but I wouldn't be me if I didn't make mistakes.

"So are you with this new baby momma? And what happened to your face?" he finally asked.

"Nah, me and her are toxic. She did this shit to me."

"You met your match, and now she's toxic?" He chuckled, but I didn't. I didn't find nothing funny about this shit. My eye was still hurting, and I couldn't even blink without being in pain.

"Back to the reason I'm here. I want to get out of the game, but you know how I feel about change."

"Yeah, but it's time. I've been waiting a long time for you to come sit down with me and tell me this. You've been in the streets for a long time, son, and it's time for you to find something else to do with your time. You should have more than enough money to make sure you don't have nothing to worry about. It's just up to you how you utilize that shit. You're far from dumb, so you're gonna be okay."

Nodding my head, I asked, "You think so?"

"Hell yeah. Now, get out there and make that shit happen."

Dapping him up, I hugged him, then walked toward the door with him right behind me. He gave me some shit to think about, as well as what I needed in order to get this shit on the move so that I could be out of the streets, which had been my goal for a long-ass time.

Chapter Thirty-five

Deion

I Wanna Know

The full day was spent with me in court going back and forth with the judge on these little misdemeanor-ass cases. At first, I was nervous and didn't think I would win them, but the judge finally saw my point and dismissed all five cases I had today after I let him know that I could go all day. In some of the cases, he was lucky that all they wanted was the case dismissed, because some of these people could have sued the city for harassment by cops. Those motherfuckers were just fucking with half these people. Now I was sitting down with the woman I thought I would never see again—my mother.

This woman did me so dirty when I was a child. She abandoned me, treated me like shit, and half the time she would act like I wasn't in the house with her. When I say that my mother taught me not to disrespect woman, I mean my grandmother. She was the one who raised me into the man I was today, but it didn't stop my mother from thinking she was the reason I was successful.

"I don't know what you want from me," I told her. She had been sitting here pouring her heart out to me for the last thirty minutes, and all I wanted to do was get up and walk out of here like she used to do to me so many times. I yearned for my mother to love me when I was a child, but she didn't. She had her sights on other shit like drugs, money, and men. She didn't understand how that shit fucked me up in the long run. I felt like women would only fuck with me because of the money I was getting, and most of the time I was right.

"Deion, please don't do me like that. I'm clean now, and I want to be in your life," she stammered while looking around like she was looking for somebody.

"After all this time why now? I'm grown now. Granny took care of me and turned me into the man I am today. She taught me everything I needed to know about life. Shit, you should have been trying to teach me, but instead you were too focused on other shit. Ma, I love you because you birthed me, but my mother is Granny. I don't need you," I let her know, and she dropped her head.

I knew my granny was a sore subject for her because it was one for me as well after she passed away. I felt like I had no one, and shit, I didn't until I met Korey and Jace. They both were the reason I stayed with my head in the books. They let it be known that I was destined for more, and Korey was the only one who made sure he was handling his business to get out of the streets. Jace, on the other hand, thought that the streets and fast money was the way of life, but it wasn't. There was so much you could do when you weren't busy running, ducking, and hiding from the cops.

I really wished he would get his mind together and actually get out of the streets.

"What I want is for you to give me a chance to be here for you. I know I wasn't a good example when you was a child, and I know Gran is the reason you're successful, but her not being here should make you want to work things out with me."

"Do you know Gran told me before she died that you might try to come back into my life after I started getting money?" I asked. I wanted her to know how much I didn't trust her or a word that was coming out of her mouth.

Again, she put her head down. "I figured, but I'm not here because I want money from you. Honest to God, I just want to be in your life, son, that's all. I told your grandmother before she died that I wanted to make things right with you. I can understand how you would think I'm only in your life for what you have and not you, but you're wrong."

It didn't matter how hard I was trying to get her to crack and tell me why she really wanted me here. She was keeping her composure. As a lawyer, I could always tell when somebody was lying to me, but for some reason I couldn't with her.

"I don't know if you're lying to me, but here's my number. I have somewhere to be, so maybe we can meet up again real soon," I said before standing up and making my way to the exit. I was going to wait outside just to see what she did while I wasn't in there. I hated to treat her this way because I loved my momma, but some people you had to form a distance from, and she was that person in my life.

Finally making it to my car, I climbed inside, started it up, and drove to the front. I was sure she didn't know what kind of car I was in, so it was easy to sit across the street and watch her get into a 2010 Impala and pull off. A part of me wanted to follow her just to see if she was still staying in the same house she had when I was a child, but instead I went the other way, toward Dreux's business.

Ever since giving her that letter, I'd been checking in on her just to make sure she was straight. I knew what this kind of information could do to somebody. She had told me not to do anything until she talked to her parents, but I did my own research on her parents and the woman who sent the letter. I didn't know if it was a coincidence that on the same day Dreux was born, a child came up missing from the nursery at a hospital in Delaware. Maybe it was me, but I didn't think that it was that far off.

The ride to her job was spent with me thinking about how I was about to break this news to her without her being mad. I couldn't keep this shit from her. Even if she did get mad at me, she had to know, and I had to be the one to tell her. When I finally pulled up, I sat in the car for a while, then sat up to get out, but she was walking out and over to my car.

"What are you doing here?" she asked, sitting in the passenger seat.

Leaning in, I kissed her on the lips, then took a deep breath and backed away. "I have something to tell you, and I know you're about to get mad at me because you told me not to do anything. I just couldn't help myself."

"I hope this is not about the woman who is claiming that I'm her child. I told you to stay out of it," she said, looking me in the eyes.

"I know, but just hear me out. A woman reported her baby girl missing in Delaware the same day you were born. It's the same woman who sent the letter to me. I don't want to be in the middle of this—"

She cut me off before I could finish my sentence. "Well, don't. All you had to do was mind your business until I talked to my parents. I'm not ready for that, and for you to take matters into your own hands is wrong, especially when I asked you not to do anything. You don't listen, and I hate for people to go behind my back and do things when I asked them not to."

I nodded my head, understanding why she was mad, but I couldn't change what I did. Even if I could, I didn't want to. She needed to talk to her parents, and she was taking too long to do so. If she wanted to know the truth, then she should have made her way over to their house the moment I told her what I told her.

"I understand why you're mad, but you need to look into this so that you can clear your parents' name. She wants me to be her lawyer for when she takes them to court."

"I'm grown, and she doesn't know if I'm her child. This whole thing could just be a coincidence. She probably saw my name and birth date and automatically thought I'm her child. You ever think about that? I don't have time for this shit," she snapped, then turned to get out of the car.

"I'm sorry I went behind your back, but I wanted to make sure you had all the facts before sitting down and talking to your parents if that was even what you were gonna do."

"I wasn't ready. You can't make me be ready to go sit down and talk to them about something like this. This shit is life-changing, not only for me but for my daughter as well because my mother and father are the only people she knows as her grandparents. I'm not about to let anybody take that away from her," she let me know before jerking her arm away from me and getting out of the car.

I sat there for a while, hoping that she would come back to the car and let me explain, but she didn't. Instead, she went inside and looked back at me while shaking her head. Putting my car in reverse, I backed out of the parking spot and made my way to my house. I didn't know if I just put a damper on our relationship by the shit I had done, but I didn't regret it. Like I said, she needed all the facts before going to sit down and talk to her parents. I wanted her to figure this out, and I wanted to be there when she did, but I had a feeling that she wouldn't be talking to me for a while after this.

Before I could pull into the driveway of my house, my phone started to ring. Looking at it, I saw that it was Breann, and I just looked at the phone while it rang to voicemail.

Getting out of the car, I went into the house and sat on the sofa. I had so much on my mind, and the only thing I could do to get it off was smoke a blunt and hope that Dreux didn't hold this shit against me. I just needed her to know that I did this shit so that she could get to the bottom of it without having to go through a roller coaster of not knowing if her parents were lying. Dreux meant the world to me, so it would devastate me if she didn't want to have anything to do with me all because I was trying to help.

Chapter Thirty-six

Dreux

So into You

I didn't know what the hell Deion was thinking launching his own investigation when I specifically asked him to let me handle it my way first. This was the exact reason why niggas were always in the doghouse. I could understand him trying to help, but I didn't ask him for that. I had to want answers before looking for them, and a part of me didn't want them. The moment I asked my parents about it, if they told me that, yes, I was kidnapped or adopted, then everything would change, and I wasn't ready for that. There already had been a lot going on in my life, and the last thing I needed was for this shit to actually be true.

"Thank you for keeping her," I told Max.

"No problem. If you need me again, just hit me." He smiled.

I didn't know what happened with the Max I was used to dealing with and this new nigga who was standing in front of me, but I guessed he was working on being a better version of himself than who he was when he was with his wife. We were getting along, he was bringing Savannah home when it was time, and I didn't have to harass him about my baby because he stayed letting me know what they were doing and where they were going. She was enjoying having her father back in her life, and that was all I could ask for.

"You know, I've never seen her this happy to be able to actually see and spend time with you again. I'm sorry I took you to court."

"I'm not. You did what you had to do, and I don't blame you. I was on some other shit, and I would have done the same thing if I were you. I guess I just let somebody get in my head and didn't think for myself."

Nodding my head, I said nothing. He was saying everything I had been saying from the beginning. Although our coparenting situation was never excellent, it worked for us, but when he got married, he switched up all the way. But we were both trying not to live in the past and actually move on.

"So I have something to tell you," I told him. We were waiting for Savannah to get her things and come back down, but she was taking forever.

"What's up?"

"Somebody sent a letter to my boyfriend saying that she was my real mom and that my parents kidnapped me from her."

"And you think it's true?" he inquired.

I shrugged my shoulders. "At first I was saying that it could be anybody, but he actually did his investigating, and it turns out a baby girl went missing from a hospital on the same day I was born."

"That could be a coincidence, though. Talk to your parents and ask them. I've seen you with them a lot, and I just don't think it would make a difference. I mean, you were loved and had nothing to worry about as a child. Do what's best for you," he said just as Savannah came back down.

"Hey, Momma, I'm ready," she said, hugging her father, then coming to my side.

"Did you have fun?" I asked her.

"Yes, I always have fun when I'm with Daddy. He took me to the movies, shopping, and he even got me a new iPad."

When she said that, I looked at him. He knew I said no more iPads since she broke the one I got her from a temper tantrum she threw one day.

"My bad." He smiled.

"It's fine. Thank you again. I'll be calling if I need you to get her again," I let him know before walking out of the house.

The entire ride to the house, Savannah talked my head off about what all she and her father did, and it made me kind of jealous. I was happy that he was spending time with her and actually doing things like that with her, but sometimes I wished that I could do the same. It was just that sometimes my job ran later than usual, and then on the weekends, she was either with him or my parents. It was like everybody had her spoiled rotten, and I had to make sure everybody spent time with her. Now, as far as what Max was saying about the whole "might be kidnapped" situation, I felt like it was time for me to have that talk with my parents, but I wanted to wait until the weekend since Savannah would be with her father. The last thing I needed was to have that conversation in front of my child.

I wasn't sure what would happen if I found out that all my life they had been lying to me, but I was starting to wonder if Max really felt like nothing would change if they did tell me I was kidnapped. They could have easily adopted me from the kidnapper without knowing the truth about where I came from, but I did feel like in order for me to be able to move on without having to think about this, I needed answers.

When we finally made it home, we got out of the car and went inside. Savannah ran right up the stairs and into her bedroom like always, and I went into the living room. Taking my heels off, I got up and made my way into the kitchen to start cooking and roll a blunt. I also wanted a glass of wine, but I thought that would be overdoing it.

Once I had the grease to smother the chicken on, I finished rolling my blunt, then put it to my mouth while cooking. Lately, I'd been smoking a lot more, and I didn't like it, but I liked the fact that it took my mind off shit if even for a little while. Sitting down at the bar, I hit the blunt a few more times before putting it out and finishing the food.

I still couldn't believe that Deion went behind my back the way he did. That shit had me so pissed off that I didn't even want to talk to him no more. I knew he was only doing it to make things easier for me, but when I asked him to let me handle it, it was because I didn't know if I wanted to bring the shit up. He had to understand that I was not his charity case or his fixer-upper. I was a grown woman who could handle her own issues. If I wanted him to do that, then I would have given him the okay.

The sound of my phone ringing made me look at it. Rolling my eyes, I just watched the phone ring to voicemail. He was gonna have to feel just how mad I was. I couldn't forgive him that easily, although I did miss him. I hadn't talked to him at all after that shit and for good reason. Now he was just going to have to wait for me to get back to him when I was ready to talk, but right now I wasn't.

Going back to what I was doing, I put the rice on, then the sides, and I sat back down. Putting the blunt back to my lips, I was about to light it when Savannah came down with her phone glued to her ear. "Who are you on the phone with?" I asked.

"My friend Lisa."

"Oh," was all I said before lighting the blunt and watching her as she made her way through the kitchen and right back up the stairs. Her little ass was acting like she was grown, and I knew I was going to have to watch her. The last thing I wanted was for her to be on the phone with a boy and think I was going to be fine with it. She would not end up like I did, and that was another reason I decided to let Max back in her life. As long as she had her father, she would never make the decisions I did when I was 17 years old. I was so in love with Max that I let him do me any kind of way, and it wasn't a good thing to do. I was blind to a lot of stuff he was doing, and I wanted my daughter to have a better pick of men than I did.

My phone ringing again made me look at it, and this time I answered, "Hello?"

"Hey, what you doing, baby?" Deion asked.

"Cooking."

"What you cooking, and why haven't I heard from you all day?"

I couldn't help but roll my eyes. He knew damn well why I wasn't talking to him, but it was just like him to ask so that we could talk about it and get over it. I loved that about him, but right now all it was doing was agitating me even more.

"You know exactly why I haven't talked to you."

"I'm sorry for going behind your back and doing that. I don't know how many more times I have to apologize, but I was doing it for you."

"That's the thing. You shouldn't have to apologize because you should have just let me handle it like I told you I was. You took it into your hands without even thinking about me and what I said, and that's a trait that made me stop fucking with Max, so you need to think before you do."

"I'm nothing like that nigga. Don't ever compare me to him again. It was wrong, and you don't have to worry about me doing anything like that again, but when has it ever been a crime to look out for your woman?" he asked.

"It's not a crime, but when I ask you to not do something, I expect you not to so that I can handle it myself. I'm going to have a conversation with my parents, but it won't be until the weekend when my daughter goes with her father."

"And how is that going? I hope he's not acting like he's good just to get you right back where he had you before."

"He's not. That I know," I let him know.

Yeah, Max and I had a fucked-up relationship, and he wasn't trustworthy, but one thing he wouldn't do was lie. If he told me he was sorry about something, then he was. He would never do anything that could get him booted out of Savannah's life because now he knew that I didn't have an issue keeping her away from him. The only reason he got off so easy was because she missed him so much, and I missed seeing her smile. This was the most she had talked to me in a few weeks. She didn't understand it yet, but when she got older, she would know that I was only looking out for her.

"Can I come see you?" he asked.

"I guess." I smiled.

He could probably tell I was smiling. He made my days much better and the nights I spent with him much better. That man could put it down in the bedroom and always had me screaming his name, which was a good thing. He made sure I knew he was the man when we were in the bedroom, and I wouldn't never play with him or make him feel any less. All I asked was that he let me fight my own battles, because not all battles are for another person to fight.

Chapter Thirty-seven

Draya

Next to You

Sitting in the office, I was waiting for the next manager candidate to walk in, but she was taking a little too long, and it was pissing me off. *I mean, damn, you knew you had an interview for a job you said you really wanted, and now you got me waiting like I'm the one being interviewed.* She didn't know it, but she was about to get a mouthful when she walked inside. I had to let her know upfront that she wasn't making a good first impression on me, and I had it in my mind to go with the first woman who walked in here. There was nothing like having a woman who used to dance be the manager. She knew her shit, and she was ready to start the same night. She was already beating all the other candidates, and I let her stay around until I had this last interview, but I was about to cancel it and tell her she was hired.

Suddenly, the door flew open, and this drag queen–looking woman walked in. She had on some heels that had her looking way taller than I figured she was. "Sorry I'm late. I had some stuff to do before coming here," she said.

"Name?" I asked with a blank stare on my face. I hadn't been showing any emotions, and I wasn't about to start right now no matter how bad I wanted to laugh at what she had on and the shoes. She looked a fucking mess, but I was going to hold my composure until she walked up out of here.

"Char."

"Okay, Char. You have already wasted my time by making me wait for you, and then you come in here and act like things are supposed to be good. Thanks for coming in, but I think I'm going to go with another candidate," I let her know while standing up and sticking my hand out for her to shake.

She just looked at it then me like I was crazy before scoffing and speaking. "I'm not shaking your hand. You act like I had the interview or like I got the job. You won't even let me interview. Just kicking people out. I swear, you give a black person money and a business, and they start acting like they shit don't stink," she snapped.

It took everything in me not to cuss this bitch out or bust her in her fucking mouth. This disrespectful-ass Juwana-Mann-looking bitch did not just try to read me. "First of all, we had money before this business, and I'm sure we will have it after. You showed up thirty minutes late, and I was even waiting for you, but when you walked in here talking about you had other things to do before coming in here, you turned me all the way off. You got it, though. I'm not about to argue with you. Have a blessed day, sweetheart," I calmly said while holding the door open for her to get the fuck out.

"Girl, what the fuck ever," she semi-yelled while walking out.

Looking out at the girls that she had interrupted, I shook my head to let them know that everything was all right, because I knew them, and they would have pounced on her ass if I didn't. Turning my attention to Loren, I motioned for her to come up to the office, and she did. As soon as she got in there, I shut the door and started moving around to grab the new-hire paperwork. There was no point in making her wait. She wanted to start tonight, and I wanted to get the fuck out of here and back home to my baby and man.

This was the best thing about having a manager. I wouldn't have to be here all the time, and I thought that I just may find another one so I could come here and check on things instead of being here regularly. The girls would miss me, and I would miss them as well, but I needed a vacation. In order to get one, I had to make sure the staff was all the way together before taking time off.

"Okay, girl, fill these out while I go talk to the girls. Were you for real about wanting to start tonight? Do you have kids?" I asked.

"No, ma'am. I don't want them right now. A man will have to be pretty special for me to let him fuck me raw." She smiled, making me high-five her.

"I don't blame you," I told her, then left her to do what she needed to do.

Stepping out onto the floor, I grabbed the mic that was on the deejay stand and spoke into it so that I could get everybody's attention. "A'ight, y'all, I have an announcement. Y'all know I've been talking about getting somebody else in here so that I wouldn't have to be here all the time, and I found her. That woman who was standing down here at the bar, yes, she will be the new manager. Her name is Loren, and she will be starting tonight. She knows everything to know about running a business, especially a strip club, so I ask that you all show her the most respect. Treat her the way you would treat me or Korey, and y'all know she has the right to fire y'all if y'all get out of hand, and both Korey and I will stand behind her a hundred percent."

I had to let them know that this was serious. One thing I knew about Loren was that she wasn't about to let them run her off. She told me that in her interview when I told her they tried me but I had to put my foot down and let it be known that I wasn't going anywhere.

The only thing I had to let her know was she didn't want to get on their bad sides. Yeah, she had all right to do what she wanted and fire them if she wanted to, but we needed to make sure the moneymakers stayed a little happier. They were the ones out there shaking their asses for cash, so the last thing I wanted was for them to feel like we were just tucking with them. I needed her to leave that stripper mentality at the door and come in here on boss shit only. I wasn't taking anything less, and if she didn't meet the requirements I set for her, then she would be out of here before she could fix her wig. I wasn't playing. I told Korey when he let me be his partner and take over this club that I was going to make sure everything was running smoothly.

He wanted me to take a step back, but I wanted to keep my promise to him, and that was the only reason I'd been working as hard as I had been. The last thing I wanted was to be the reason his club got shut down. We already changed the dress code, and everybody had to be patted down before being let inside. We weren't about to have any incidents that caused us to be on a stand or have the cops in our shit. Although we were not doing anything illegal, cops always found a way to fuck with you, so that was something we didn't need.

"We're gonna make sure she feels right at home," Minnie said, and I had to look at her to make sure she wasn't on no bullshit. That bitch could make somebody drag her through the club and down the street. Her mouth was dangerous, but after I told her that I wouldn't hesitate to take my shoes off and beat her ass, she stopped fucking with me.

"Minnie, I'm serious. If she fires your ass for fucking with her, then you can't get your job back."

"I'm serious too, boss. You won't hear nothing about me being disrespectful to her or nothing. I've heard about her, and she will slap anybody for any disrespect."

"Exactly, and that's something we don't want. The way you all respect me is the same way everybody needs to be when I'm not around. We've been doing good and haven't had any mishaps, so let's keep it that way," I said and put the mic down.

Going back up to the office, I grabbed the paperwork from Loren and started to put it into the computer, then told her what her job would be. I also let her know that I was looking for an assistant manager so that she wouldn't have to work all the time.

"Thank you so much for this opportunity. I swear you won't regret it."

"I have a feeling that I won't." I smiled and stuck my hand out for her to shake, but she hugged me instead. "Whoa, okay."

"Sorry. I'm just really excited. I've been looking for a job that don't require me going back to dance, and this is perfect for me." She beamed.

"You'll do great," I told her before walking her out. When we got to the floor, I made the bartender pour us both a shot to celebrate her coming on with us. We took them back, and I ran upstairs and gave her the quick rundown. "You don't have to do anything but watch the girls. If they even remotely look like they're about to fight or argue, break that shit up. We had an incident at the other club that could have gotten us shut down, and we don't need that here," I let her know.

"You don't have to worry about that. I got you," she said, and I grabbed my purse and car keys before leaving.

I was gonna make it my business to stop by Korey's mom's house so that I could talk to her. I never wanted her to think I had anything against her. Like I said, when I didn't want to see or be around her son, she was there for me, so it was a must that I let her know just how much she meant to me.

When I pulled up to her house, she and KJ were outside, and he was playing while she was watching him like always. I put one foot down on the pavement, and KJ shot over to me and reached for me to pick his ass up like always. "What's up, baby boy?" I asked, and he just smiled and kissed me on the cheek. "Hey, Ma," I said.

"'Hey, Ma,' my behind. Why haven't you been over here to see me? You and my son get back together and you just forget about the person who was there for you?"

"I didn't know you were feeling a way until Korey told me. I'm sorry. I've just been busy. It's not on purpose. I would never intentionally treat you like you don't matter when you mean a lot to me."

When those words left my mouth, she smiled. She was just as spoiled as my son. I treated her like my mother, so I could see how my not coming around would make her feel like I was blowing her off or like I wasn't fucking with her, but she wasn't just a mother to me. She was my best friend. I could tell her just about anything about me and her son, and she wouldn't judge. She gave me advice, and she didn't go back and tell him what I said. She was the reason I actually decided to talk to Korey instead of having her play middleman. I knew she didn't like that.

We had a good relationship, so of course I didn't want anything to get in the middle of that, and I hoped she knew that.

Chapter Thirty-eight

Korey Sr.

Stability

I sat in the office overlooking everything that was going on and all the money that was being thrown. Draya was right about this costume night, and I was happy that she didn't mind me using it. These niggas was eating this shit up, and we were seeing way more money. I wasn't going to just steal her idea and not give her props for it. Each night I announced it was a new costume night, I made sure I let everybody know my wife came up with the theme or idea.

"You good?" Kaylen, one of the dancers, asked, peeking through the door.

"I'm good. What's up?"

"I just wanted to know if it was okay for me to take off a little early. I have to go pick up my son from my sister."

I just looked at her because she knew I didn't play that, but since the club was raking in money tonight, I didn't really need her. "I guess, but next time find a babysitter for your whole shift. If I keep letting you out of here early, the other girls are going to think I have to do it for them as well," I let her know. She was really lucky that I didn't want to hear Draya's mouth. She had to remind me a few times that some of the dancers were mothers and a lot of them didn't have any help with their kids.

"I got you. I'm sorry."

"It's good."

When she walked out, she closed the door behind her but not fast enough, because it opened right back up, and this time Jace and Deion stepped in. "What's up, bro?" Jace asked, dapping me up.

"Ain't shit. Making sure shit look good before I get out of here. What y'all got going?"

"Shit," Jace responded.

"Dreux a little mad at me, but I think she back on a nigga's side," Deion said.

"What happened?"

"I went and did my own investigating about her parents and the woman claiming to be her real mother. She didn't like that, so I'm on the way to her house to make up for it. Just thought I would stop and check on you."

"Shit, I'm good. I'm ready for all this shit to fall into place so that me and Draya can start planning the wedding. I don't plan on going into another year without her being my wife."

I noticed Jace not really saying anything and looked at him. I knew my nigga was miserable without Junie, but he had nobody but himself to blame for that shit.

"Jace, what's wrong, bro?" Deion asked, picking up on his silence as well.

"I want to get out of the streets. It's time. I'm about to have two shorties, so I have to make sure I'm here for them at all costs," he said.

It felt good to hear him say that. We'd been waiting for this day for a long time, so now all he had to do was figure out what he wanted to do to replace the streets. "It won't be easy. You're going to have to find something that will keep you occupied and not thinking about the streets. What made you come to this decision?"

"Man, just thinking about the lives I'm putting at risk: mine, my daughter's, my unborn son's, Junie's, and Vicky's. I don't want none of them to suffer on behalf of me. I've already hurt them enough."

"Listen, if you think you're ready, then you can work here until you figure out what you want to do. Although you have enough money to sit home, it's not a good idea. The more you sit at home, the more you're going to want to get back out in the streets to make some noise," I advised him. Both Deion and I went through the same thing when we first got out of the streets. *As long as he knows why and who he's doing it for, I don't think he'll go back.*

He nodded his head. I stuck my hand out, and he shook it.

"What am I going to be doing?" he asked, rubbing his hands together like he was Birdman.

"Not talking to the dancers. I've been looking for a manager to take over for when I'm done for the day, because having dancers blowing my phone up all night is not going to work out," I stressed. I didn't want to put a lot on him, but he might want to open a club up, and this was the perfect opportunity for him to see what it was like to run a business. I already proved Draya wrong about how much it took to do this shit, because for some reason she thought all I did was sit around this bitch and throw money, and that wasn't it. I loved showing people that this shit wasn't easy work and that you had to have a lot of patience to put up with the shit I'd been putting up with.

"I think I can handle that. So I'm just watching from here?"

"Something like that. All I can say is watch closely, because these bitches will keep you on your toes. I mean, fighting, arguing over little shit, nagging about shit, and they will try to get over on you. Being new, you have to show them that you're not one to be played with, so I advise you to not get sexually involved with any of them." I kept it real with him. I would be here to train him to be just like I was. When I first opened this club, I used to be fucking these bitches all the time until I lost my girl. That shit was dead after that. Yeah, he was single, but it still wasn't a good idea. I needed him to understand me when I said not to get involved with them by any means.

"A'ight, so I'm guessing you're going to be training me and watching my every move?" he asked, and I shook my head.

"I will be showing you everything you need to know and what you need to do when I'm not here, but I will not be watching your every move. I'm nobody's babysitter. If you get involved with one of the dancers, just keep that drama away from my club. At the end of the day, you're grown, and I know you're going to do what you want to do."

"You don't have to worry about me bringing no drama to your club. Shit, I may not be fucking with any of them on a serious level, but I also won't disrespect your spot and be fucking all of them. I know how much drama that can start. I just want to help you take this club to the next level."

I nodded my head. I knew my nigga was going to do good up in this bitch. All I had to do was talk to Draya about it, and it would be on and popping. She really didn't have a say-so in who I hired, but I wanted to at least let her know that he would be working with me at the club so she wouldn't be surprised when she saw him.

That was the last thing I needed, especially when I knew she already felt a way about that nigga. If she didn't have to be around him at all, she wouldn't be. I could understand what she was saying, but like I told her, I wasn't about to sit up there and make it seem like he wasn't my nigga. I knew him before I even got with Draya, so wasn't no way I was about to stop fucking with him as long as he never disrespected her.

"A'ight. You can come back in the morning, and I'll show you everything. Right now, I'm about to get out of here, but I'll be back later on to lock up."

"So you're leaving them unattended in your club?" Deion asked.

"I don't have a choice. I don't have a manager right now."

"Damn, I can stay back and watch them. It's not a big deal," Jace said, and I looked at him to make sure he was serious. When he looked back into my eyes, I handed him the club keys.

"I'm trusting you, Jace."

"I know, and you don't have to worry about me fucking this up. You can count on me. I won't let nothing happen to the club, bro," he assured me, so I dapped him up and left.

Walking out of the club, I got into my car and started it up. Backing out of the parking lot, I headed straight to my mother's to pick KJ up, but my phone started to vibrate. Looking at it, I saw that it was Draya and quickly picked up. "What's up, baby?"

"Hey, are you on your way home?"

"Nah, I'm going to get KJ first."

"Don't worry about it. He's spending the night with her."

"I'm guessing you two talked?"

"Yeah, and I had to apologize to her for having her think that I just used her until I got back with you. I never want her to think that."

I knew Draya and my mother were going to work things out. Those two were like best friends, so I knew that was the only reason she was feeling the way she was feeling.

"I'm on my way home," I told her, and we hung up.

It didn't take me long to make it home, and I was so happy when I walked in and smelled the food that she was cooking. This was the shit I was missing. "Baby, how was your day?" she asked.

"Long, but good. The club was seeing almost two million dollars before I left."

"That's amazing."

"Uh, babe, I wanted to tell you this before you found out from somebody else or when you walked in the club and saw him there. Jace is working at the club until he figures out what he wants to do. He wants to get out of the streets, so I'm trying to help him out in figuring himself out."

"How many times are you going to look out for Jace, bae? I mean, I know he's like a brother to you, but he needs to figure it out on his own the same as you and Deion did. You didn't have nobody take you to their strip club and help you. You literally had to do it alone," she informed me as if I didn't know that already.

This was the shit I hated. She was acting like because I had a successful business, that meant I had to turn my back on my brother, and I wasn't about to do that. If he wanted to get out of the streets, then the least I could do was help him out.

"I get what you saying, but listen to me when I say that if it weren't for me sitting down and telling Jace that I wanted to do this and him telling me that he knew I could, I would still be in the streets just like him. I loved the fast money as well, and it took me some time even after being with you and listening to you tell me all the time that you didn't want me in the streets before I actually decided to handle my business as a grown man and got out of them for good."

I didn't see a point in having a club if I didn't use it to show my niggas what they could have if they weren't in the streets anymore. I wanted this shit for Jace the same way he wanted it for me, and that was what a real friend would do, so she was just going to have to deal with it.

"I hear you, and you're right. I think it's a good idea for you to help him out, and I'm happy he's finally getting out of the streets. It's time to let that go with him having two kids. I believe in him, and if you need help with anything, just let me know." She smiled before kissing my lips and getting off the couch.

Grabbing her hand, I pulled her back down. "I love you, ma," I let her know.

"I love you too. Go take a shower. I'll have your plate fixed for you." She smiled and made her way into the kitchen.

Chapter Thirty-nine

Junie

Trust

After the night I spent with Ace, I didn't want to get up and go to work the next morning, but he wouldn't let me sleep in either. Now I was sitting here looking stupid and really wanting to go home. That man fucked me beyond crazy. He did things to me that Jace had never done. He had my toes curling, my back hurting, and my pussy yearning for his touch. I had never been fucked like that before, and I wanted it more and more.

"Hey, girlie, you good in here?" Dreux asked, walking into my office, which prompted me to sit up and try to act like I was doing something.

"I'm tired as hell."

"Nobody told you to be out fucking like you was last night," she joked. "Ah, you fucked Ace. How was it?"

"It was fucking amazing." I beamed.

"It's about damn time. I was tired of you walking around here with that dust on your pussy. Ace likes you, and you need to start thinking about your happiness instead of not doing it because you're scared of what people might think about you." She gave me the perfect advice.

"You're right. I've been thinking about everybody for far too long, and now it's time for me to actually get out there and start thinking about myself. I don't know if I ever thanked you for this, but thank you for giving me the chance to actually work for you. I know that we had our issues with the whole Victoria and Jace thing, but I didn't care about him being with her. What I cared about is the fact that you knew and waited to tell me. I understand why you waited and held her secret though, so I had no reason to really be mad at you."

"You really mean that? I've been around here thinking, and I don't ever want you to think I don't have your back. It's just when a situation involves both you and my sister, I'm stuck in the middle, so I felt like if I didn't say anything, I wouldn't have nothing to worry about."

"I know and that's fine. Just next time, tell me whatever you may know about Ace. I like him a lot, and the last thing I want is for him to play with me the same way Jace did. I'm not talking about him putting his hands on me. He told me that he would never do that, and I believe him. I'm talking about if you ever find out he's cheating on me, tell me," I stressed.

"I got you. If you're tired and want to go home, you can. I mean, I'm about to get out of here in a second."

"I'll probably at least try to get through half my work. I have two houses to do this week, and I want to make it as easy as possible on me and the other girl who's teaming up."

"I feel you on that. I'll continue my work at home. I have to go pick Savannah up from my parents and make dinner."

"Girl, you'd better start cooking enough to last y'all a few days. It's just you and her unless Deion is over there as well." I smirked. I knew she and Deion were getting serious about each other because she was always with him. I just wanted her to be careful and make sure she actually got to know him before jumping too quickly into a relationship, just like I was doing with Ace. We said we were making it official, but I knew in the back of my mind I was going to always think about the shit Jace put me through, and I was not going to want to put up with it again. The cheating and lying—I couldn't do it anymore. *I'm getting too old to be worrying about what another nigga is doing, so Ace had better come all the way correct, or his ass gon' get left quick as hell.*

All the problems I had with Jace were not making their way into this new relationship. We were either building something together or not at all, because I was not looking to be a main bitch. I was looking to be the only bitch, and he was gonna find that out real soon. All I asked of him was just to respect and treat me like the queen he promised to treat me like and we'd be good.

"Deion did come over last night."

"And you've forgiven him for getting into your business, right?"

"Yes, I just told him to make sure he don't do that shit again or I'm not fucking with him at all."

I knew she was telling the truth because if there was one thing I knew she hated, it was a nigga doing something she specifically asked him not to. It didn't matter if she really liked him. She would cut him off the same way she did Max, and she was madly in love with that nigga.

When she walked out of the office, I leaned my head back and just thought about all the shit that I had put myself through trying to make Jace happy. In the midst of being with him, I forgot what it was like to be genuinely happy, so now I could say I knew what my sister was feeling about her and Korey's relationship. At first, I really couldn't speak on it because I didn't know what that feeling was like, but now that I thought about it, I had been feeling it for a long time. I just put it to the back of my head the way I did everything else. If I had spoken up about the shit that Jace was doing to me, then I wouldn't have been in that predicament. If it weren't for Ace, I would probably still have been there getting my ass beat on every day, so I was grateful for him, and in a way, that made him my knight in shining armor. He didn't hesitate to stick up for me, and he didn't mind going against Jace to show him that he was wrong.

That was the kind of man I wanted beside me each and every night. He had me feeling on top of the world when we were together, and that was everything to me. I had never been treated the way Ace treated me. He took me out, showed me off, and showed me affection in public, although I wasn't very big on PDA. He didn't care. If he wanted to hold my hand, he did. If he wanted to kiss me, he did. And the best part was that he didn't care what other people had to say, just like me. Our relationship may have started off as us just being friends, but I had to admit I was really liking him, and I hoped it stayed that way.

Closing the Mac laptop, I slid it into the bag and stood up. I figured the only way I was going to actually be able to do some work was if I went home and did it. I needed a blunt, some wine, and to relax, and since Montana was at my parents' for the night, then I could. I never got to thank them for all the help they'd been giving me since finding out everything. They didn't want me to send Montana back over there for fear that he would do something to her, but I had to stop them at that point because I knew Jace. One thing he would never do was hurt her. He loved her more than he loved himself and, shit, more than he loved me as well. He had told me that on so many occasions, and instead of me being mad, I would just say that he was supposed to and I felt the same way about it. I would never be jealous of the love Jace had for our daughter, nor would I try to keep her away from him for my own selfish reasons.

She needed him, and in order for Jace to be a better man, he needed her as well. She actually changed him. He used to be even harsher to me before I gave birth, but when she came, he slowed down a lot. It wasn't until he felt like he was going to lose me that he started back up. He thought that if he beat me, then that would scare me into staying with him, and it did for a long time but not now. I refused to let any man think that he could just scare me into doing what he wanted me to do. I'd dealt with that shit for too long, and I thought that was what had me so scared to make it all the way official with Ace, but that shit was out the window. I'd dealt with it, and I was ready to move on with my life. *If that includes him for a long time, then so be it.* There was nothing that anybody could do or say to me that would make me feel any differently from the way I felt right now.

The only person who could mess up what we had was Ace, and if he did, then that was it. I was not giving any more chances after this shit. I didn't care how much I liked him. He had one time and one time only. *I'm too old to be going through the same shit repeatedly.*

Finally getting all my stuff together, I got up and walked out of the office. Shutting and locking the door behind me, I walked out to the main sitting area, and they had a woman waiting, and she looked like she was getting pissed off.

"Hi, how can I help you?" I asked since no one was in the front.

"I'm looking for Dreux. I had an appointment with her at three," she said with an attitude, and I looked at my watch. She was super late for that appointment, and she was about to be even madder when I told her that Dreux wasn't here.

"Oh, she's gone for the day, but I can call her if you would like. I don't think she thought you were coming, because it's after four and she just walked out the door."

She shook her head and popped her gum at the same time. "You tell her that she has less than an hour to reach out to me before I tell all her clientele that she's unprofessional," she snapped at me.

"Will do. You have a nice day," I told her, then opened the door for her to exit. I did the same. Some of these people would really make you want to slap their asses, and she was the prime example, but she wasn't my client.

Rolling my eyes to the top of my head, I started the engine to my car and left.

Chapter Forty

Dreux

Down for You

The day was finally here for me to talk to my parents. Savannah was with Max, and I was on the way over there. I wasn't about to wait another day. It was time for me to get this shit over with so that I could move on with my life after letting this woman know I wasn't her daughter. I still didn't understand how she just figured out of the blue that I was her daughter. She had to have done her research on me before coming to that conclusion, and even if she was my mother, I wouldn't know what to do. I was grown now, so what could we do for one another? The only thing that would happen was that she and I would be friends. She would get to see Savannah and get to know me, but that would be about it.

When I drove up to the house, I gave myself a quick pep talk so that I wouldn't be nervous. Opening the door, I got out and went inside. They were both sitting on the sofa, watching their show and eating some crackers and soup.

"Hey, pumpkin," my father said.

Walking over to him, I kissed him on the cheek. "Hey, Daddy, Ma." They kept their eyes glued to the TV. "I need to talk to both of you about something real serious."

"Okay?" My father paused the TV and looked at me, giving me his undivided attention, and my mother did the same.

"What's wrong?" she asked.

I thought about how I was about to say this shit, and I had it figured out, but sitting in front of them, I knew that this would be hard as hell for me to actually say what I needed to say without hurting their and my feelings. "A woman sent a letter to Deion stating her baby got kidnapped when she gave birth, and she believes that I'm her daughter. Do you guys know anything about this?"

They looked at one another, then me, and shook their heads. "I knew that this would come back to haunt us one day," my mother said, making me look at her.

I didn't know what she was talking about. I damn sure wanted her to go into details, but she didn't. "You knew *what* was going to come back to haunt you? Please don't tell me that this woman is right and y'all kidnapped me."

"We didn't kidnap you. Somebody left you on our doorstep, and instead of calling the cops, we just kept you," my father said.

I couldn't believe that they actually just told me this. I was really hoping that they would tell me this woman was lying, but to hear that I was actually kidnapped . . .

"Wait. So y'all knew I was kidnapped, and instead of calling the cops, y'all kept me? Why?"

"Because at the time I didn't think I could have kids. I mean, we tried time and time again, and for some reason it just wouldn't happen. I thought that you being brought to our doorstep was a blessing, and I didn't want to let you go. You mean the world to me, Dreux, and although we should have told you the truth, we kept it a secret for a reason," my mother tried to explain, but I didn't understand how or why she thought that she could really explain this situation. I was taken from my own mother, and yes, they raised me right, but what if they hadn't?

"I'm so disappointed in both of you. I thought that y'all would always keep it real with me, but this situation just showed me how real y'all don't keep it. Why not just tell me?"

"We didn't want you to hate us. We didn't know how you would react, and neither of us was ready for that. All we wanted was to keep you close to us and never lose you, and we knew if we told you, you would have wanted to go find this woman."

"That woman is my real mother, and because of you, I now feel bad that she lost out on all my years of growing up because somebody decided to kidnap me and leave me on your doorstep and y'all didn't call the cops. That's foul!"

"Now you ain't gon' be yelling in our house. We understand you being mad, but what you are not about to do is make it seem like we did it intentionally, because we didn't. We did it because we had already bonded with you and we wanted to keep that going. There wasn't anything malicious behind it. Your mother and I love you, and we gave you and your sister a wonderful, happy, worry-free life."

"I know, and I'm sorry for yelling, but I'm just so upset. I know that y'all gave me and Victoria the best life, and I don't know what my life would have been like with this other woman, but she's talking about taking y'all to court."

"You're grown. What can she do now?"

"I don't know, but she wants Deion to represent her. I should have a say-so in this whole thing, right?"

"Yeah, but this is our battle, and you have to let us fight it the way we need to. If she wants to take us to court, then so be it," my mother chimed in.

I didn't know what kind of shit they thought this was, but there was no way I was about to allow this stranger to take the two people I loved most to court. I was going to make sure this shit didn't make it beyond this household and Deion. *He wants to help so much? Now is his time to actually help, and I'm not taking no for an answer, so he'd better suit up for war.*

When I left the house, I made it my business to stop by the store on the way home so that I could get some cigars. I knew both Junie and Draya were probably busy, so I would be in the house by myself until Deion came over. It was just a matter of what time that'd be. He'd been so busy with his firm that it seemed like I had to make plans to see him when I was a spur-of-the-moment type of bitch. I liked to pop up on my nigga just to see what he was up to and maybe get some surprise dick.

After I got what I needed from the store, I went home and straightened up downstairs and my bedroom before taking a shower. By the time I got out, it was going on seven o'clock, and I couldn't wait to get in my bed. I didn't know why, but for the last few weeks, I'd been exhausted and only wanted to sleep. One thing I knew for sure was that I wasn't pregnant. Couldn't be. Shit, I still had my birth control in place, so wasn't no way. Walking around with nothing on, I sat at my vanity and brushed my hair up into a ponytail before rolling my blunt and putting it to my mouth. This was the best thing about having my own business. I didn't have to answer to anybody, and I didn't have to take a drug test. I could do what I wanted, leave when I wanted, and go to work when I wanted as long as I got my job done and the customers were satisfied. That was all that mattered to me.

As soon as I put the blunt to my mouth to light, the doorbell started to ring, and at the same time, Deion was calling. Taking it as that was him at the door, I didn't pick up the phone, just went downstairs butt-ass naked and pulled it open with a big Kool-Aid smile on my face.

"Oh, um, sorry. I must've caught you at a bad time," a woman said, turning her head.

"No, I'm sorry. I thought you were somebody else," I replied before shutting the door and running back up the stairs to grab my robe. Once it was on, I went back down and pulled the door back open. "Who are you?" I asked, not meaning to be rude, but the old woman who stood before me had to be lost.

"My name is Maria. I'm the one whose daughter was kidnapped."

"How did you know where I lived?" I asked, peeking out the door to make sure she was alone. I didn't trust this shit, and if she tried anything, I wouldn't spare putting two bullets in her ass for trying me.

"I looked it up. Now I didn't know if this would still be your residence, so I went out on a limb and just showed up."

"You do know you could have gotten shot if this was anybody else?"

"I'm sure, but good thing it wasn't, right?" She chuckled, but I didn't find anything funny.

First of all, I didn't like the fact that she was showing up at my house like everything was good. I didn't know this woman from a can of paint, and although I was mad at the way my parents went about keeping me, I didn't blame them for what they did because they gave me a wonderful life to where, like they said, I didn't have to worry about anything. They covered everything that I had going on, and they never made me feel any different. I was their first child.

"Come in," I told her before moving to the side.

When she stepped in, I shut and locked the door behind her before leading her into the living room so that we could talk. "You're doing good for yourself."

"Thank you, but can we get to the reason why you're here? I know about the letter and you saying you're going to take my parents to court for me, but I'm grown, and I would like for you to leave them out of this. They didn't know that nobody kidnapped me. They said somebody left me on their doorstep, and they took it as somebody in the neighborhood, a teen maybe, had a baby and she didn't want it, so she set me at their door. They didn't know, and I would really like you to just drop whatever case you may think you have against them. I had a wonderful life. I have a daughter, and I love my parents more than anything in the world."

"I can understand that, but what they did was a crime. They never reported you to the cops or nothing. If they had, then I wouldn't have missed out on your life the way I did."

"I get that, but you're here now, and the only way you get a relationship with me is if you don't take them to court. You can take them and you will lose me, so it's a lose-lose situation for both of us. They also have another daughter who's about to have her first child, so she's going to need me as well as our parents. I know that this may be hard for you to hear because of what they did, and I told them about themselves, but at the end of the day, they raised and loved me as if I were their own, and I will always love them for that."

She didn't say anything, so my guess was she was thinking about it. It really didn't matter what she had to say. I said what I said, that the only way she would have a relationship with me was if she dropped whatever case she thought she had against them, and I meant that shit.

Chapter Forty-one

Draya

Nothing in This World

The last few days had been busy as hell for me with running the club and making sure I planned the wedding. I was exhausted and barely had any help. My mother was helping and so was Korey, but he didn't know anything about shit and always asked me instead of figuring it out. He knew what we both liked, or he should have known anyway. All I wanted to do was relax, and that was exactly what I was about to do on the weekend getaway my man promised to take me on last week. The day was finally here. I could pack and get ready to go have some fun in the sun if he didn't come up with some kind of excuse to change all of it. The clubs had been busy, but Jace and Loren were actually doing a good job keeping everything in check, so I thought we could both manage a weekend away without everything getting out of whack. We had both been on edge for a little while now, and I knew all we needed was a little time away from everything and everyone.

"Hey, bae, my mother is going to be joining us on vacation so that she can keep KJ. I know you wanted him to stay here, but I want him to be with us so that I can keep my eye on him."

"I understand, and that's fine as long as it don't take away from the relaxation I want to deal with. We both need this."

"You're right about this. You don't have to worry about it though. She told me that she won't invade on us unless absolutely necessary, and she will be on the other side of the villa. You can go see him at nighttime before he goes to bed."

"Yeah, of course. So when do we leave?"

"Right after we go check on the clubs, we can get on the jet and get the hell out of here."

"Well, let's go. I already packed the bags," I let him know, and he leaned down and kissed me on the lips. I knew that was him thanking me for doing that because he hated packing. He would rather go and shop wherever we went for vacation, but I wanted to make sure we both had everything we needed so that we didn't have to worry about going into the mall or any boutiques and shopping. This was so much easier. We wouldn't need to go far from the house, especially since the beach was right outside our villa.

He grabbed the bags and made his way to the car, and I was right behind him. After helping him put them in the trunk, I got in and buckled myself in. He got in right behind me and started the car, backing out of the driveway. We headed to my club first, and I couldn't wait for him to see all the work Loren was putting in. He was skeptical about her working there because of her prior job being a stripper, but I wanted him to know that she actually was the best fit for the job because she knew how to handle strippers and she knew what the men liked.

As soon as we pulled up to the club, we both got out and made our way inside. It was semi-packed, and it was still daylight out. I couldn't have been more impressed to see they had flyers everywhere about the club. Loren was doing everything she could to make sure we had men and women lined up and possibly around the building waiting to get in. She was doing all the things I was planning on doing. I just didn't have the time to actually sit down and do it.

"Hey, boss," she said and walked over to me and Korey.

"Hey, Lo. This is my fiancé, Korey," I introduced them, and she stuck her hand out for him to shake, which he did.

"Nice to meet you. I've heard nothing but good things about you. Although I was skeptical about you working here, you seem to be doing a good job," he told her.

"Thank you. I'm trying to do the best I can. I don't want to lose my job. I love working here already, and the women are amazing and go-getters," she said, and I could tell she was happy just by the way she was smiling.

"I told you she was good at what she does. She hasn't been in any trouble, and she has actually been helping me with keeping the women in line so that I don't have to deal with arguing and fighting."

"Good. I'm proud of you because you knew what you were doing, and although I wasn't on board with it at first, I am now. I'm happy that you made sure you put some-body in charge who knew what they were doing," he told me, and it felt good that he was actually acknowledging what I was doing.

Smiling, I leaned in and kissed him on the lips before letting him walk around and get a good look at everything that was going on. While he did that, I went into the office just to see how much money the girls were making. When I saw the amount, I was amazed. We had made over $3 million just for the day, and I couldn't have been prouder. "Thank you for all that you're doing. You're amazing, and I'm so happy that you're working with me," I let Loren know.

"You don't have to thank me when I'm just doing my job. I should be the one thanking you for hiring me on," she said before hugging me.

She was super cool, and I knew I would have to set up a day so that she could come chill with me, Dreux, and Junie. I knew they would like her because I did, and that was a fact. My girls didn't like anybody if I didn't like them, so if I brought her around, then they would surely hit it off.

When we left the club, we got into the car, then made the last stop, which was his club. We had to let Jace know that Loren would be popping in on him just to make sure everything was running smoothly. He had an attitude about it before I let him know that we trusted him, but she knew what she was doing, and we just wanted to make sure they both had each other's backs. We had to remind him that this was a family business, not every man or woman out for themselves. We all had to be on the same page if we wanted this shit to work out the way it was already. They had too many people trying to see to it that the clubs didn't do good by opening one up, so we had to be on our toes.

As soon as we finished with him, we headed to pick up Korey's mom and KJ. The entire way there, my mind was on one thing and one thing only, and that was relaxing with my man and possibly having my legs in the air. I thought I was pregnant a few weeks ago because my period hadn't come, but when it did show up, a bitch was happy. Lord knows I was not ready for no more kids. Shit, KJ was only a year old, so I had to be more careful.

When we finally arrived at the jet parking lot, we got out and boarded. I had so much on my mind that I knew I wasn't going to get a wink of sleep while we were on here. I still had to think about the wedding and wedding dresses that I had found but hadn't been able to decide on.

"When are we making this wedding happen?" Korey asked.

"I don't know."

"I'm not trying to wait any longer to marry you. Why don't we just get married in the Bahamas?"

"Because we would have to invite everybody back home, and my parents are not going to fly. Junie is busy, Dreux is busy dealing with her own shit, and I want everybody there," I pouted.

"A'ight, but I want to make it happen soon. I need you to have my last name before I put another baby in you," he said, making me look at him like he had grown two heads.

"Korey, I'm not having no more babies until KJ is at least five years old, which means we have four years to go."

"Nah, you saying that now until you end up pregnant. I want more kids and before he is that old, but right now, I just want to focus on making you my wife. It's been a long time going, and I'm ready."

"I am too." I smiled and turned my head to face the window.

When we finally landed, we got off the jet and climbed into the family car that was waiting for us. Once we got in and Korey had the bags in the trunk, the driver started the car up and took off toward the villa we were staying in. Looking down at my phone, I texted Junie, Dreux, and my parents to let them know we made it before turning my phone off for the entire weekend. I wasn't taking any calls. Anything that happened would have to wait until I got back.

Not even thirty minutes later, the car pulled into the double gates of the home, and KJ was screaming at the top of his lungs.

"Where is his pacifier? I know I packed it!" I grimaced, tearing up the diaper bag looking for it.

"Uh, it's right here," Korey said, holding it up. It was attached to KJ's shirt, making me feel stupid.

"Oh."

"Yeah. You need this vacation," his mother said, grabbing KJ and taking him right up the stairs. I knew it wouldn't be long before he went to sleep, so I went upstairs and took a shower, which was much needed after that flight.

"Babe, I'm gonna grill us some steaks and shrimp," Korey said through the bathroom door.

"Okay, fill us some blunts, too. I'll be down when I get out," I yelled loud enough for him to hear. I was standing in the shower just letting the water beat on my body in all the right places before grabbing the shower gel and bathing. After rinsing, I got out and wrapped a towel around my breasts before walking out and dressing in a nightgown. I made sure I didn't put on any panties because I wanted to smoke and fuck. I didn't care where. All I knew was that I wanted my back broke.

When I got downstairs, Korey was already on the balcony smoking, and the sun was getting ready to set. Walking out, I sat on his lap, and he handed me the blunt. Putting it to my lips, I took a long pull from it and held the smoke in before blowing it out.

"This was much needed."

"Hell yes. We've been putting in so much work that we needed some time alone."

I handed him the blunt back, and we smoked, ate, then retreated to the bedroom. As soon as we got in, he took a shower and came out naked as the day he was born. His dick was hard, and he was licking his lips. I motioned for him to get in the bed. He did, and we made love all night.

Chapter Forty-two

Deion

Can't Get Enough

Running out of the building, I jumped into my car and sped all the way to Dreux's house. I received another letter from Maria, and she said that she knew where Dreux lived and that she was going to show up there because she didn't want to wait. I was trying to make it there before her, but when I drove down the street to her house, I saw an unfamiliar car sitting in the driveway. I quickly parked and got out. Making my way to the door, I knocked and waited for Dreux to open it.

When she did, she was smiling from ear to ear.

"You good? Maria said she was coming by here, and I wanted to make it before she did. I don't think it's a good idea," I said, almost out of breath.

"It's too late. She's already here. Keep it down before she hears you. We talked, and I talked her out of trying to take my parents to court. I want to keep it that way, so I don't want you coming in here and saying anything that could possibly make her change her mind. I need her to be on the same page as me, and right now she is, so promise me that you won't say anything?" she asked, and I couldn't help but look at her like she was crazy.

Without saying anything, I nodded my head, and she moved to the side to let me in. Walking through the house, I came upon Maria sitting in the living room. She had some food and wine sitting in front of her.

"Hey, I'm Deion, Dreux's boyfriend," I introduced myself, and she smiled.

"Nice to meet you. Thank you for giving her the note like I asked you to. I want you to know that I'm not going through with any charges against her parents. She loves them, and it would be wrong for me to take them away from her and her sister. I may have missed out on a lot, but at least I know the kind of woman she is, and I couldn't be prouder of the way they raised her."

I could tell she wasn't being truthful. I didn't know what she thought was going to happen, but I wasn't handling any cases for her. If anything, I would be on the opposite side of this. Anyway, I had the recording showing that she didn't want to go through with the charges, so the case would be dropped.

Recording people without their knowledge was against the law, but I had to make sure I protected Dreux at all costs. When Maria left, I would let her know that she was lying about not pursuing the charges. I would never let her play my woman for dumb, and I didn't care if Dreux got mad at me, but at least she would know.

I was dead ass when I said that I would do anything to make sure she had nothing to worry about, and I meant that shit. I would always have her back and make sure nobody got over on her, and that was exactly what Maria was trying to do. She didn't care about what Dreux wanted. All she wanted to do was make them suffer.

"Did y'all do a DNA test?" I asked, and Dreux looked at me like I was crazy.

"Deion, stop," she mouthed.

"What? I just thought that you two would want to know if y'all were really related before sitting down and talking. This is backward, Dreux. You need to get a DNA test as soon as possible."

"I'm sensing you don't like the fact that I'm here. I'll go, but I know deep down that she is my daughter, so I don't have a problem with taking a DNA test." Maria smiled, but I could see deep down that I had gotten to her. She wasn't about to play my girl, not while I was around.

Sitting on the sofa, I watched as she walked to the door. Dreux showed her out before coming back into the living room and standing directly over me.

"You have a lot of nerve. First you get in my business when I asked you not to, and then you show up here saying all this crazy shit about a DNA test like I'm dumb." She put on a pair of gloves and grabbed the glass that Maria had used. She used a swab and rubbed it around the glass before doing the same to hers and putting them both in a package and sealing it shut. "I want you to let me handle things myself from now on. I know that you want to help, but you could have made things worse."

"You do know I can read people, so I know when they're lying and shit?"

"Yeah, and?"

"She's lying. Not about being your mother but about dropping the case against your mother and father. She's going to pursue it."

When I said that, she really looked at me like I had lost my mind, then sat down on the sofa next to me. "She gave me her word."

"She lied, babe. You know I wouldn't lie to you about nothing like this. I don't want to see them go to court, but she wants to make them pay, and she's going to use you to do that. I don't condone nothing that she's doing, but to be honest with you, she might have a chance at winning if your parents don't know who actually kidnapped and put you on their doorstep. I don't know if you want to keep talking to her, but I can tell you now I'm going to be handling the legal part of this shit, which is putting a judge who owes me a favor on the case. I need him to take it so that he can throw it out as soon as it comes to him."

"Do you think he'll do that?" she asked.

I guessed now she was starting to actually believe me when I told her that I would always have her back. I would never lie to her about anything ever, and if I didn't like somebody, it was because of something. I didn't know what kind of woman Maria was at the moment, but she was rubbing me the wrong way with how she was lying, and I damn sure didn't want her in my presence.

"Yeah. Although Maria may think she has a case, she doesn't," I let her know.

Pulling her into me, I kissed her on the forehead, and she sighed, "I really thought I had persuaded her to not do anything, but she was playing me the whole time. Asking me how my parents were to me when I was a child and what I loved about them. She didn't really care. All she was doing was thinking she was going to get some kind of information about me that would help her case."

I could tell she was down about this whole situation, and I knew there wasn't anything I could do to make it better except try to help her out with it. I could get in touch with my judge friend so he could pick up the case, and when I played the recording for him of her saying she wasn't trying to take them to court, then he would throw the case out before anybody could go to court.

"I know that this is hurting you, but I got you, and you don't have to worry about it. I have everything under control. I have your back."

"I know you do, and I love that about you."

"You love me?" I inquired, and she just looked at me. I knew she loved me because I was having the same feelings toward her. I just didn't think either of us was ready to say the words. She had me feeling like a king with the way she treated me, and I always tried to make her and Savannah feel like the queens they were. I'd never felt this way about anybody before. I didn't know how she did it, but she had me falling deeper for her each time we were around one another, from her feisty attitude to the fact that she was a loving woman on the inside.

"If I do?" she asked.

"I would tell you I love you too." I smirked and kissed her on the lips.

"Oh, so you saying you do love me?"

"Shit, I wasn't supposed to tell you that yet. I don't want to scare you off by loving you too much. I know that when I fall in love, I become crazy as hell, and the last thing I want is for you to run away from me. If we do this, I'm going to be for you and only you."

"And I'm going to be for you. There is nobody I would rather be with than you. You mean the world to me, Deion, and I love the fact that you treat my daughter like she was your own. You don't try too hard, and it makes her happy that I'm happy. All I want is for you to always be honest with me like you are now, and don't cheat."

"Oh, you don't have to worry about that. I will never cheat on you, and you know that. As for you, you'd better not ever entertain another nigga."

"Oh, please, I will never do that."

"Mm-hmm."

"You want to have some fun since Savannah isn't here?" she said, standing up and removing the robe she had on. When she dropped it, my heart skipped a beat like it did each and every time she stood before me with no clothes on. Dreux had the body of a goddess, but she was slim thick, with just enough ass and a handful of breasts that had me enticed with her. Pulling her closer to me, I sat her on my lap and kissed her lips. Sliding my tongue into her mouth, I moved it around while she sucked on it, and her hands made their way to my shirt, and she started to unbutton it.

When she moved back, she opened my shirt up, but I pulled her back to me and kissed her lips again. Raising her a little bit, I pulled my slacks and boxers down and let my dick hang freely while she ground her pussy on me. "Mm, put it in, daddy," she purred in my ear, and I did just what she wanted.

Grabbing my dick, I slid her down on it and started to slowly bounce her up and down while sucking on her nipples. My hands roamed down to her ass, and I grabbed it. Hanging on to it, I pumped my dick in and out of her as hard and fast as I could. "Fuck," I groaned.

"Shit, that feels good."

Whap! I slapped her ass and kept ramming my dick inside of her.

"Ooh, yessss. Oh, my God."

"Damn, I'm about to nut, baby."

"Me too. Don't stop, daddy," she moaned and threw her head back. She had her mouth open, and I could tell she wanted to scream but it wasn't coming out, so I decided to help her out. Picking her up, I bounced her up and down as hard as I could. "Yes! Oh, my God!" she screamed while fucking me back. Feeling my nut build up, I laid her back on the sofa and kept sliding in and out of her until it reached the tip of my dick. Then I pushed deeper inside of her before cumming.

I wanted her to get pregnant for me so bad. She was such a good mother to Savannah that I knew if we had a baby together, that baby would be in good hands. There was nobody else I wanted to have my child besides her. I just hoped she was ready for all that came with me falling in love.

Chapter Forty-three

Jace

No Love

"Jace, I love you so much," Junie panted as I hit her with those deep strokes that she loved so much. Pulling her closer to me, I kissed her lips while sliding my tongue into her mouth. She sucked on my bottom lip, which had me speeding the deep strokes up. Rising, I started to pound her while she moaned and screamed out my name.

"Fuck, I love you, Junie," I groaned in her ear.

Slowing my strokes down, I pushed even deep into her and kept the pace steady so that she could catch her breath. She started to fuck me back, and that shit had me feeling in heaven. She had the best pussy I had ever been in, and the way she loved me was enough to make me want to give her all of me, but I didn't know how.

Leaning down, I kissed her neck before making a trail of kisses down to her breasts. Sucking on one of her nipples, I licked and flicked my tongue on it while using my hand to make love to the other one. The sounds she was making were enough to make me nut, but I was holding that shit back. I never came without making her bust twice first.

"Oh, my God, don't stop."

"I got you, ma. Keep that shit going right there," I said to the way she was rolling her hips. She opened her legs a little wider for me, and I bit down on her nipple softly while digging deeper inside of her.

"Fuckkkkkk," she screamed, and I covered her mouth with my hand so we didn't wake Montana. This was the first time we had been able to actually get it in like this since having her, and the last thing I wanted was for her to wake up before I got my nut.

"Jace, did you hear me?" a voice asked, snapping me out of my thoughts.

Looking up, I saw Loren standing there with her hands on her hips. Draya and Korey had us working with each other to make sure we kept things straight and stayed on the same page. Sometimes she would pop up on me, and I would do the same to her.

"What you said?"

"If you stop daydreaming, then you would hear me. You need some more bottles of Ace of Spades, and Draya said they're in the storage unit. Walk with me down to grab a case."

I got up. Not wasting any time, I made my way out of the office behind her, and we both went down to the storage room.

When we stepped into the warm room, I turned the light on, and we both started scanning the room for the case. "Found it," I said, picking it up and making my way toward the front. When I noticed she wasn't behind me, I set the case down and went to the back where she was. She was going over the inventory sheet while I stood behind her. She had a body on her, hips and ass for days, and it didn't help that she had on a little-ass skirt that rode up each time she bent down.

Licking my lips, I moved closer to her and stood directly behind her. When she stood up, my manhood was hard, and I knew she felt it just by the way she jumped.

"What you think you're doing?" she asked.

"Nothing. Just counting bottles." I smirked, making her roll her eyes.

"You a damn liar, and that had better be a bottle of liquor I feel." She grimaced but backed her ass up a little bit more to get a good feel. Reaching around her, I grabbed her breasts through her blouse and started to massage them. "We can't do this," she panted, but that didn't stop her from grinding her pussy on me.

"Why the fuck not? Can't nobody come in here and see what we're doing, and I know you've been feeling me."

"I can't stand you, so how do you figure?"

"You a liar," I chuckled, leaning her forward and raising her skirt above her ass, exposing the fact that she didn't have on no panties. Nodding my head with a smirk on my face, I unzipped my jeans and slid a condom on while rubbing her slit up and down. She was dripping wet, and that was how I knew she wanted me the same way I wanted her. Not wasting any time, I slid my dick deep inside of her and held on to her hips while pumping my thick shaft into her.

"Shitttttt, fuck," she moaned out while throwing her head back.

She was resting it on my shoulder, and I picked up one of her legs and stroked her as hard and quickly as possible. I knew we couldn't be gone for long or the dancers would get suspicious. A few of them bitches was mad because I didn't want to touch them, but that was a given. Them bitches wouldn't have been able to handle a nigga like me, and the other half of them had ass shots, and the last thing I wanted was to fuck a bitch too hard and her ass cheeks deflated.

"I'm about to cum," she whined while I kept feeding her my dick, never letting up. Reaching my hand up, I pinched and rubbed her clit until I felt her juices sliding down my dick. I stroked her a few more times before filling the condom up with my seeds and pulling out of her.

"Whew, that shit was good," she let out while pulling her skirt down. "But now I have to go clean myself up. Go put the bottles at the bar and meet me in the office for round two." She smirked and kissed me on the lips.

After putting the bottles at the bar and the second round we had in the office, I was drained and just needed to catch my breath. I never had a female work me the way she did, and she wasn't ashamed of it either. I thought she took pride in how she had me moaning like a bitch.

"Tired?" she asked.

"Nah, I just need to catch my breath," I let her know before getting up and walking around. Once I had my breath, I put my shirt back on and walked out of the office so that I could see how everything was running.

Korey liked for us to see but not be seen, but I needed to make sure niggas knew the ladies had somebody in here who wasn't afraid to make his gun clap on anybody. Too many of these niggas had gotten away with being disrespectful to the women, and as long as I was here, that shit was not gon' flow.

Walking through the crowd, I sat at the bar and enjoyed a drink before getting up when I saw one of the dudes manhandling one of the strippers. Shaking my head, I made my way toward him and stood directly behind him while giving the dancer a look to assure her that she was good. He was dead-ass trying to drag her to the bathroom, like that was finna happen.

"So you don't know how to keep your hands to yourself?" I asked, scaring the shit out of him.

When we looked back, he put his hands up while letting out a chuckle. "That's you? I didn't know, my man."

"Nah, she ain't for me, but it's the principle. You're here to throw money and see ass, not fuck, or rape in your case."

"Man, I threw all my money at this bitch. I've been coming here for the past two weeks only to see her."

"In hopes of what? My nigga, she's here earning her money. She's not here to fuck you just because you're throwing money. This ain't that type of party, bitch nigga." I mugged. He was so lucky I wasn't trying to have the cops in my nigga's spot, or I would have laid his ass out for even thinking it was okay to distress shorty.

"It's not that. She told me that she would fuck with me, but she never called."

"So the fuck what? Find another bitch, because this one is spoken for by Lady Rouge, and that's the way it's gonna be. Get the fuck outta here before I push your shit back," I snapped, and he hurriedly headed for the exit.

"Thank you so much for that."

"No problem, but you need to let them niggas know what it is. Half of the men who come in here think they're about to get the pussy, and it's best to shut that shit down. You don't want to have no issues when you leave and one of them follows you home. Come get me when your shift is over so I can make sure you get home safe," I let her know, and she nodded her head and went about her business.

Making my way back up to the office, I sat on the sofa while Loren stood in front of me. "What was that about?" she asked.

"A nigga got too rough with one of my dancers, and I shut that shit down."

"I see you acting like you care for the dancers, but nine times out of ten, if he was trying to get her to go to the restroom with him, then she must've told him something."

"It doesn't matter what she told him. The fact is he was too rough, and she didn't want to go with him, so he couldn't make her. Like I told him, he can't make her do nothing that she don't want to do. I can't even believe that as a former stripper you can stand here and say some shit like that. We both need to make sure the girls feel safe," I let her know.

She was really throwing me off with the way she was thinking, and I couldn't believe that shit. I could understand that money was being thrown, and the stripper could make whatever promises she wanted to make, but that didn't mean she had to go out and really fuck that nigga. She said what she needed to say for him to throw that money, and that was exactly what he did. It was nobody's fault he threw all his money.

Standing up from the sofa, I made my way to the desk and picked up the pre-rolled blunt that was sitting on it. Putting it to my mouth, I lit it and took a long drag off it while looking at the girls and what was going on. Feeling a hand on my shoulder, I looked over at Loren, and she licked her lips while winking and smiling.

"What's up? Why you all over me?"

"Don't act like you don't want me as bad as I want you," she said.

"I don't know about all that," I said, pulling her in front of me and wrapping my arms around her. She leaned her head down on my chest, and I kissed her on the cheek while handing her the blunt. We stood there for the longest time until her phone started ringing, and then she grabbed her things and left. My guess was she needed to go to the club for something.

Sitting down, I smoked the blunt, then went over the books for the night so that I could get out of there. I was ready to get home, shower, and get into bed. It felt like I had been working my ass off. Korey had given me the idea of what I wanted to do, and that was open up a *club* club, not a strip club. I just had to execute it the right way if I wanted it to be as successful as this one I was standing in right now.

Chapter Forty-four

Korey

I'll Be Yours

Draya and I were sitting on the balcony, smoking a blunt and watching the sun rise. There was nothing like having peace with the one you loved right next to you. If I could have married her right now I would have, but I knew she was not having that. She wanted her whole family to be there. Meanwhile, the only family I had besides Jace and Deion was my mother, and she was the only one I would want at the wedding. She had never done anything to make me cross her out of my life, which surprised me because, when I was younger, she used to stay getting on my ass about everything. That was just because she didn't want me to turn out to be a street nigga. Although it didn't stop it from happening, when I got older and started seeing all the stuff she told me about, I had to step back and go legal. I saw too many of my niggas get buried, so instead of chasing that bag, I chased another bag.

Draya came into my life shortly after that, and she had been my one and only since then. I loved this woman more than life itself.

"Babe, thank you," she said, snapping me from my thoughts.

"For what?"

"For this, being here with me and your son. I thought that when we got back together, nothing would change, but you are actually showing me that you're not the same man I was engaged to. Now you're the man I knew you could always be." She smiled.

Not saying anything because I believed she had said it all, I pulled her to me and kissed her on the lips. We spent all night making sweet love, and I was hoping I actually put another baby in her. I didn't care what she was talking about. We were having another kid. *The sooner the better.*

The way I felt about this woman would never change. I had been wanting her to get that through her head, and it seemed like she finally had. She didn't have to worry about me ever playing with her heart again. I would never again be that man she despised. I had too much to lose, and no bitch was worth me losing the prize I had in front of me right now. I didn't know how I did it, but I knew for a fact I would always do whatever I could to make my woman happy.

"I love you," I whispered in her ear.

"I love you too. This place is beautiful, and I want to come back here to get married," she let me know, and I nodded my head. I would make that happen. As long as she had my last name by the time it was over with, that was all I cared about.

Grabbing her hand, I led her back into our bedroom so that we could go down and join my mother and KJ for breakfast. When we made it down, both my mother and KJ were already eating. Draya went over to the counter and was about to start fixing my food, but I stopped her. "I got it, baby. Go sit down," I told her, and she did just as I said.

After fixing her plate first, I set it in front of her, then fixed my own and sat down. Putting my head down so that I could say a quick prayer to the Lord for not only waking me up but for blessing me with this food, I dug in immediately after.

My mother spoke up, breaking the silence. "I'm so happy that you two worked out your issues and now we're like one big family. It feels good to actually be in the room with both of you without worrying about the bickering or the nasty looks."

"Yeah. We both know that things aren't going to always be good, but I'm willing to work through whatever with Korey. He means everything to me, just like this little handsome man," Draya said, tickling a laughing KJ.

"I feel like as long as we know that, then we'll be good. All I'm waiting for is the day she takes my last name. Then I will truly be the happiest man on earth. It took us a while to get here, but I wouldn't trade this shit for nothing in the world. I have never been this happy before, and I know that if I hadn't fucked up so much when we were together, then she would have my last name, but maybe it wasn't our time."

"Yeah, I will always say that. You two needed to see what life was like without one another to determine if y'all wanted to get back together. I'm happy it all worked out, because for a second, I was scared. I didn't know what was going to happen."

"True that," I chuckled.

Me and Draya worked really hard to get to this point in our relationship, and I knew that as long as I stayed faithful and always kept it real with her, I wouldn't ever have to worry about us having major issues like that again. I would have a whole lifetime to make up for the way I did her, and I was going to spend that time showing her how much she meant to me and how much it meant to me that she actually gave me a second chance. All she had to do was sit back and let her man handle everything, and she would never have to lift her finger to work ever again.

After we ate, I helped my mother clean up the kitchen. Then I went upstairs and changed into some shorts and a white tee. Sliding my feet into some Nike slippers, I walked out of the bedroom and downstairs, where Draya was waiting in a bikini and some sandals. "So you just gon' go out on the beach naked?" I asked, looking her up and down.

"I'm not naked. I have on a bikini."

"Men gon' be staring at you, and you know I don't like that. I can see myself acting a fool already."

She rolled her eyes to the top of her head and blew air out of her mouth. "You need to slow ya roll and just have fun. I don't need you controlling what I wear, bae. You know all this belongs to you and only you. Niggas can look, but they'd better not touch," she assured me, making me smile.

"You're right about that shit."

When we walked out of the house, it didn't take us long to be on the beach since it was right behind the house we were renting. I wanted to make sure we didn't have to drive or nothing. I was tired of it all, so you know a nigga just wanted to relax. As soon as we got to the chairs that were out there, I sat down and put a pre-rolled blunt to my mouth while watching Draya as she went to the water and put her feet in. She looked so exotic that I had to take my phone out and take a few pictures of my wife-to-be.

When she looked over at me, she smiled and posed for some pictures, making me smile until she turned around and poked her booty out a little bit more. "A'ight, now you making me want to pick you up and take you back in the house."

"And do what?" she asked, strolling over and sitting in my lap.

"Do you even want to know? Or you just gon' let me do it to you?"

"Both." She smirked, then leaned in and kissed me on the lips. When she did that, she rose a little bit and put her hand on my dick.

"You'd better stop before you get into trouble out here."

"I do wanna fuck you on the beach." She winked at me.

Taking another pull from the blunt, I handed it to her and watched as she hit it. The way her lips wrapped around the blunt had my dick jumping for some attention, but I knew that would have to wait. She knew just what she was doing, too, because she kept looking at me, but I was about to make her ass wait like she was doing to me.

"You want some dick?" I asked, and she nodded her head. "I got you later on."

She handed the blunt back to me just as some females were headed our way. "Hey, did y'all rent out that big villa?" one of them asked.

"We did," Draya answered for me.

"Do y'all mind if we have a party there tonight?"

When the girl asked that, even I had to look at her like she was crazy. "Nah, our son and my mother are in there. Y'all can rent it out when we leave," I replied, and they all dropped their heads and walked away.

"What the fuck?" Draya asked.

"I know, right?" I chuckled.

They had no right to be asking us no shit like that, and they should be ashamed.

"Anyway, why you got me tonight? Why I can't sit on it right now?"

"Because I said so."

"Hmph," she pouted, then got off my lap. I watched as she walked down the beach, but I didn't get up. I knew she would be back eventually. This dick wasn't going anywhere, so she needed to stop acting like a baby. Shit, I fucked her all night last night and when we got up this morning. A nigga needed a break.

When she finally came back, she had two drinks in her hand and handed me one. "It comes from the cabana down there," she said when she saw the confused look I was giving her. You know you can't be too careful taking drinks from people.

"Oh, a'ight."

Grabbing it, I set it down and kept smoking my blunt when she climbed back on my lap. Wrapping us up with a blanket, I held her, and we just lay right there for a while longer. "If you want to, once we eat and get KJ down, we can come back out and fuck on the beach," I suggested.

"Okay." She smiled, getting up from my lap, then reaching her hand out for me to grab on to.

When we got into the house, my mother was sitting on the sofa watching TV, and KJ was playing with the toys we brought for him. There was no way we were coming out here without his favorite toys because he would have cut a flip behind his shit. Draya got on the floor and started playing with him while I stood back and watched. My family was beautiful, and I couldn't wait to add more kids to this equation.

Chapter Forty-five

Junie

For My Baby

Ace had been showing me a good time all weekend, and he even took me and Montana to an annual fish fry his parents had every beginning of springtime. That was the most fun I had in a long time. He showed me a really good time that was short-lived because of Jace popping up. Obviously, Ace's parents didn't know about his and Jace's falling out, so when they found out I was his baby mother, they tore into not only his ass but mine as well. I didn't even have time to explain to his mom what he did to me or why Ace was in the picture. She just made it seem like I was a ho for jumping from homeboy to homeboy, and then she made us leave.

It was the worst experience I had ever gone through, and I never wanted to go through that shit again. I told Ace that I would never go back to his parents' house, and I meant every word of it. I never wanted to disrespect anybody's parents, especially not after the way he spoke so highly of his mother and father, but she had me fucked up with the way she had done me. To have that done to me in front of everybody was embarrassing to the point where I was going to work and home only. You couldn't pay me to go out in public.

"You good in here?" Ace asked, walking into the bedroom.

"I'm good, just thinking about what happened at the fish fry."

He sighed. He was probably tired of me talking about it, but he had to know that I wasn't used to somebody talking to me or about me the way his mother had, and that shit really fucked with me.

"I hope you don't let what my mother said get to you. When I went back over there, I had to put her in her place without telling your business. I didn't think it was my place," he said, and I nodded my head.

"I hear everything you're saying, but I can't not let it get to me. She basically called me something that I'm not, and I don't like that. I would have never disrespected her, but you need to understand that I'm not used to going through anything like that," I explained to him. I wanted him to know that shit was dead and that maybe his mother was right. Maybe we were moving too fast.

"Do you think she's right about us moving too fast?" he inquired, but I could tell that he was hoping I told him no.

"You know I would never lie to you, right? I told you from jump we were moving too fast and how I didn't want people to think I was a ho, and that's exactly what happened. I feel like you should have explained who I was to them before just bringing me and Montana around them. Not only did she disrespect me, but she did it in front of my child, and now I don't want her around them at all."

He shook his head. I knew that he wouldn't understand where I was coming from.

"I don't know why you let what other people think get to you. We're grown, and we should be able to do what we want to do without having to worry about what other people think. Me, I don't give a fuck what she was talking about. I love my mother to death, but sometimes she says things without thinking about them, and that was one of those moments. You can't let shit like that get to you, because I would never let what Jace tells me get to me. That nigga can't tell me shit about you because I feel like I already know everything there is to know about you."

"But she still thinks you two are friends, which tells me that you didn't let her know that you had fallen out."

"You're right. I didn't let her know only because I didn't think she would remember. She don't even like Jace. She just don't like disloyalty, and she feels like I was being disloyal and so were you."

"Yeah, but nobody knows the things I went through with that man besides you, my sister, Dreux, and my family. I try not to put our business out there because I know people talk, and the last thing I want is for our business to be in the streets. So I don't talk about it with anyone other than the people I know I can trust. The only way I would ever go around your parents again is if she apologizes for what she said. I don't care if she thinks she was looking out for you. She's wrong about me, and you need to let it be known, Ace," I told him before getting up and making my way out of the bedroom and downstairs so that I could start dinner before Jace arrived with Montana.

He wasn't supposed to know where I stayed, but I didn't want to leave the house, so I decided to give him my address. It wasn't like he would come in or make it past the threshold, but I needed him to bring her. I just wasn't feeling leaving the house at all, and he knew that. He thought what happened was funny, but when I told him that some of Ace's family was referring to me as a ho or the bitch who jumped from dick to dick, then he wanted to go over there and slap everybody who said it. He apologized because he said he didn't know I was going to be there, but when I asked why he was going, he made it seem like Ace's sister invited him, but I knew that was a lie.

His ass showed up because he knew that things were going to take a turn for the worse.

"Baby, I just don't want you to think that we shouldn't be together all because of what was said or how it was said. I know my mother didn't mean any harm when she said that shit, and I hoped that you would take that into consideration instead of writing off what we're already building. The last thing I want is to lose you. I like you so much already, and I haven't felt this way about a woman in a long time."

"I know, and I like you as well. The only other man I've been with is Jace, so I don't know how to handle situations like this. His mother wasn't in his life, and it shows. A mother is always saying she knows best, and maybe your mother does."

"What are you trying to say?"

"I'm saying, do you really think you're ready to deal with somebody like me on a daily basis? I mean, I'm not the type to take the bullshit and not speak my mind. The only difference between you and Jace is that I know I can say what I need to say and won't have to worry about you putting your hands on me, and I like that about you. You don't get insecure when I do certain things, and your sex is off the charts." I smiled at him.

"I know it is, and it's all yours. I'm ready to do whatever with you. If I weren't, I wouldn't have pursued you as fast as I did. I didn't care about the fact that you and Jace had just split up, but because I knew you needed time to actually get over it is why I never pressured you into wanting to be more than friends with me. You're an amazing woman, and I want you to know that. Shit, I want to be the man to treat you like that. You deserve somebody like me, and I think I deserve somebody like you in my life as well. When I tell you I have never felt like this for a woman before, I'm not lying, and for me to fall this easily is telling me that you're the one for me."

"You really believe that?" I asked, but he didn't get a chance to answer because somebody started knocking on the front door. Getting up from the bar, I made my way to the door, and Ace grabbed me.

"We need to continue this conversation."

"We will, but my baby is at the door," I told him, and he let me go.

Walking up on the door, I pulled it open, and both Jace and Montana was standing there. "Hey, Stink, did you have a good time with Daddy?"

"Ya." She smiled and walked into the house.

"What's up, Ace?" Jace said, and Ace just threw him a head nod while following Montana into the kitchen. "Damn, you got that nigga sprung," he joked.

"Jace, thank you for dropping her off. I've had a headache all day long," I told him while taking her bag out of his hand.

"It's cool. I'll be back to get her this weekend if it's cool with you."

"It is, just hit me before you come."

He nodded his head before walking away and getting into his car. I hated the feeling that came over me whenever he and I were in each other's presence, because I knew I had no business feeling this way, but I missed him a lot. I thought I had gotten over him, but it was obvious that I hadn't. I would never go back to him after what he did to me, but I did wonder where we would be if he hadn't done what he did.

"You okay?" Ace asked, wrapping his arm around my waist.

"I'm good. Where is Montana?"

"She's in the living room watching cartoons."

"Okay. Thank you for sitting her down. I'm about to start cooking. Are you staying for dinner, or do you have other things to do?"

"I don't have nothing to do if it don't include you and Montana. I know that this is kind of soon, but I think of you two like y'all are my family."

"I like that. I mean, it's very rare to find a man who will accept a child you had with another man and treat them like their own, and I have to say that's one of the things that really turns me on about you," I told him before kissing his lips. Pulling me closer, he pulled back just a little bit.

"Let's sneak off." He smirked.

"I wish, but my daughter will come find us, and the last thing I need her to see is me and you having sex. I got you later on tonight."

"Shit, and I'll be here waiting. You want help cooking?"

"Sure."

We made our way into the kitchen, and I started the food while he helped. He didn't really know what he was doing, so I knew I would have to teach him a few things, or he could just leave it to me to do all the cooking.

"You're cutting them all wrong." I laughed, grabbing his hand and showing him how to cut it. "I think you got it now."

"Thank you for teaching me, baby. I think I can learn a thing or two from you, and you can do the same. I never really thanked you for giving me a chance to show you that I'm nothing like the other niggas you had in your life. I want to love you, but when the time is right, shit, I want to make you my wife. As beautiful as you are, ain't no way you shouldn't be nobody's wife right now."

"I know, right?" I laughed and laid my head on his shoulder.

He turned his head in my direction. I kissed his lips, and he put the knife down and sat me on the counter. Easing his way in between my legs, he moved closer while I sucked on his tongue. "Mm," I moaned while grinding my pussy against his dick. He didn't know how horny he was making me, and I wanted him to be the only man I even thought about marrying. It was odd as hell for me to be falling for this man as fast as I was, but it wasn't a surprise after all the attention and love he showed me. I could see this going somewhere far as long as he always kept it real with me and never turned his back on me.

Chapter Forty-six

Dreux

Always

The shit I was going through with this woman was out of fucking hand. She was pissing me the fuck off. To hear that she had actually gone down to the precinct and tried to press charges on my parents killed the fuck out of me. I could understand her being hurt, but to drag them into a precinct after I asked her not to told me that she didn't care about anything I had to say. So now I was about to sit down with her for the last fucking time and let her know that I didn't want to have anything to do with her. Not now or ever. She ruined everything. Any chance she might have thought she had at getting to know me or my child was out of the question now. *I don't care how hurt she may be or seem. Some shit you just don't do. It's not like they abused, beat, or mistreated me my whole life, so why does it matter who raised me? I'm grown and can make my own decisions.*

I felt like it was a blessing in disguise that I got taken away from her and dropped off to my parents' home. They were obviously the better choice.

"Hey, I was surprised when you called and said you wanted to see me," a voice said, making me look up.

As bad as I wanted to look at her with disgust on my face, I didn't. Mustering up my best fake smile, I stood and hugged her. "I don't know why you're surprised. Please have a seat." When she did, I just looked at her.

"What's wrong?"

"You. Why did you go to the cops when you told me you wouldn't?"

"Because although you think they gave you a good life, they took you away from me. I was supposed to give you this life. I was supposed to make sure you were good and became the woman you are. They took years away from me. Shit, decades. And you think I was just going to be okay with that?" she asked.

"I don't care what they took from you. What should matter is the life they gave me. Something we both know you wouldn't have been able to give me. You were sixteen years old. Your parents didn't want you to have me, but you decided that you would, knowing you had nowhere to go. Yes. I did my research on you. I would never let somebody like you into my or my child's life, and that's why as of today you no longer exist to me. You keep it moving, and I'll do the same. We can act like this meeting never happened. People like you are the reason kids get taken away from their parents every day. If you take them to court, I will hate you so much," I said, not even noticing the tears that streamed down my face.

My parents were all that I had, and I refused to let anybody take them away from me or vice versa. No matter what, Deena and Frank were my parents and always would be.

"I don't understand how you're mad at me. You're a mother, so you should know what it would feel like to have a child ripped from your hands without any say-so in the matter. That hurt me to the core, and the fact that you're sitting up here defending the two people who could have given you back, filed a police report, or anything says a lot about your character."

"Yeah, and the fact that instead of you taking your daughter's word about what great parents they were to me and the fact that I had nothing to worry about says a lot about your character. I said what I came here to say, and I don't want to keep having this same-ass conversation. You did what you felt like you needed to do to get some attention, and I'm replying to you. This relationship or whatever we thought we could build is over with," I said, standing up and grabbing the coffee cup that was in front of me. Deion would probably be at me for coming and having this conversation, but it was what it was. I had to get this off my chest, and I couldn't do that with anybody but this woman who sat across from me.

Walking out of Starbucks, I got into my car and headed to work. I had a long day, and all this did was delay me and my thinking. I had to get two houses finished so that the families could move in without having to wait any longer, so the last thing I wanted to do was spend any of my time thinking about this mess that was going on in my life.

Pulling up to my office not too long after, I got out, went inside, and got straight to work. Once I had what I wanted the house to look like on my computer, I sent my team out to find all the things we would need and told them to make sure it was all delivered before the day was over with. I was about to throw myself into work so that I wouldn't have to think about what was going on behind the scenes with this whole shit. I just hoped that Deion came through like he promised he would.

I never thought that I would have somebody like him in my life, somebody who loved me for me and not what he could get out of me. To have a man who made it to where I didn't have to worry about anything was everything to me, and the fact that he was a beast in the bedroom made things so much better. I wouldn't trade this man for anybody, although sometimes he did piss me off by overstepping his boundaries. He did it because he cared about me and because he didn't want me to have to worry about it, though, so he would always get a pass for that shit.

Once the house was finished, I couldn't but smile at it. *We did that.* Now all I had to do was wait for the family to come home and look at it.

"This house looks good, sis," Junie said, standing beside me. She had been here for the whole process, and we weren't leaving until it was all the way finished.

"It'd better. All the work we put in to make sure they love it, they'd better come in here with a big-ass smile on their faces," I joked and giggled.

"What you think about me opening my own interior design business?" she asked, making me look at her.

"I think that would be a good idea. I mean, you got everything down pat, and I think you have the mindset for it. All you have to do is make sure you have a team of people who want to satisfy the clients' needs, and you're good to go."

I would never get tired of seeing people I worked with actually move forward and decide that this was something they wanted to do. Junie had the hustle for this shit, and I would have loved nothing more than for her to find her own way. That was why I wanted her to come with me. I knew how hard it was to pick yourself back up after the horrible relationship she went through with Jace, but she did it.

"You know I never told you how proud I was at the fact that you finally picked yourself up after that situationship with Jace. You don't let him get to you, and I think it's amazing that you actually found the courage to let somebody else in. I know it's not easy, but you're getting there, and I'll be there the whole way."

"Thank you. It wasn't. I didn't think I would ever be able to give another man a chance, but Ace is different, until he proves to me that he isn't. I don't want to go through what I went through with Jace ever again, and Ace keeps promising me that he's nothing like that, but only time will tell."

I nodded my head just as the front door opened and the Classic family stepped through. Looking from the wife to the two little girls to the husband, I could already tell what he did for a living. *Drug dealer.*

"We love the house. Who do we make the check out to?" he asked, and they never looked.

"Dreux and Co."

"Here you go, thanks." He smiled, handed me the check, and showed us out.

I didn't say anything until I looked at the check and saw that he had paid us way too much. "This is too much money."

"Nah, it's not enough for all the work that you did. My wife loves it already, and I'm sure the rooms look even better. Thank you." He smiled once more, then walked away from the car.

Chapter Forty-seven

Draya

Ride for You

When we made it back home, I was exhausted and ready to go to bed. It was still the middle of the day, and all I wanted to do was go to sleep. As soon as we got back, we dropped KJ off to my parents so they could spend some time with him, and me and Korey were on our way back to the house. "Did you have fun?" he asked.

"I did, and I wouldn't mind doing that again. I want to go to Dubai next."

He chuckled, "I got you, bae. I don't care where we go as long as I got you next to me," he replied, making me smile. This man knew just what to say to make me feel good on the inside and out. I never thought that we would be back in this place, but he was making me happier and happier each day. Moving in together may have seemed like we were taking a big step that neither of us was sure about, but it was working out.

To be in love with someone as long as I had been in love with this man was something I wasn't ready to give up on. "About this wedding, I'm ready to make it happen."

"When?"

"Shit, in the next week."

"Don't play with me, Draya," he said in a serious tone.

"I'm not even playing with you right now. I'm ready to have your last name, and I'm ready to be your wife forever. I don't have time to be waiting when I know that we're not going anywhere. You're meant for me, and I'm meant for you and only you. I don't have no reason to be scared anymore."

"I don't understand why you were scared in the first place."

"Because of everything that went on with us. It wasn't a good place for me back then, but I want to forget all about the past and focus on the future we have in front of us. I never told you how proud I was of you for getting out of the streets and actually becoming a legal man. You actually got Jace out of that shit as well, which tells me that you're a good example for our son."

"Of course I would never steer him wrong. That's my seed, so I have to make sure he makes all the right decisions for the future because I can't have him in the streets."

"True."

"But on a more serious note, I want you to know that you don't ever have to worry about me taking your love for granted ever again. I felt like because I knew you was here and wasn't going anywhere, that gave me a pass to do what I wanted, and I don't ever want to put you through that hurt again. Not being able to call or work things out was hard for me. I felt like shit without you, so the fact that I have you back is enough to make me never want to go through that again."

"And you don't ever have to worry about me jumping to conclusions again unless all the evidence adds up. I know that I may have done that when I left, but that's because it just felt like you was doing something. You were never home, and you never answered the phone for me when I called you."

"I was working only. I know I never gave you much of a reason to think I wasn't cheating though, so that was all my fault. I hate that I put you through that, and that's what I wanted to tell you, but you wasn't fucking with me."

"I know, and I know that I should have been a bigger person and actually sat down and talked to you, but I was just so in my feelings that I didn't think I had to give you the chance to explain yourself. I wasn't happy at all."

He didn't say anything, just looked at me, then leaned over and kissed my lips. "I know, and I promise to never put you through that again," he assured me, which he didn't have to do because I knew for a fact that he learned his lesson, and he knew that I would leave his ass in a heartbeat. The only thing I was happy for was the fact that we actually had this conversation. I had been wanting to tell him that I wasn't happy when I was with him, but I didn't want to hurt his feelings.

I should have been grown about the situation at hand and told my man how I felt, and maybe we could have worked things out earlier instead of things being the way they were. They say when you have a baby your feelings change for the person you're with, and I thought that was what it was more than anything, because I was still in love with him. It wasn't like I hated him or wanted him to drop off the face of the earth. Yeah, he hurt me, and I knew a few women may think I was weak for taking him back, but it was what it was.

As long as we knew where we stood and what we both expected from one another, that was all that mattered to me.

This was the man of my dreams, and I would do anything to keep him. The next thing up for us would be the wedding. Then I would maybe give him the child he swore he was going to get. I wasn't going to tell him that though. All we had to do was keep communicating and making sure we understood each other's feelings, and we would be fine in my eyes, because there was no me without Korey.

Chapter Forty-eight

Korey

Forever Yours

The fact that Draya was sitting here telling me that she wasn't happy did something to me. I did some fucked-up shit, but one thing I knew I would never do was make her unhappy. When we finally made it back to the house, she got right in the bed, and I left. I had to go check on my club to make sure shit was running good. I trusted Loren and Jace, but I knew I still had to check on things just to make sure he was doing what I knew he could. All he needed was a push.

When I pulled up, he was sitting outside, having what looked like a meeting with the bouncers and the security guards, and my antennas went up. Parking, I got out and made my way over to him.

"What's up, bro?" he asked, dapping me up, then giving me a brotherly hug.

"Shit, just made it back. What's going on?"

"We had a little mishap. One of the customers tried to pull a stripper in the bathroom without her consent."

"What you mean?"

"What you think? He was gon' try to rape her. He said she promised him something, so he threw all his money at her."

I couldn't do nothing but shake my head. *These niggas really be taking this shit too serious.* My dancers would tell them whatever they wanted to to make sure they threw that cash their way, but I also told them they had to beware because some of these niggas were really sick.

"You handled it?"

"Hell yeah. I tossed his ass outta here, and now I'm letting them know to never let him back in."

"Good shit. Let me holla at you," I said, and we stepped off to the side. My nigga was doing a good job, so I wanted to see if he wanted to partner up with me on this next project. It was gonna be a hookah lounge. "What you think about linking up on another project with me?"

"Shit, what kind?"

"A hookah lounge. You know that shit make bank."

"I'm with it as long as you make me equal partner."

"I got you. That's why I'm asking. There's too much money to be made out here to just be sitting on these two clubs."

"You ain't lying. I was thinking about opening up a club."

"No shit?"

"Dead ass, bro. Doing this shot for you let me know what all goes into it, and I think I can handle it. It's time for me to get out of these streets, and I mean it. This shit has kept me occupied and on my toes."

"I told you, all you needed was a little push, and I'm happy I'm the one who gave it to you. You got this, and you know whatever you need, I'm here."

"Good, because I need help finding a building. I want this shit together as soon as possible."

"Say no more. I got somebody who'll get you right, and I'll even help. That way, we can knock your building and the building for the hookah lounge out," I told him, and he nodded.

Once we had that squared away, we went back into the building, and I started going over the books and everything. We made way more money that weekend than we had seen in a while. He had been doing his thing, and as I played back the tape and saw what happened with the girl, I was proud of him for stepping up and letting it be known that wasn't about to go down.

I was a little scared about leaving my business in his care because I didn't know if I was going to come back to a building standing, but to see that he actually handled business, the money was right, and he didn't let nobody get over was the best feeling ever. Now I had to focus on this hookah lounge and make sure I found a manager who could handle this kind of work. When I first opened my club, I didn't know how it was going to go, but I was happy to say that I had one of the best strip clubs out here.

It took me a while to get where I was now, but I wouldn't trade anything for this shit. It made me money and made sure I was able to take care of my family without having to do much. I would take a step back from this business as soon as I found that manager and just let the money pile up. I wanted to be on some "I only sign the checks" type of shit, and I had a feeling that time was coming. I had streams of income about to flow, and that was exactly what I needed: something that I could leave for my kids just to secure their money bag without them needing to be in the streets for anything, because they wouldn't have that to do.

To sum up my life would be to say that I was a black man who made a name for myself, and I had my woman next to me. Just like in all relationships, we had our issues, but we worked through them, and hopefully we wouldn't ever have to worry about something like that ever again. I knew for a fact that I would be working extra hard to make sure I kept my woman happy and let her know how much I loved and appreciated her.

When I couldn't have her, that hurt my soul. It had me feeling like I would crumble into nothing and never find another woman who could give me what she could. The moment when God gives you a second chance to right your wrongs, it's time to make different decisions to make sure you keep that woman or man next to you.

Epilogue

Draya

Me and Korey were finally married and were about to welcome our second baby into the world. I finally got my little girl and couldn't have been happier about it. The moment I said "I do" was the day I went to my doctor and had them remove the birth control from my body. I knew I wanted to give my man another baby. It was just a matter of when. But the second he put that rock on my finger, I decided it was time. I'd never been so happy that I had a second chance with my man, and I knew for a fact that he wouldn't fuck this up.

Instead of me running the second club, I left Loren in charge and just stayed home with the kids. KJ was now 2 years old and going to private school. He was growing smarter and smarter every day, and he loved having his father around. I could only hope that life kept treating us this good so that we wouldn't have to worry about anything coming in and shaking our lives up. Trust and communication were what got me and my husband to where we were, and we were gonna keep going until the day we died.

He wouldn't ever have to worry about me going any-where as long as he kept it honest and told me everything he had an issue with so that we could work it out. That was the only way this marriage was going to work. Yes, we may have had issues, but what married couple doesn't? As long as he was willing to work them out instead of finding his way to another woman's bed, then I was all the way in with him. That would never change now. This man came back into my life and, without a doubt, stole my heart all over again.

I didn't think either of us could have truly seen ourselves without each other, and I was happy I came to that agreement with myself. For so long I fought myself on being with him because I told myself I wasn't happy, and I wasn't, but he came in and showed me that he could make me happy. I hadn't cried or been upset with him to the point where I wanted to pack up and leave again.

Korey

Draya had made me the happiest man on earth. When she said, "I do," I cried, knowing this was it for me. There wasn't another woman I would have wanted to marry if it couldn't be her. I fought hard to get back to her, and I would keep fighting for the love we had for the rest of my life. I took my vows seriously, so she'd better be ready for this lifelong journey we had ahead of us, because I wasn't letting her go anywhere. She was stuck with me forever, and that was a fact that would never change.

With the way things were going with us, I had to say that the effects of me not having her really showed me that I needed her more than anything in the world. She never made me feel like I was less than a king in her eyes. It just took me a while to start treating her like the queen she was.

The love I had for this woman was something that didn't come around often, so I had to make sure I cherished it while I was here.

Jace

After all I had been through and all the shit I put Junie through, I was finally able to say I was happy with where I was in life. I had my own club, Loren and I were official, and she never let up on me. She pushed me to be the best man I could be, and I would forever be grateful for that.

Our relationship had its issues, but I was trying to stay faithful to her. I didn't want to start over with anybody new because she left her mark on me. I didn't know how she did it, but her aim shot straight for my heart, and now I didn't want anybody else to have it.

As far as my children, Vicky and Junie and I were making the coparenting thing work, and it was actually going better than I had thought it would. I didn't have to beg for time with my kids, although Vicky was trying. She thought that we would work things out when she had the baby, but I was already in too deep with Loren and didn't want to risk losing her. I had to let Victoria know that she was young and had her whole life in front of her.

I wasn't looking for a toxic relationship. I was looking for one with a woman who would help me grow into the man I could be and the man I knew I needed to be, and that was something I could only do with somebody like Lo. She knew everything there was to know about me, and she never judged me for anything I did in my past. She made me wash my hands of that old nigga and welcome the new one. I was all about her, my kids, and my money, and that was the way it was going to be. I would never want a woman to stay with me because she loved me when I was wilding out and putting my hands on her. Junie stayed. Vicky stayed, but when Loren told me I had one time and she was gonna bury my ass, that was all I needed to hear to keep taking my medication and going to therapy. Shit, she came with me, which was one of the things that made me fall in love with her.

Junie

Life for me was going well. My relationship with Ace didn't really work out the way I thought that it would, but he was still in my life as a friend. We just didn't see eye to eye on certain things, and instead of him seeing things my way, he tried to manipulate me into seeing them his way, and that wasn't working out for me. I knew he didn't know what he was doing, but it reminded me too much of Jace for me to go through it.

I was happy for Jace and Loren. She was a nice girl, and I had nothing against her. She loved my daughter as if she were her own, and that was the only thing I could ask of any woman he had in his life. My relationship with Jace was friendly. I still didn't want him in my presence all the time, but on important days like Montana's birthday, we did the party together so that she could see that her father and I were good.

I had so many things going on in my life that I couldn't afford to fight with anybody or be off my A game. My daughter was the only person I needed in the world to make me happy. She was the reason for the grind I put in to open my own interior design company on the other side of Houston. I never thought I had it in me to want to work all the time, because when I was with Jace I didn't have to worry about that.

Now, my company and Dreux's were collaborating on this huge mansion for the mayor, and if he was impressed with the work that we did, then we could be getting more clients, and I couldn't wait for that. I had been pushing my business for the last six months, and it was doing well. It wasn't as big as Dreux's, but it was getting there.

I may not have gotten my happy ending like everybody else, but I was happy with the decision I made to want to get myself together for myself and not a man. I didn't need a man to make me happy, and that was a fact, but Ace and I did fuck around from time to time just so I wasn't out here fucking with other niggas. I knew that someday we would get back together, but for now I was happy where I was, and that was alone and just having my daughter to worry about. When it was time, God would send the man I needed in my life, whether it was Ace or somebody else. I wasn't rushing it.

God had me, and at the end of the day, as long as I knew I could count on that Man, I didn't need another one. He opened my eyes to a lot of stuff I was blind to for so long, and I was grateful for that. I learned from my situation with Jace, and now I knew what kind of man I didn't want.

Dreux

My relationship with Maria was nonexistent. I had nothing for her. I was so serious when I told her that if she tried to go through with the charges against my parents, she would never hear from me, and she decided to do just that. Although Deion got the case thrown out, it still made me feel a certain kind of hatred for her. She had been calling for the past few months, and I never answered her. I didn't have a vested relationship with her, so there was nothing for me to actually say. I didn't want to have anything to do with her, and I cut her off. My relationship with my parents never changed, and I let them know all the time that I loved them and that was the way it was going to always be. Me and Vicky talked, just not as much. I always got my nephew and helped her out when she needed me to or when Jace was busy working. I loved her and my nephew so much that I was willing to do whatever for them as long as it didn't interfere with my own children and my fiancé.

My relationship with Max wasn't any different. We coparented and that was it. We didn't have anything else to talk about. The only thing we could do was talk about Savannah and how we could make this coparenting situation better for her. She was the only one who mattered to both me and him.

Deion and I were always on good terms. He actually learned how to let me fight my own battles when it came to things I could handle. Now if I felt like I couldn't handle it, then he could step in. Us being engaged gave him access to everything, and that included my legs. I was four months pregnant with his first child and my first son, and I had to say I was happy about my decision to actually keep the baby. I had my issues with Max, and he made it to where I didn't want to have any more kids, but Deion came in and swept me right off my feet, making me want everything with him. Soon I would have his last name, something I had been wanting for a long time. I knew it was going to be hard to find a man who would love me and my daughter, and after all the failed attempts, I just knew I wouldn't find it at all until he stepped into the picture.

I never had to worry about him cheating on me, lying to me, or trying to manipulate me. He had me head over heels for him, and that was something that I would always adore about him. I loved the way he treated me and the way he treated Savannah, and I just knew that our little boy was going to be just as spoiled as both of us.

The side effect of loving Deion was that I would never have to be depressed or sad because he kept a smile on my face.

Deion

When I say my life was going good, I really mean it. I had my first child on the way, my law firm was booming, and I had some of the best lawyers working for me. We had become the biggest firm in the last year. It made for a lot of work, but it wasn't a bad thing. I loved what I did for a living and wouldn't change that shit for nothing in the world. I had something to prove to all the people who doubted black lawyers or tried to pay us less than what they paid the white ones, and now I had most of them trying to get on with my team.

Dreux was the one who made all this possible. If it weren't for my lady, I wouldn't have even thought about running a full law firm. The day I popped the question and she said yes, she made me the happiest man in the world. I would spend the rest of my life making her, Savannah, and our son my first priority, and nothing would ever get in the way of that. Never did I think she and I would hit it off the way we did when we first got together, but I had to say I wasn't against it either. I knew what I wanted and so did she. It was just a matter of making it happen.

The time we spent together was us building our foundation, and the fact that I made it my business to help her in any way that I could was me showing her that, no matter what, if she called, I would be there, and I thought she got the picture. After that, I knew that she was destined to be my wife and carry my children.

I didn't have a relationship with Breann. I heard she got engaged and married to some big-time dope dealer, which had always been her go-to. I also heard that he was beating her ass, but that wasn't my problem anymore. She cheated on me with those kinds all the time, so maybe it was her karma, although I wouldn't wish that on anybody. But she had a good dude when she was with me.

I never tried to be someone I wasn't, and Dreux accepted me for the smart-ass I was. We were in the process of moving into a bigger house out on some land I purchased before we got together. This was the beginning of something that I knew would last forever.